SCORING OFF THE ICE

ICE KINGS, #2

STACEY LYNN

Scoring Off The Ice

Ice Kings, #2

Stacey Lynn

Copyright © 2020 Stacey Lynn

Content Editing: My Brother's Editor

Proofreading: Virginia Tesi Carey

Cover Design: Shanoff Designs

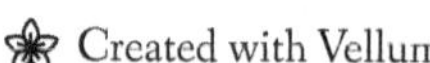 Created with Vellum

To Lauren
May there be many more
girls trips and dance nights
in our future.

CHAPTER ONE

Mikah

"LUTZGO."

I pause midway of tugging down my Ice Kings T-shirt and meet Coach Woods's gaze. He's over twice my age, shorter, rounder. His gray hair is always side-swept and he looks like a kind man.

His kind, happy-go-lucky looks fooled me when I met him. After several conversations and meetings, I thought I'd met the man I always wished my own dad could be. Then I stepped on the ice with him. He yelled so much I was certain my butt was on the first plane back to Denmark. I've learned since it's just his way. He fools us with his kindness, grows us with his fierce need to make us be our best, and in return, he earns our loyalty.

"Yes, Coach?"

"You work out this season?"

"Often."

"Good. Good." He slaps my shoulder as he passes me. "You're good. Fast. This will be your best season yet. Promise you that if you keep up the hard work."

A wash of relief warms me to my core.

He's not a man to give compliments easily but I *felt* the way I skated today. I was one with the ice. Fast. Quick releases on the puck on the pass. Fast catches on the bad ones sent my way. It was grueling.

I live for it. Always have since the first time I slid onto the ice. Literally. My dad put me on skates and plopped me on the ice. I did the splits and landed on my ass. Thirty minutes later, I was speeding around the small rink in our smaller town almost right in the middle of Denmark's central region. It came to me naturally, but I still worked my ass off to make Denmark's International hockey team in Europe. The Danish team isn't the best team in Europe and only one or two a year get drafted to America's National Hockey League.

It's been my father's goal for me since before I was born. It's been mine since I was five.

Sweat still drips down my back as I bend down to grab my pants. T-shirts. Athletic pants. All embossed with the Ice Kings logo because the marketing and promo departments are constantly shoving new gear into our hands. I have dresser drawers full of shirts and pants and baskets filled with hats. I have enough boxer briefs to last for a year without once doing laundry if I want the Ice Kings logo slapped all over my ass and balls.

A jolt slaps my shoulder and my hands slip from my waistband.

"You coming out with us tonight?"

I turn to Sawyer Chauncy, one of our team's first line

defensemen. The guy who slapped my shoulder. His long brown hair hangs to his shoulders, soaking his shirt. "What? Where?"

"Out. Want a few drinks but in quiet. You in? Maddox is coming and Taylor might too."

"Which one?"

Jude and Jason Taylor are brothers, four years apart in age. Both are our starting wingers and two of the best men I have the honor of knowing.

"Jason. Jude already took off. Said Katie has the weekend off work and doesn't want to be away from her."

Where Jude fell in love with his college girlfriend during last season when he was injured, for the three years I've been on the team, Jason's had a parade of women rotating in and out of his life.

Which is more than I can say for me. I've had one woman. One incredible weekend.

One weekend where I put aside the focus I've had on hockey since I was a little kid and took an opportunity that literally, fell into my lap.

One weekend where I decided after being a virgin until the age of twenty-three, one-night stands are not my thing. Don't get me wrong. I loved every second of learning how to work a woman's body. Putting my fantasies to real-life experiences is something I'll never forget.

But in the end? I want to learn what *one* woman likes. Learn her body so well I can get her off and make her come and scream my name with an easy touch, knowing exactly what she craves and how she wants it. I at least want to know it means something to the woman I'm with.

Which means, since the weekend I lost my virginity to a puck bunny who didn't care at all when I gently kicked her out of my condo a couple days later, my weekend of fun over, I have not been with another woman.

Honestly, I want what Jude has with Katie.

What Chauncy has with his longtime girlfriend Debbie.

And what Byron Maddox, our goalie, has with his wife, Hannah.

"Yo, Lutzgo!" Speak of the devil. Maddox walks around the corner, fresh from the shower and wearing nothing.

Maddox wears clothes so infrequently it's possible I've seen his dick more than I've seen my own. "You coming tonight? I'll swing by and pick you up later. Around eight."

"Yeah. Yeah, I'm in. Sounds good."

I can drive myself, but if Maddox is offering that means he won't drink. Something not a lot of guys do much of anyway during the season. But that means I can. And I have stress to kick to the curb.

The beginning of the season is always the worst. The stress of wondering who improved more than me over the off-season—hint, not many, but it can happen. Which new players will be called up from the farm leagues. Who will be sent down. Who will still be traded, or their dreams destroyed completely. The first few weeks of training camp and exhibition games which are only a few weeks away has everyone on edge.

Me more than most.

My VISA allows me to stay in the United States as long as I stay on a professional hockey team. And there is no way I ever want to return to Denmark.

The coach's compliments feel good, but they're not enough. His opinion of what the team needs is not the only one that matters.

"I'll see you at eight, then."

"Where are we headed?"

"George's. A night to chill."

Some night the guys go to clubs. Loud music. Sore throats the next morning from having to scream to be heard. Fans. Puck bunnies. I do not want that tonight. He must see my shoulders slump with relief.

"Hey. You okay?"

Out of everyone on the team, I'm closest with Maddox. When I showed up, fresh off the plane from Denmark, I was only twenty years old and Maddox was already one of the best goalies in the league. He's also the largest guy on our team, the meanest looking and his personality is not much nicer. The man is gruff. A boar in the most fragile of tea shops. The first six months on the team, I was certain he hated my guts. Over time, he started treating me like his younger brother, Seth.

"I am fine." I grab my gear back and shut the oversized locker. "Busy. Sore from working out."

Not all are lies.

"You look good out there. Gelled well with Hendrix. You have nothin' to worry about, eh?"

"Thank you." I slap his shoulder and start to head out. If he's coming at eight to get me, I have enough time to get home, throw in an additional bodyweight-only workout, eat, and shower before he gets there.

"See you later."

I'm looking forward to it. My teammates are my family. Not built by blood and expectations, but mutual respect.

Plus, George's bar is great. He's never let it leak that's where we like to hang when we want to be with the team and their wives or girlfriends even though it could mean a huge jump in business for him. Which means we can relax, have a few drinks, talk about whatever we want and not have to worry about fans demanding our time and attention.

George gives us that. He's either old and seen too much to care about a bunch of pro athletes, or maybe he's a fan of the Raleigh Rough Riders and doesn't care about hockey. We show him our appreciation in large tips and not being complete slobs.

CHAPTER TWO

Paisley

IT HAS BEEN A *DAY*. Actually it has been a *week*. That kind of bone-weary, exhaustion-settling sensation that occurs at the end of the first week back to work or school after an extended absence kind of week.

I barely have the energy to scan my key fob that gets me access to my private and well-secured loft building in the epicenter of Charlotte. Waving to the afternoon manager takes herculean effort but I manage the task and give Pierre a faux-happy *hello* on my way to the elevator banks.

Thank goodness for my uncle Trent, though. He elected to take a three-year position in the Philippines, creating new centers for the tech company where he's based in Charlotte. His moving out of the country and not wanting to sell his fancy loft in his upscale building gave me the opportunity to housesit for him while I attend graduate school and do my student teaching at an inner-city school.

Trent refused to allow me to contribute any money for

rent while he's gone which means my meager finances stretch a lot further. Plus, since it's in Uptown and close to everything, including my school, my car is currently being stored at my parents' house through the school year.

By the time the elevator reaches my floor, the tenth floor where there are only two apartments, I'm dragging the nylon bag that carries my lunch leftovers and the leather office satchel my parents gave me as a gift. I should take more care with it since I know it cost a lot, it's hard at the moment to care.

My eyes are barely half-open, my hair styled so nicely earlier this morning in an attempt to look decent my first weeks of school is now tangled. Sweat is dripping down my spine and probably staining the blouse I'm wearing in that same attempt.

Not that it matters or went noticed. Most graduate students still dress in rumpled sweats and tees, not caring about their appearance. We still spend hours in class, more hours in the library doing research and even more hours writing and researching after hours. I was always taught to dress for the job you want, not the job you have, and I want to excel in teaching, not slump my way through school.

I might not have come from money, but I do come from a family with a lot of pride and honor in who we are.

I unlock my door and enter, dropping my satchel inside the door. After flipping on a few light switches, I drag my feet to the kitchen and plop down my lunch bag. My mouth is parched since I forgot my water bottle on the kitchen counter this morning when I left. It's ninety-eight degrees outside and my last classroom of the day faces west and has broken blinds. I just spent hours where it felt more like one hundred and twenty. Every minute I spent in my chair increased my exhaustion exponentially.

But it's Friday. Four o'clock. I have survived my first two weeks of my second year and now I have the entire weekend to do nothing but study, research, do laundry, and clean.

"Thank goodness," I mutter. I empty the earlier forgotten water bottle, refill it, and as I'm chugging the water in my desperate need to rehydrate from all the sweat I lost today, I pull open the freezer to decide on tonight's dinner.

Frozen fire-grilled steak and rice bowl? Enchiladas? Spinach ravioli?

"Ugh." I close the freezer door and pull up Uber Eats instead. I'll eat the frozen meals when I'm desperate or when my bank account is on its last breath before a stipend check arrives. I'm not quite there yet.

After I order my meal, I head to my bedroom where I strip out of my skirt and blouse into a much more comfortable pair of yoga shorts and a tank top with a built-in bra.

In the bathroom, I wash off my half-ruined makeup and reapply moisturizer. My hair that looked so cute this morning, curled in loose beach waves now looks like I spent hours rubbing balloons all over it before jumping into the dryer without a dryer sheet. And that's with it being pulled up halfway through the day into a bun.

Thanks North Carolina, for the humidity that never quits. I pull my hair back into a low and loose ponytail.

The corner soaking tub silently calls to my tired limbs and I promise myself after I get food in me, I'll spend the rest of the evening taking a bubble bath while having a glass of wine and reading my new romance novel. I've been waiting all week to dive into it.

"Soon, dear friend." I lovingly pat the edge of the tub on my way out. I'm a bubble bath lover to the extreme and weeks like this are exactly why. There's nothing more relaxing than soaking in hot water until the knotted stress at my shoulders and lower back from sitting all day long melt into the tub.

The very idea and reminder that I get to spend days relaxing pushes a pep in my step as I head back down the long hallway to the living area.

Trent's home is absolutely gorgeous. Not only does it have a stunning view of Uptown, but the horizon casts a beautiful glow at sunrise when the sun rises above the endless trees in the distance. I'm lucky to have an uncle who loves me enough to offer me up his place instead of having to commute into Charlotte from a suburb, the only place I could afford rent, or live in a cramped apartment with other grad students. Living with my girlfriends in college was one thing, but they're now all starting their careers while I continue to get a Master's in Education, and I don't want to be studying while they're out having fun.

Essentially, life is good, better than I ever expected I could have growing up the daughter of a plumber and a dental hygienist. And it will be fantastic once my sushi and noodle bowl arrives.

Give me all the carbs. I'm a hungry girl.

A loud thump echoes from the hall and my brows furrow before my feet quickly take me to my peephole. Yeah, it's possible I'm a stalker, but my neighbor across the hall is to die for gorgeous.

He's young like me and I've seen him wear a pinstripe suit looking mouth-watering sexy. It's a debate I have with myself whether he's sexier in the suit carrying a weekend bag when I see him come and go or if it's the black athletic pants, skintight T-shirt he wears while carrying a large duffel bag that's even more glorious.

Honestly, the man is too beautiful for words, and while I've never gathered up the courage to say hello to him, I can't say I don't semi-stalk his departures and arrivals whenever I hear his door close.

By the time I get to the peephole, there's a blur of movement in front of my door and then my cell dings with a text. I grab it quickly only to roll my eyes. Pierre is super nice, but he's not exactly the *best* doorman in our building. Which means the blur of movement outside my door is the delivery man.

I should be notified before they reach the elevators, but Pierre gets distracted easily.

Without thought, I open my door, thank the boy who looks only a year or two younger than me for my dinner and give another wistful look at my neighbor's now closed door.

Someday I should gather up my courage to go say hello. Maybe ask him for a cup of sugar or an egg. Bake some cupcakes for him or find *some* excuse to introduce myself instead of the hellos we exchange as we cross paths in the hallway or elevators.

He always seems to be leaving when I'm returning home or vice versa.

Further, unfortunately, I've never successfully baked a thing. I'm allergic to eggs, and when it comes to courage? Well, I'm not sure I got the lion's share of that growing up.

Maybe someday I'll think of a viable excuse, but until then, there's sushi, noodles, and bubble baths to keep me company. I flip on Netflix, drown out to the afternoon evening news, something I find equally depressing and intriguing while I eat my dinner. When I'm full, I pack away half of it for leftovers. Then I fill my wineglass and grab my Kindle. It's bath time, and then a night of solo Netflix and chill for me.

As I make my way down the small hallway to my bathroom, my ears perk up at a soft, odd noise. I give a quick scan around the living area and entryway and I double check that the television is off. It's not sirens from outside, at least not that I can tell, but it seems to be coming from inside my apartment.

Like someone screaming, or crying, but far away. It's muffled and soft, but it has to be loud for me to hear it. Other than his door slamming when he comes and goes, my unknown and hot neighbor is usually quiet. The strange sound grows louder, and I can't brush away my curiosity. I set down my glass of wine and peer out the door.

What in the heck? My jaw almost hits the wood floor surface at my feet. I pull back and rub my eyes. There has to be a mistake to what I've seen.

Without further thinking, I throw open my door and hurry to his. A blanket draped over the car seat sitting outside his door moves. The ear-piercing squealing sound is no longer unknown.

It's a baby. In a car seat. Left outside my neighbor's door and there's absolutely no one else in sight.

What in the hell is going on?

This baby can't keep screaming like this. Its cheeks are already bright red, turning purple and huge tears fall down its cheeks, so I fling off the blue and white checked blanket, figure out how to unstrap the straps from his chest and gently lift him out. I'm guessing it's a boy based on all the blue. Hard to tell when babies are so small, and he *is* small. It's been awhile since I babysat infants, but I worked afternoons at a daycare when I was in high school and always loved being in the infant room.

"Shhh. Hey, little guy," I croon in his ear and gather him up. My body has gone lava hot and I look back down the hall toward the elevator. There's not a single soul in sight, but he was left here for a reason. "It's okay."

I bounce the baby in my arms and readjust the blanket wrapped around his legs. When I do, an envelope flutters to the floor and I grab it without thinking.

Mikah.

It's the name scrolled on the outside of it which makes my brows pinch. Have I finally figured out the name of my hottie neighbor? Or the baby in my arms?

Only one way to figure it out.

I turn toward the door and lift my hand to knock. I definitely should have stopped by before to ask for that sugar or egg.

This is not the way I want to meet the guy who makes me wet on sight.

CHAPTER THREE

Mikah

WATER RUNS down my arms and drips from my hair. I'm wrapped in a towel at the waist, clinging to it at the hip as I race down the hallway. The incessant pounding on my door began when I was in the shower and hasn't stopped since I finally got sick of trying to relax and ignore it.

There's no reason for it either since the building has security. No one should be allowed inside without me being notified. But it doesn't always work perfectly even though the security is one of the main reasons why I bought the place.

My thighs burn from the quick movements. I probably shouldn't have put in the extra time once I arrived back home, but I'm determined to be the best. Always. Despite the sacrifice. Still, I need ice, a heating pad, and a gallon of water to rehydrate.

I reach the front door, tighten my fist at my hip where my towel sits and fling the door open.

"What is wrong?"

The pretty girl I have seen ducking inside her apartment across the hall whips around. Her blonde hair comes first, tied back at her neck and her green eyes are huge.

She is so pretty. No. That word does not say enough. She is *verkelig smuk*. Very beautiful. *Vidunderlig*.

Immediately catching my gaze is a squished up, red face, with huge dark eyes and an odd-shaped nose. That is all I can see peeking out from beneath a blue and white striped hat.

I have never seen her with him before. She seems so young. Around my age, I thought. My mouth drops open and I point. "You have a baby?"

She is snuggling the baby close to her and at my words, she moves the baby away. Her expression changes into something I don't like. Not even a little bit.

It feels like doom.

Like the look on my father's face the day I didn't make the junior league hockey team despite being the only kid my age invited to tryout—two years younger than anyone else.

That look should not be so familiar on a stranger.

Whatever it is. It is not good.

"No," she says. It's the first word she's ever spoken to me other than *hello*, but it's as pretty as the rest of her. "I think... well, I think he's yours?"

"What?" I'm already stepping back. I had only opened the door far enough to poke my head through but as I move back my door opens. "I do not have a baby."

"I'm guessing the note I found when I heard this little guy crying out here is going to say you're wrong about that."

What note crazy neighbor lady? Before I can ask, a white envelope in one of her hands is held directly in front of my face. I reach for it, and at the same time, get a drastic waft of cool air across my waist.

"Oh shit," the woman says, holding a baby... gaze dropping to my—

"Shit!" I crouch down and grab the towel, holding it in front of me. I am now naked in front of a woman claiming I have a baby. I'm pretty sure I passed out in the shower. I had to have slammed my head into the marble tile and this is all a dream.

Everything since I opened the door is entirely impossible. Plus, I'm now naked. If I could write a list of top ten worst first impressions to make on a pretty woman, I'm pretty sure this will take the number one slot.

Not to mention my naked state.

"Oh!" She spins, putting her back to me. The baby in her arms starts crying and I am speechless.

One weekend. I was careful. She claimed she was too.

What in the world am I supposed to do? There is no playbook for situations like this. And that's all I know. Studying hockey. Studying games. Being better. Faster. Stronger. People... they are not where I succeed.

"Sorry. I am so sorry about that. But that—" I point at the squished up face. "But this cannot be my baby."

Her blonde hair sways as she bounces the baby who is now crying louder. "Well, there was a note in the baby's blanket. He was crying outside your door and there is a diaper bag next to it. And like I said, he was outside your door, not mine, so..."

"I haven't..." I close my mouth.

I am not admitting to this girl who I've always thought is so pretty that I have only had sex with one woman.

One weekend. My twenty-third birthday. The weekend

my teammates finally convinced me to let go. It was no secret before then I was a virgin. I've played for the Carolina Ice Kings since I was twenty. Hockey is my life. Always has been. It's been my sole focus. But our season was off to a rocky start. I wasn't playing well. And for the first time, I allowed myself to be pulled into the mayhem of after game partying. I allowed Newman and Maddox, my teammates, to drag me to a bar... and then I brought a woman home with me.

Angela. She taught me what she liked, and I was a quick learner. Then I realized I liked it a lot of different ways. She was more than willing to let me experiment, let me figure out everything I liked and how to please her.

Two mornings later, she woke up, and after I told her thank you, she smiled and laughed a gentle laugh. There were no promises.

But I also did not think there would be consequences. Not of this magnitude.

"I..." I have no idea what to say but quickly scramble. First, I need to get dressed. In lightweight clothes because I'm sweating like I've finished a workout. As I tighten the towel around my waist, I realize I'm shaking. "I don't know what to do."

Her pink lips spread into a smile and I'm momentarily distracted from the fact I'm naked and there's a strange baby screaming in my hallway.

Her smile is that distracting.

"Well, you could go get some clothes on. Take the note and the baby and let me get back to my Friday night."

Right. The note. The baby. Possibly *my baby*. This cannot be.

She does have a point.

"Come in? For a moment? Please?"

I do need to get dressed so I step back and hurry down the hallway hoping like hell she does come in, then I send up more prayers that this is a joke. A horrible prank by a teammate. Newman would do this to me because he would think it's funny.

But where would Newman get a baby? And *why?*

I am in trouble. Big trouble. Too many thoughts jumble in my mind as I reach my bedroom. I drop the towel and grab the first pair of sweats and shirt I can find, tugging them on, fearing for an attack of my heart. It is too fast. Racing.

I might need a doctor.

I need to get control before I see the pretty woman who I am certain might also be crazy.

Who brings a baby to my door and tells me it's mine?

Crazy people. That's who.

This is not happening. It cannot be. My season starts soon. Training camp. Pre-season. Six months of games, three nights a week, traveling.

I cannot be a father.

My hip bumps my dresser as that thought hits and I settle my ass to it, barely holding myself up. My knees might give out. I might faint.

Father.

I cannot be a father.

"Shit." I scrub my face, heel of my palms press into my closed eyes. I cannot be a father. A dad. *En far.*

But there is also only one way to find out. From outside the door, the cries of the baby, who is definitely *not* mine, have quieted. I make my way toward the woman who might need to see a doctor for making up such a story to scare me.

Perhaps she wants money. I will give her all of mine to take the baby away.

As I think it, another pain hits my chest.

If it *is* mine... do I want it to go away?

I reach the living room and pull to a stop. The girl is swaying slowly, hips swishing back and forth. Her back is to me, but as she moves, I see the blue and white blanket swish with the rhythm of her body.

It is quiet now, which is good.

"Who are you?" I don't like calling her the woman. I've wondered her name for months since she started appearing in that doorway so close to mine.

She turns to me and in her arms is the baby. She's holding a bottle and the baby is drinking. Quiet little sounds come from it and she grins down at the baby in her arms before tilting her head at me.

"What?"

"You. What is your name?"

"Paisley. Are you Mikah?"

She must want money if she knows my name. Perhaps she's a fan. A puck bunny—that's what my teammates call the girls who follow players and only want one thing from them.

"How did you know?" I wish she wasn't so pretty. Sometimes it hurts to talk when all I want to do is look at her.

She points to an envelope on the table. *The* note.

"It's on the outside. I didn't know if it was your name or the baby's, so I took a guess. Are you... are you okay?"

"A stranger shows up at my door with a baby in her arms, saying it's mine. How okay am I supposed to be?" I wander to the table while I ask. I'm surprised by her gentle laugh.

"I suppose this isn't your typical Friday night."

She is funny. If I didn't think I might throw up, I might laugh. No. This is not my typical Friday night. Mine are for resting. Not life-changing drama.

I say nothing and grab the envelope. I stare at it for a moment. Perhaps if I do not open it, I can pretend this didn't happen. My fingers shake as I tear it open.

The envelope is larger than normal and thick and I'm careful as I pull out several folded papers.

The top one is the most important though as I instantly see my name, written in scrolling black ink.

MIKAH,

His name is Angelo.

EMOTION PUNCHES me in the chest. Angelo. I turn, see the woman. No, I see Paisley still rocking back and forth. Her gaze is on me, hand on the bottle still in the baby's mouth. No, Angelo's mouth.

A boy. I might have a son. My jaw tightens and I turn back to the letter that is now burning my fingertips.

HE IS YOURS. I promise, even though I'm sure you won't believe me. I've done the best I can. I'm sorry. I can't keep him. I thought I could, and I tried. I can't do this. So Angelo is yours. All yours.

I found out I was pregnant in December and I debated contacting you and then I wondered how much you'd hate me, or if you'd want to do the "right" thing and make us a family. And I didn't want either. We had a weekend, and I enjoyed it, but the family life... I'm sorry, but that isn't what I want. So I tried to take care of him on my own but I don't think I'm cut out to be a mom.

I'm easy to find, but as painful as this is to say, and how horrible of a woman, a mother this makes me, I don't want him back.

I have included his birth certificate and social security card. If you need to contact me, my name is on his certificate.

Angela

ANGELA. A hockey puck lodges in my throat and the paper in my hand crumples. She knew. She never said. She didn't come to me. Not even for money.

I ball the paper in my fist and as I do, I see the paper beneath it.

Birth Certificate. It looks legal even though my name is not on it and I'm not sure how I feel about that. Does it give me hope that she's lying? Or does it piss me off that she didn't even allow him to claim me in name?

Angelo Martin.

If he's mine, it should be Lutzgo.

Another swell of emotion tightens my chest, prevents my breathing. My breaths come in short spurts and I press my hand there as I turn, remembering Paisley is still here.

Holding my son.

"What the hell am I going to do?"

Her eyes widen and my knees buckle. Thank God for the couch that is right here because I grip the armrest before I go down and move to the couch.

"His name is Angelo," I tell her, although I don't feel like it's my voice saying these words. It certainly doesn't *sound* like my voice. "And he was born in July."

And then I stare at the both of them.

I believe the woman who wrote the letter and what it says. The woman in front of me looks so comfortable, so beautiful holding my baby, and I have never held one in my life. I have no idea what to say.

CHAPTER FOUR

Paisley

MIKAH. Angelo.

The bundle in my arms squirms but I can't pull my eyes off the guy on the couch who looks approximately point three seconds away from passing out right where he's sitting. He's gone from looking at me like I'm crazy to gaping at me like I'm an alien.

"Angelo," I murmur and the bundle in my arms kicks his legs. He's so sweet and easily takes to the bottle. When Mikah took off to his bedroom to get dressed, a visual I am intently trying to forget I ever saw otherwise I won't be responsible for my actions because good Lord... *wow*... that was a pretty sight, I dug through the bag I'd dragged in and found bottles with a note typed and taped to them saying he drinks four ounces of formula every four hours. I filled the bottle with water, dumped in two scoops of formula and while I shook it, the baby stopped crying, like he already recognized the sound.

He took to it easily, but now he's shoving the nipple out of his mouth, so I pull it back and hold him for a moment.

"Do you want to hold him?" Mikah is frozen on the couch like he's turned into a statue and who can blame him.

A birth certificate is in his hands and while the note he read is crumpled into a ball and on the floor, he clearly must believe whatever it said.

I'm dying of curiosity, but it's not my place.

"I don't know how." He sounds so tortured my heart hurts for him.

I don't know this man at all and I've fantasized about him more than neighborly appropriate. But can I leave him alone with this baby? Does he *want* to be alone with his baby?

"I can show you," I say and my voice is almost a whisper. In my arms, Angelo lets out a low grunt and I remember what I was doing with him. Lifting him, I gently hold him so he's upright, chest to my shoulder. I rub his back from his bottom toward his shoulders, pressing lightly in the middle. He needs to burp, and Mikah hasn't moved to help.

"I don't..." Mikah shakes his head and then laughs. It's an airless sound that sounds like he's choking. "I don't know you. I don't know him. I didn't know... I know... I know nothing."

"Hey, hey," I repeat to get his attention. At my shoulder, Angelo burps and I hold him there, patting his bottom. There are diapers in the bag and he should be changed. The man on the edge of a possible panic attack in front of me is more important.

Why I feel so invested is the weirdest thing. Perhaps because I can't just leave a *baby* with a stranger who has admitted to knowing nothing.

How did this bizarreness become my life? All I wanted for tonight was a bubble bath and a romance novel. For a moment I question why I bothered checking out my peephole, but then I imagine what could have happened had I not and I shiver. No, I'm glad I found him, and I'll go home soon, once Mikah is calmer and able to think of a game plan.

"Is there anyone you can call? Someone who can help, I don't know... get you settled?"

My knowledge of babies is vast, and I'm suddenly no longer tired. I blame the adrenaline and fear and craziness of the last twenty minutes for the energy burst, but I can't *leave* him looking so lost. For a moment, awareness brightens his brown eyes that are closer to gold than brown and he falls back into the couch. He rattles off a few guys' names, lets out a word I don't think is English which makes me more curious. He has an accent, not heavy, but it's obvious and the more he mutters in what I'm certain is another language, the more attractive he becomes.

A man with a great body and an accent? I'm done for.

He pushes off the couch. "Maddox. He's supposed to be here soon, anyway. He has a kid. He will know what to do. My other teammates... not so much."

"Teammates?"

Mikah stops moving like I've paralyzed him with my question and then he blinks like he's forgotten I'm standing here, holding his son... the same son he hasn't looked at, or reached for, or touched yet.

"Teammates," he confirms and steps away grabbing for his phone on the kitchen bar. His apartment is not surprisingly an exact replica of my uncle's, only flipped in reverse so it's strangely odd standing in his living room filled with black leather furniture, feeling so at home and yet in a strange land compared to my uncle's creams and browns and more lavish, formal furniture.

He says nothing else but grabs his phone. As if his son and I are a last-minute thought, he turns to me. "Can you stay here? Hold him until I make a call?"

He seems so uncertain. With his pulled in thick, blond brows and those sparkling blue eyes, I'm a sucker for him already. "Sure, Mikah."

He grins then and nods, takes a step toward me. His hand raises and for a moment, he moves to touch Angelo and pauses. "I know nothing of babies. Nothing."

"You won't hurt him by touching him." Since I've already burped him, I resettle him in my arms and move the blanket from his face. He's probably warm in there, so I gently unwrap the blanket and give Mikah a better view. "He's really cute."

And he is. Chubby cheeks. Cutely pursed lips. He's making that sucking motion with his mouth even though he has nothing to suck on. His eyes are closed and he's sleeping, probably a milk coma from the bottle. He becomes even cuter when he lifts his fist, turns toward it and sucks on the edge of his thumb.

"Angelo," Mikah mutters. "Good name. Strong."

He comes forward and soon he's so close to me, peering down at his baby for the first time with such rapture on his face it makes my eyes turn wet.

He brushes a thumb over his cheek and the guy looks so young and so scared. Angelo shifts toward him and Mikah jerks his hand back, grinning at what appears to be an embarrassed little smile at the surprised motion.

"He's my son." He swallows thickly and I drag my gaze to his eyes. He sounds so surprised. So scared. My heart squeezes in my chest. "Angelo."

He clears his throat and returns to focusing on his phone. "I need to make a call. You will stay?"

It comes across more like a command than a question. "Sure, Mikah. I can stay."

"Good." He presses a button on his phone, hurries toward the hallway and at the last moment turns back. "Thank you, Paisley."

I grin and then Angelo squawks in my arms, dragging my focus back to him.

"Hey little guy," I say to him. Mikah vanishes down the hall and Angelo's noise-making becomes louder. I go to the diaper bag and take it to the kitchen bar, jostling and bouncing him to keep him quiet. While he fusses, eyes still closed, I dig through the monstrous bag, setting out everything I can find.

It appears whoever dropped him off came prepared because on many of the items, there are typed notes taped to them. I lay out stacks of burp cloths with a warning *He doesn't spit much but when he does, have several nearby.* It would make me smile if it didn't make me think of a woman who could abandon her baby while cracking jokes.

Fury rolls through me. How can someone do this? How can someone be so callous to not even have the guts to hand a baby off personally and explain herself? She births a baby and leaves a *note?* What would have happened had I not been home? Or if Mikah had been gone?

Anger makes my limbs tremble. I don't even know any of the players in this, so I shake it off and continue setting out everything she has. Perhaps if Mikah can see he has a decent start; he will feel better.

There are two cans of formula, six bottles. On top of the burp cloths there are the long sleeve sleepers that snap all the way up. Way too warm for August in the south so I dig until I find short sleeve onesie shirts. Some pants. The tiniest socks I've seen in my life. There are pacifiers inside a plastic bag with the note *loves when he fusses*. Consider the *he* in question is still squeaking and sucking on his fist, I tear open the bag and hand him a pacifier, guiding it to his mouth. He latches on immediately and sucks to his heart's content. While he's happy, I grab his car seat and lower him down into it and keep it on the floor at my feet. It gives me two hands to use so I can easily empty the rest of the bag. I find wipes and diapers, but he'll need more. So many more diapers than the dozen she provides with a note of brand and size and weight limits.

Which makes me wonder how big the little guy is. I haven't even seen his body. He's been so snuggled in the blanket and since he's happy, now is probably a good time to check him out. I pick him back up and grab a small travel pack of wipes and a diaper and take him to the couch. I unwrap the blanket from his body and grin at his chubby legs that kick and flail as soon as I lay him down on the blanket.

"Hey there," I croon, holding onto his chest with one hand so I can prepare everything else. "You're a kicker, huh? Will you be a runner when you get older? Maybe a soccer player? Hmm?"

I smile down at the little baby with blue eyes so dark I'm sure they'll change to a different hue. I imagine him growing up, a spitting image of Mikah possibly, but that's ridiculous.

He could end up looking like his mother for all I know. It's not like I'll be around to see him grow up.

Goodness.

"I'm going kind of nutty, Angelo." I'm rewarded with a gummy smile that peeks out from the edges of the pacifier. I tickle his tummy and then his chest. He squirms, wiggling beneath my hand and pulling his legs up.

"There you go," I say, tickling him more. He's so itty-bitty which makes sense if he was born in July. It's late August, so at most he can only be seven, maybe eight weeks old.

I make quick work of the diaper change, saving the fun of that job for Mikah for later. He's wearing lightweight pants and socks, so I tug both off and unsnap his plain white onesie, pushing it up to his tummy.

"You're so cute," I whisper. I have the sudden urge to kiss his tummy, inhale his sweet baby scent and I barely restrain myself and finish up the diaper change.

Once he's re-dressed, I lift him back into my arms and relax into the couch, lifting him so his face is again on my shoulder and I run my hand up and down his back. He's so small, my hand is almost the same size as his back but mostly I love the tiny size of his bottom.

There's something about babies I've always loved and adored. They're so sweet, just needing love and food and sleep and even though some are difficult, this little guy in my arms seems to be a very relaxed and happy baby.

He burps again as I hold him and lifts his head.

I smile down at him and I'm struck by the beauty in his eyes and wrinkled face with cheeks barely starting to fill out, but man... is he cute.

"Hey there." I run my finger along his hairline and his baby fuzz eyebrows. He wiggles and I support his neck with my hand. "Are you happy? I hope you're easy and sleep really well. Sounds like your daddy might not know what to do but I promise, I'll help in any way I can."

Not sure how that's possible considering I have school

and work and research, but this little guy is tugging at my heart in a foreign way.

Maybe because I *found* him. It's the caretaker in me. I need to know people around me are happy and healthy and my friends constantly tease me that if anyone gets sick, I turn into mom mode and run them chicken noodle soup or have it delivered. I wash their laundry and keep their places clean. I'm the one Maggie calls to watch her cat when she goes to Ohio to visit her parents at Christmas. Occasionally, I do the grocery shopping for Mr. Tolken downstairs when his wife visits her sister in Florida.

Angelo starts kicking his legs and squirming against me, so I stand and rock him again. He seems to like it when I sway back and forth, but now when I do it, he fusses more so I bounce him, walking laps around the condo. I sing him "Twinkle, Twinkle, Little Star" as I bounce and roam, my eyes taking in everything in Mikah's apartment. The walls are bare and there's essentially nothing outside the black leather sectional and an oversized black leather chair. There are black metal coffee tables and side tables with glass tops. I cringe at the sharp corners. Then there's the television stand with the same metal and glass and exposed cords, bundles of them, hooked to what looks like multiple gaming systems with a massive big screen planted on top. It's a baby hazard palace once this guy will become more mobile.

"You'll need to tell Daddy those are unsafe," I say, smiling and kissing Angelo's head. It can't be helped. Baby smells are yummy and tempting. "He'll need to put bumpers on the table and corners so you don't bang yourself around and get hurt. Yes, he will. We don't want you getting owies now, do we?"

A snickering sound comes from behind and I freeze. How long has he been there?

I turn slowly. Mikah is several feet away, arms crossed over his chest and head ticked to the side.

"Owies?" he asks and I swear I see him fighting a grin. Or a laugh.

"Well, yes. He can bonk his head on all the sharp corners and get hurt."

"I do not know much of babies, but I do not think he can move."

His smile pops through and it's as beautiful as the rest of him. Mind-scrambling.

"They also grow quick." I mean to tease him back but his smile falls.

He dips his chin toward Angelo. "I have a friend coming to help. He and his wife, they have kids. Will you... will you teach me how you do that?"

"Hold him?"

"I should learn before he's able to run away, yes?"

I laugh at his joke, spoken in that heavily accented English and move to him. "Sure, Mikah. I can help teach you."

CHAPTER FIVE

Mikah

WHEN SHE OFFERS to help me, I want to pull her into my arms. I have no idea what I would be doing if I would have been the one to hear the baby screaming, and it scares me to think of how long he was crying before Paisley heard him and knocked on my door.

From the memory of when I opened it, now seared into my mind forever, his face was red, almost purple and he had giant tears on his cheeks.

I made that happen by not hearing him. My shower is loud, yes, but apparently, I am a father. I should know when my child hurts. It only makes sense, yes?

I have been a father for less than an hour and I am already failing at it. Which is logical since my own father was not a good dad unless I was excelling on the ice rink. Even then, I was never good enough.

Enough. My lungs burn as I blow out a heavy breath and lift my arms. I do not want Paisley to go. I like seeing her with Angelo, rocking him, talking to him in a sweet voice like he can understand every word and I have no idea how to do anything.

"How do I?" I gesture to how she's holding him, laying in her arms and she smiles at me.

"It's easy, Mikah. Just bend your arm so you can support his head with your arm and elbow and then hold him with the other arm."

I do what looks like she's doing and then she settles the bundle in my arms. He's so light.

The heaviest thing I've ever held even though he doesn't weigh much. How can something be so small and big at the same time?

His large eyes are open and he blinks, kicks his legs while I adjust him until he looks more comfortable.

I am anything but that.

How is it possible that I am now a father to a baby when I have never had a girlfriend? I am twenty-three years old and I know I'm not normal in that, definitely not in the United States. But even in Denmark, it is not common.

Although I would venture it would be if more children were raised in my house with my father's strict standards, lack of caring words, and a mother who kept quiet.

"Angelo," I murmur and I can't help it. My smile begins before the muscles follow as I look down at him. He smells nice. Looks funny with a big forehead and smooshed nose but he smells nice. I repeat his name, smiling, and glance up.

Paisley is there. Still close. She has his blanket in her hand and she drapes it over his body. "So he stays warm," she whispers, still smiling. Eyes shining.

"Thank you."

I barely remember the time since she showed up at my

door. I don't think I have been very nice to her. "Thank you for your help."

"I can stay until your friends get here," she offers.

I should *man up* like my teammates tell each other and *grow some balls*. I am now a parent, I am certain he is mine. And yet, I'm clueless.

"What is all that?" I ask and nod at the mess now piling up all over my kitchen counter.

"Oh, I emptied the diaper bag while you were on the phone. I thought it'd help to know what you have, what you need."

"Thank you." It leaves me in a heavy whoosh. What I need? I have no idea. There's a chair-like contraption on the floor and an empty bag with a mess on the counter. I know nothing of baby stuff except whenever my teammates have had babies, they constantly complain about how little they sleep. "Will you help explain them?"

"The baby stuff?" She smiles, and I can tell she wants to laugh.

Being clueless is embarrassing and yet I don't care. I don't think she's laughing at me.

"And stay," I tell her. "Please stay. You can meet my friends? Byron is bringing dinner with him."

"I've already eaten, but I can stay and help, Mikah. I don't have plans tonight."

No date. This girl home alone on a Friday? For a brief moment, I wonder how many Fridays we've both spent alone and ignore it as quickly.

I'm a dad now. And the season is starting soon. I don't have time for women even if they're beautiful and kind and helpful.

"Thank you."

She heads toward the counter and I follow her, the baby

still in my arms and so quiet I look down at him. He's sleeping again, a lump the weight of a sack of potatoes in my arms.

And yet it feels like the weight of the world.

"This is his formula," she starts, pointing to two cylinder containers next to bottles. "The instructions for filling them are on the sides and Angelo's mom left several notes."

"How kind of her." She gives him her name and then ditches him. Another round of anger punches my gut. I can find her easily and I will, if only it is to yell at her for this.

"That's what I thought," Paisley says. If I am not mistaken, she has anger in her eyes, too.

She then continues explaining everything and I'm trying to listen. I really am. Mostly I'm lulled into an over-whelmed catatonic state by the sound of her voice. She smiles at me often, raises her brows as if she's asking if I'm following her, and her voice is so sweet and playful, easy to listen to. She has a great voice, not a terribly good singing one from what I overheard, but when she speaks, it still sounds like a beautiful song.

What she doesn't realize is I quit understanding half of what she's saying almost as soon as she started. I learned English from the time I was young, but some words are still strange especially when I don't understand the context. Anything related to anything to do with babies is definitely not something I have the context of, but I nod and pray Byron brings his wife Hannah with him.

Not only do they have kids so they can help, but they also live close. They cannot get here soon enough. When I called Byron, he first gave me a hard time about being in a hurry to go out.

When I said, *"There's a woman here. With a baby.*

Saying he's mine," he said nothing else other than *"I'm on my way."*

He hung up before I could ask for him to bring Hannah.

"Are you lost?" Paisley asks, and I squeeze my eyes closed before opening them.

"I'm right here."

She huffs a quiet, playful sound and shakes her head. "I meant, do you understand, or have I confused you?" She's holding up an outfit with snaps that go from the top all the way down one leg to the foot area and I have no idea what she was saying.

How am I supposed to focus on anything?

"I am lost." I might as well have been dumped on a baseball field for as much as any of this means to me.

My phone rings with the ringtone that says it's the desk downstairs and I jump at the noise. It has to be Byron but I'm holding Angelo and I glance at my phone then the bundle in my arms.

Paisley appears in front of me, arms outstretched, smiling so kindly. "I can take him while you get the phone. You'll figure out how to do both soon."

"Thank you." This shouldn't be so difficult, right? People parent babies all the time. Except they have notice, I suppose. Time to prepare. I have nothing except from what Paisley said, enough diapers to get through the night. I hand him off and grab my phone.

"Now the desk calls and tells me I have visitors," I mumble.

Behind me, Paisley laughs.

I answer the phone, allow Pierre to send Byron up to me and when I set the phone down, Paisley is doing the rocking and swaying thing. I have to learn how to do that.

"Have you spent time with babies?" I ask. It seems such a natural thing for her.

"I worked at a daycare center in high school and usually worked in the infant room, so yeah, a little."

"You know what to do." I cringe. I must seem so dumb to her, and I don't like looking dumb in front of her.

Her green eyes soften and that sweet smile appears. She has a dimple on her right side. It makes her prettier.

"You'll figure it out. And the most important thing about babies is that they need love, feeding, changing, and sleep."

Four things. I can do four things. She makes it sound so easy but it's a *human* I might now be responsible for by myself with a life that is not meant for this. It's anything but simple or easy.

There's a quick, loud knock at my door and our gazes swing in that direction before I return to her...

"You can get the door," she says, reading my thoughts. "I've got him."

I let out a relieved breath. Byron is loud. He's going to give me so much shit for this, but this is his fault.

Well, not the baby-making part, but he was part of the crew who insisted I get out and experience life and the benefits of being a pro hockey player. I can't blame him for the rest but if I would have stuck to hockey, none of this would be happening right now.

I open the door, standing in the doorway, Byron and Hannah are both there.

"Thank you for coming."

He practically shoves me out of the way and he squares his large form up to Paisley. I barely have time to step back and allow for Hannah to step in right behind him, *thank goodness,* when Byron barks out an evil sound.

"Sweetheart, if you think you're getting money from this man here, you're barking up the wrong tree. No way in hell that baby is yours."

Oh. Oh no. He read that wrong. Or maybe I explained it wrong. I flip back to what I said on the phone but can't remember.

"A baby?" Hannah says on a breath.

I step in front of Byron, hands out. Paisley's face has paled and then scrunched.

"It is not hers." I lower my voice. He was with me on my birthday. "Angela," I say quietly. But I'm also pretty sure I shorten her name to one syllable.

Louder, I continue. "She left him here. In the hallway. Paisley, she is my neighbor. She found him."

"Oh," Hannah gasps and her fingers fly to her mouth. "That's so..."

"Shitty?" Paisley snaps and again I am struck by the anger in her too.

"What the fuck?" Byron glances at me. His eyes are steel like he's facing down an opponent and I know with the way he's looking at the woman holding the baby behind me that she is his new target. "How much is that bitch paying you to lie about this?"

Hannah slaps his chest. "Stop it," she hisses. "Don't be a dick."

It took me almost a year of living in the States to stop thinking of my penis when someone called someone a dick. English slang sometimes makes no sense.

"Paisley didn't do anything. She lives across the hall and heard him. I believe her. Angela left a note."

"No shit?" Byron mutters.

"Wow," Hannah croons and I swivel my gaze off Byron to her. She's already hurried over to Paisley and she's peeling back the blanket, smiling down at him. "He's so cute, Mikah. Are you sure he's yours?"

"That's what the note says."

"This is un-fucking-believable." I am really going to need Byron to do or say something more helpful soon. It's the whole reason he's here.

"It was just that weekend." I don't need to elaborate. It was all his and Newman's idea in the first place. "But why would she lie?"

"Why would she drop off a baby at your door? Where is the note?" Hannah is scanning the place like it's going to float from the ceiling and land in her hands.

"I threw it somewhere, but his birth certificate is on the table." I point to the coffee table and Hannah snatches it up. Her brows furrow and I imagine her planning on hunting down Angela and giving her a piece of her mind.

I hope she brings me with. I have a few things to say myself. But then her lips press together and I can almost see her mind working.

"July," she says softly. "Timing fits. Birthday weekend, right?"

She grins at me and I burn straight to the tips of my ears. Does everyone know when I lost my virginity?

"Yeah." I clear my throat and I'm fascinated with Paisley who is still standing there, holding my *kid*, looking like she wants to run.

It's probably time I *man up*. I go to her and hold out my arms. It feels awkward. Like I'm made of wood but in truth, the only time I have ever felt comfortable is on skates and on the ice. "I'll take him."

"I should go. Let you have time with your friends. It's good you have help though." She chews her lip and her eyes bounce to all of us in the room. I don't think she knows who Byron and I are, and I like that almost as much as her voice.

It's nice to not be recognized sometimes.

I don't blame her for wanting to leave, either. Byron is still glaring at her, like he doesn't believe her.

"I'll be around all weekend," she says again. "If you need anything. Don't hesitate to walk across the hall, okay?"

"Thank you." A pressure in my chest releases. I'm going to need her help. But I don't know if I will ask. I laugh then and it's strained and ridiculous. "It was nice meeting you. Finally."

I smile and hers appears too. She shakes her head, brushes a finger down Angelo's cheek. She peers up at me through her lashes. *Gud.* She's so pretty I want to kiss her. I bet she'll taste sweeter than she looks.

"You too, Mikah. Finally."

She lingers on the word and it gives me hope. As does the blush rising on her cheeks.

Her hand drifts away from Angelo and if I wasn't holding him, I would reach for it. The thought of her leaving me makes my heart jump. Byron and Hannah will leave and go home and then I'll be with Angelo alone.

She must see the panic in my eyes, the racing of my heart because she giggles. "All weekend, Mikah. If you need anything, come get me. And maybe I can come check on you?"

"Please." It falls through me in a rush, before I can be embarrassed about it.

"Okay then." She steps back and lifts her hand toward Byron and Hannah. "It was nice to meet you."

"You too." Hannah smiles at her and then she's in front of me, whisking Angelo out of my arms before I can blink.

At some point, I'll need to hold him for longer than a minute or two. I hope I don't break him.

Byron grunts at Paisley as she walks by him, but that is his way with most people.

As soon as the door shuts behind her, Byron turns to me and smirks.

"Knocked someone up the first time you have a go, hey slugger? That's my man."

He slaps me on the shoulder, jolting me forward. He's a big guy and even though I'm six feet, he's much bigger.

Hannah tells him to shut up and then he grabs Angelo from her and holds him tight to his chest.

It's that moment, seeing another man more comfortable with him than I am that I break down.

"What in the hell am I supposed to do, guys?"

CHAPTER SIX

Paisley

IT'S time I call the cops on myself for being a stalker. Has anyone actually tried to get a restraining order against themselves? My eye has been glued to my peephole for so long since my awkward and weird return to my apartment, it's surprising it doesn't stay stuck to the door when I finally turn my back.

It's been noisy though, and who can blame me for being curious.

It seemed like not long after I came home, glass of wine in hand and all thought of a bubble bath evaporated, the door shut and then an hour later, I heard another noise and saw Byron returning. With *boxes* and *boxes* of things.

The pictures on the sides as he made trip after trip showed he'd done some serious shopping. Pack'n'Play was in one. Stroller. Car seat. Diapers. Large red bags from Target proving how many items and how large some of them are and when he opened the door to Mikah's, I heard a lot of laughing come through.

I wish I was still there.

Stupid. It's a stupid thought and an even worse idea. He doesn't need a stranger in his way as he gets settled and holy cow... what he must be thinking. How scared must he be? What's he going to *do*?

Mind your own darn business, Paisley. I scold myself and sip my wine before heading to my living room where I pull up Netflix and toss the remote to the table and sit on the couch. I am anything but relaxed.

Man. What a night to end the longest and hardest week.

My imagination runs away with me and it can't be helped. I held Angelo almost for the entire time I was there earlier. And Mikah mostly looked scared.

What will he do tonight when he cries? How will he handle it when he spits up or when he has to be changed?

I can go over and offer to stay the night. To help. To ease him into this.

I slap my forehead. He has friends. A lot of them considering he named several before deciding on Byron, and man... that guy is big and angry looking.

At first I thought he was going to grab me by the throat and string me up by my toes. Hannah, on the other hand, I thought was going to rip Angelo straight out of my arms if she didn't get her baby fix. I'm so crazily invested in this entire, wild situation, I zone out to the Netflix logo on the screen. I haven't bothered turning on a show I won't focus on watching.

"Get over yourself," I mutter and take a sip of my wine.

It's none of my business. So the hottie next door is now a dad. So I finally know his name. So I also now know he has an accent that I can't place and speaks a language so easily he's definitely not originally from here. So I know more about him than I did before and I might see him again in passing, or maybe drop by tomorrow to see how he's doing.

Big deal. He's still only my neighbor.

Sighing, I grab the remote again and pull up the medical drama I've been streaming for the last several weeks. Whatever is going on across the hall from me isn't my business. I'm glad I was home earlier to help, but Mikah will figure everything out. We'll go back to passing each other in the hall with a smile and perhaps now a polite word or two.

Other than that, it's best I focus on me and my schoolwork and what I need to do this weekend like laundry and research. Speaking of, I should probably get started. I set down my wine and head to my bedroom where I grab my laundry basket.

A quick sort and a few minutes later, I have my first load in the washer, humming from the small laundry room closet off my hallway.

I'm just about ready to sit back down with my wine and television drama when a soft knock hits my door.

Mikah. It's scary he's my first thought but who else would be here? I hurry to the door and open it without thinking, surprised when Hannah is standing on the other side, hand still raised in a fist like she's preparing to knock again.

She drops her hand to her side and smiles. "Hey... Paisley? Do you have a minute?"

I step back, stunned. She's here? Why is she here? I give a quick glance to the closed door across the hall. "Is everything okay?"

"They're doing well. Angelo is sleeping. Byron and Mikah are setting up the bassinet and other furniture we went out and got him. But I'd like to talk to you if that's okay?"

"Um. Sure." I step back slowly, wary at the look on her face. "Come on in."

I close the door behind her and go to the bottle of wine on my counter. Something tells me I'll need it. "Would you like one?"

"Oh my gosh, yes." She laughs and shakes her head. "What a night, right? I mean, I swear my head is still spinning from all of this. And Mikah, the poor guy. He's so utterly and adorably lost."

She babbles on while I grab a glass and fill it for her, but I'm stuck on adorable.

To me, Mikah is anything but adorable, except for maybe his embarrassment when he admitted he doesn't know what he's doing. On a scale of one to ten for awkward actions with a strange neighbor I'm pretty sure the hug I wanted to give him at that moment would have reached a twenty.

"Anyway" —she flips her hand in the air— "that's all, well that's sort of why I'm here. Byron wanted to come talk you, but I convinced him it'd be better coming from me."

A chill runs through me at her words, the way she's smiling at me. It's not exactly friendly and I'm not sure what to do with it.

"Okay..."

"Well, here's the thing and I'm just going to say it." She takes a sip of her wine and licks her lips. "You haven't told anyone about tonight, have you?"

"No." I haven't even considered it. It might help my friends are all out partying and my parents and I, while close, aren't exactly the kind of parents I dish about boys with. "No. I haven't said anything."

"Okay good." She sighs and presses her hands to the countertop. Her eyes harden and I'm not even sure I know how I recognize it but the happy babbling woman vanishes. She's so much more serious and I'm stunned again when she asks, "You don't know who he is, do you?"

"Know who, who is? Mikah?"

"Yeah. I take it you don't watch hockey?"

"Hockey?" It'd be fantastic if I could stop answering her questions with questions but I'm not sure where she's going. Everything she says confuses me. "I don't really watch any sports," I admit.

At my answer, Hannah's smile widens and she returns to being friendly.

"Okay. See, that's good. Great even, I think. But Mikah and Byron, well, they play for the Ice Kings."

"Ice Kings?"

She laughs so hard she snorts and covers her mouth. "Sorry. So sorry. I'm not laughing at you, I promise, but yeah. Carolina Ice Kings. The local professional hockey team? Ever hear of them? Because their games are like three blocks away from here."

I pay attention to hockey as much as I pay attention to golf, which is to say not at all. And that includes all sports. My father is more of a NASCAR fan but Mom and I usually left the house when races came on. Like either of us wanted to sit around and scream at cars zooming around the track.

"Um. It sounds familiar, but I'm confused why this matters I guess?"

"Because, if word gets out Mikah has had a baby dropped on his doorstep that'll make the news. It'll be all over social media. It can distract the team before their season ever begins and it won't be good for any of them, or him."

My throat tightens and that chill I felt earlier turns to a rolling heat. "I wouldn't do that."

"That's good. Good. Great, really, it's just, I'm not trying to be mean, but I care about the guys and the team. We're like family. Mikah's going to get enough attention once people find out he has a kid. Fans will go absolutely nuts. I want to help him as much as possible. And to be honest, we're the only family he has here."

"I do too." Yes, I blurt that out before I can stop it. "I don't, I mean, I don't even know him but I wouldn't hurt someone. Not intentionally at least."

"And I'm not saying you would, but I also wanted to come over here and double check. Mikah said before tonight you two had never met, so he doesn't know you. We're dealing with a rather large unknown."

My lip curls at not only her insinuation, but by calling me an *unknown*. Like I'm dirt. Or someone not worth knowing here. She must see what she's done by my expression because she throws her hands up.

"I'm not trying to offend you. Or hurt you. Maybe I'm not explaining everything clearly and for that, forgive me, it's been kind of a whirlwind few hours."

"Tell me about it."

She cracks a smile and takes a drink. "You seem nice, Paisley. But can you understand why one of us would want to come over and at least *ask* you to keep this news to yourself? Let Mikah get settled. He'll have to announce it at some point. He's known as rather, well... he's known on the team at least as this, well, innocent kid. Byron and the guys who have been playing for awhile like to think of themselves as his big brothers. We're just looking out for him."

He is young. He's never once seemed innocent to me though. Way too handsome and hot to be that. And yet there's his blushing and uncertainty.

I can see her point. It's not like I've ever paid attention to professional athletes to know how big of a deal they are, but I'm not stupid. I know they get attention.

"I won't say anything. You can reassure him, and I will too the next time I see him."

"He's called the team lawyer. Byron insisted. I'm pretty sure he should call the cops or something, maybe DHS? I'm not really sure so to be further honest, I'm not sure we're handling it the most *legal* way. Mikah wants to keep it quiet so the lawyer said he'll see what he can do."

She doesn't owe me further explanations. Yet, she has a point.

"I get it, Hannah, and I promise. My lips are sealed." I mime a zipping motion across my lips. It's less offensive to think of it this way and she has a point. Should I have called the cops or something? But how was I supposed to know? I was so thrown by the sight of a random baby in our hallway my only real thought was to get him to stop crying.

"Thank you." She sighs and takes another sip of her wine. "It was really nice of you to help him out earlier. I have no idea what he would have done if he would have found Angelo first." Another pause and then, a bigger smile. "He's really cute, isn't he?"

I'm assuming she's talking about Angelo. But my mind first goes to Mikah.

"Yeah." Regardless of who she means, they both are. And seeing Mikah hold Angelo the first time? Ovary explosion!

Enough.

And a professional hockey player? I come from such a

small upbringing I can't even fathom what his life is like. Trent's the first person from either of my parents' side who actually left Blandsford. It's a small town closer to the coast, much more farming and trade schools than high rises and big cities and even bigger paychecks.

Perhaps I've been swept away with the luxury of Trent's living and have forgotten myself. When I finish school, I plan on returning to Blandsford where I can make a difference in the small, farming community schools.

What in the world do I have to offer someone like Mikah?

"Thanks for stopping by." I've surprised her by my abrupt tone and change in subject, but it can't be helped. The realization has knocked all the wind from my sails. It's probably best for everyone if Mikah and I go back to occasional nods while we duck behind our doors.

Hannah licks her lips like she has something else to say but whatever she must see on my face stops her. She takes one more sip of her wine and nods. "Thanks again for being there for him. I'll see you around?"

"Sure." Most likely, absolutely not.

I walk her to the door and tell her good night and when the door is closed behind me, I settle my back against it. All the insanity of the evening slides from my body and if it was visible, it'd be a pool of emotions jumbling at my feet.

I need sleep and to forget tonight ever happened.

The problem is once I do finally fall asleep, hours later, after tossing and turning, I swear I'm awakened by the quiet sounds of a baby crying and my dreams are filled with strollers and diapers and baby laughs and handsome smiles that come from the guy across the hall.

The guy who I've crushed on for months, and who now, will probably never be mine.

CHAPTER SEVEN

Mikah

I SUCK at everything parenting and baby related. I'm still in the clothes I threw on Friday night in a hurry. I haven't had time to take a shower. I'm not sure when the last time I ate was... probably when Byron and Hannah brought food. I'm certain I haven't brushed my teeth since yesterday.

Angelo hates me. He has to with the way he cries regardless of how I try to take care of him.

Hannah was nice enough to stay Friday night. She slept in my guest room in case I needed her and three times she came in when he was crying. But I was already awake because I seem to wake up every time he makes a noise. And he makes a lot of them.

When she left Saturday, she could not hide the worry on her face. She was worried about leaving me home alone with my son.

And isn't that a slapshot to the face without a mask on?

Byron called yesterday afternoon on the rare occasion

Angelo was sleeping, but I was too tired myself to answer. I laid on the couch, too sore and worn out to move. My muscles ached. I didn't have the energy to lift my arm to reach my cell phone two small feet away.

Since then, I've been on the phone with my agent, the team coach, and a lawyer. Conversations that are hard to have with a baby who cries all day long.

He does like the swing sometimes. It's a huge contraption. Navy blue seat with yellow ducks on it and sometimes a thing that spins around above his head grabs his attention. He likes his pacifier.

The note Angela wrote is correct. He doesn't spit up much after he eats, but when he does... well, there is a stain on my living room rug and my home now smells like sour milk.

That could also, maybe be me, because he cries and spits when I hold him, and he cries when I set him down.

I am failing at this.

I am also angry that Paisley hasn't come and checked on me. Perhaps she has plans. Maybe she works. But she said she'd be here all weekend and I haven't seen her. Haven't heard her leave, and I have spent time by my door, bouncing and swaying Angelo like she did so easily but all it does is make him cry harder.

I can't even calm my baby correctly.

I am currently a sweaty mess, angry with my lawyer who says I'll need a paternity test to determine he's mine before anything else can happen... like getting me on his birth certificate and tracking down Angela to *hurt* her for doing this to me.

I am an ass for thinking such things but some warning... some help... that would have been nice.

Angelo is in his swing, unhappy at the world, perhaps

screaming because he can't stand the sight of me, and I'm trying... and failing... at getting some carrier contraption onto me. The straps keep twisting and my arms do not bend behind my back enough to fix them. Hannah said her kids loved being carried in this *thing* Byron bought me. I remember him carrying his babies like this when they were littler, so I figure I'll give it a shot.

For as much as the instructions that came with this thing make sense to me, they might be written in Swahili... not one of the three languages I know.

I need help.

I need to go to the team's doctor and have my head examined. How big of a fool am I for thinking I might be able to do this? And this is all I've been thinking of this weekend. Can I do this with Angelo? Alone?

His mother couldn't.

What makes me think I can? Especially once the season begins.

Hannah has already called me with the name of a babysitting service she hired when her babies were little before she stayed home full time. She said they're highly reputable. Some nannies live-in, some don't. Some have flexible schedules and can stay while I travel.

I have no idea what it comes to needing to do what's best for Angelo. The only needs I have in front of me are getting him to stop crying, take a shower, and figure out this damn carrier.

I fling it off my shoulders and slam my hands to my hips. In his swing, Angelo is settling and as I move closer to him, hesitantly because my mere presence seems to piss him off, he hiccups. It's followed by a smile.

Everything around me melts to the floor.

When he's not screaming, he's cute.

"Mine," I grit my teeth. He's mine. I point at him, although his eyes are quickly closing. "I will figure this out, Angelo. Swear it to you. And I will not be a giant jackass like my *fer* is to me."

Shit. I haven't called them to let them know what's going on. Which isn't surprising. I don't speak to them much at all these days. I send them money every year. I don't know if they spend it or invest it and I don't care. My relationship with my father ended the day I signed my contract and boarded a plane for America.

He never said congratulations. He didn't slap me on the back. He stood next to me in the airport, holding one of my bags before dropping it off at my feet and said, "Do not screw this up. We have worked too hard."

As if him screaming at me, punishing me after losing a game by forcing me to spend another two hours once I got home practicing wrist shots in our indoor hockey net area made me who I am.

Perhaps it is. I like to think it's my constant hard work, my love of the game, and talent I didn't get from him because he could never play past the eleven-year-old travel leagues that makes me who I am, but perhaps there is a part of me that owes something to my father.

That doesn't mean I'm in a hurry to call them and tell them they might now be grandparents.

My father will be angrier than a volcano preparing to erupt.

My mom will take her cues from him.

"It's you and I, Angelo," I say, as that settles on my shoulders. I have friends. Teammates who feel like family, but when it comes to blood family... "It's me and you. I will figure this out. I promise you."

With that, I grab the carrier thing from the couch where

I threw it and I stomp back to him, gently unbuckling him and lifting him into my arms, careful to support his head like Hannah and Paisley taught me so he doesn't smack it on the animals hanging on the machine. I leave my keys on the counter and head for the hall.

I need help and Paisley said she will. Anytime.

That time is now.

Hopefully I can take her help and forget all about how pretty she is and how much I still want to kiss her lips and see if they're as soft as they appear.

Angelo squirms in my arms and I hold him tighter, adjusting him so his cheek is on my shoulder.

He burps and it reeks like formula, but I'm getting used to the smell. It's the smile he always gives after that makes my chest warm in a strange way.

Angelo's smiles are better than scoring a goal in a game and it's odd I feel so much for him when he does this.

Maybe it means I like him enough to make sure I don't mess this up.

"Be good, okay?" I whisper, holding his cheek to my shoulder and whispering in his ear. "We don't want to scare Paisley away again, right?"

He burps again and smiles. It looks so freaking weird to see a toothless smile.

It makes me laugh too.

"All right, flirt. Do your thing then."

I knock on her door and drop my hand to the side. I'm holding the carrier in my hand that's resting beneath Angelo's bottom. He's as light as a bag of flour and every time I hold him I get a fear of him flopping backward and me dropping him. Or breaking him from holding him too tight.

When I said something like this to Byron the other

night, he'd sighed and ran one of his fat fingers across Angelo's forehead in a gentle way. Didn't know he had in him.

Then he'd said, "Yeah. Man, I get it. Good news is they're stronger than you think."

But I don't think he was thinking about me or Angelo then. His face went soft and Hannah had sniffed. I knew then he was remembering his own two kids, a girl and boy who are so loud and always moving and in school now. I'm pretty sure he was imagining them when they were as small as Angelo, wondering where the time went.

I want to hurt Angela and scream at her and make her pay for doing this to me so abruptly. Mostly, I think I'm more pissed she didn't tell me right away. That I've already missed so much.

But I will not miss another moment.

"I swear it," I whisper and kiss his cheek. His weight settles on my chest and mine warms again. How strange, that holding him seems to calm me when he usually hates it.

I knock again, louder this time. Angelo is starting to get fussy again, squirming and whimpering which tells me he's getting closer to a full-blown wail at any moment when the lock clicks.

The door opens a few inches and this time, it's my turn to be surprised at what I see.

"What is on your face?"

Paisley is wearing something pink. On her face. It wrinkles at the edge of her nose. It looks like she took a sheet of hot pink paper and glued it to her face.

For a moment, I swear her eyes seem even more green with the pink goo all over her and she glances at Angelo, smiles, and it falls when she meets my gaze. "It's a face mask."

It doesn't look like any face mask I've ever seen. Or worn.

"Mikah. Are you okay?"

She steps back, opening the door, and I'm struck by a déjà vu moment from Friday. Except this time it's Paisley fresh out of the shower and she's not holding a towel with her fist at her waist like I was, but she's in a fluffy, light green robe that covers her from her chin to the tips of her toes.

And I want to strip her out of it so I can see the shape of her curves I've thought about so much.

If only she would accidentally drop it to the floor like I did to her. I'm not even embarrassed about it. I liked the way she blushed when I saw her glance down at me.

"I'm fine. Angelo is fine."

As if he disagrees with me, because he disagrees with everything I do, he lets out a loud squawk sound that grabs both of our attention. She smiles at him.

It's a smile that hits me in the place that caused this mess in my arms to begin with.

"I think he hates me," I admit and I mean it as a joke but there's truth in it. It comes out in the gravel in my throat and Paisley catches it.

"Mikah." Her shoulders slump and her smile reappears. "He doesn't hate you."

Angelo fusses again, kicks at my chest with his tiny feet and his face scrunches. "I think he's saying you're wrong. Can you come help me?" I lift and drop the contraption in my hand. "I was trying to get him in this carrier but it's twisted and not working."

She laughs softly. "Sure. Can you give me ten minutes? I can be over as soon as I get this" —she circles her face, pointing with her finger— "off my face and get some clothes on."

I'll take her in the robe. Mentioning that will probably get the door slammed in my face.

"Ten minutes?"

"I'll make it seven."

Thank goodness. Ten minutes seems like forever. "Thank you."

CHAPTER EIGHT

Paisley

MY RESOLVE TO stay away from Mikah crumbles as soon as I see him. I almost yanked the door open and kissed him myself when I saw the way he grinned down at Angelo through the peephole. I've spent the entire weekend trying to ignore him, which is in a direct internal war with my crazy desire to want to help him. I have spent entirely too much time at my door, squinting with one eye in hopes of catching the smallest glimpse of him.

I might need a new life. At least a hobby that doesn't involve stalking the hockey player in real life and on the internet.

Because yes, I've done this as well. I've tried telling myself it's pure curiosity. I mean, who is this guy that is with a woman and then gets a baby dropped off at the door. And why would he trust her?

I consider all of this, not questioning why I'm willing to scrub my face before my face mask is done and throw on some cute, but still relaxing clothes, when I've planned for today to be a day where I rest and recharge. Something tells me being around Mikah isn't going to relax anything. I predict the opposite if seeing him rumpled, looking exhausted, and possibly wearing the same clothes he was wearing on Friday jumpstarts my libido in a matter of seconds.

I haven't seen any action since last spring, and I've been okay with that. Mikah's accent alone threatens to awaken parts of me I haven't concerned myself with lately without battery aided assistance.

Unwrapping my hair from the towel I scrunched it up in after my shower, I pull it back into a braid so it looks halfway decent. Then slather on a tinted moisturizer and grab my keys and phone. At the door to my condo, I slide into a pair of leather, flip-flop sandals.

I'm not even at his door when his opens. He's sans baby, shirt wrinkled, hair a mess and he has dark purple circles beneath his eyes.

A twinge of regret pierces me. I should have come and helped him or at least offered earlier. Still, I hate him a little bit for how he looks when he's such a mess.

It's official. Mikah Lutzgo, whose last name I learned from my internet searches, looks good in a suit, sweatpants, wrinkled and overwhelmed, and possibly, no... definitely, better when he's wearing nothing at all. A visual I still haven't forgotten.

"Good. You're here."

"Waiting for me?" I ask, laughing at the way he sounds so *desperate.* I can't lie to myself. I like that he's desperate for me, even if it's for baby help.

"Yes." He nods and steps back so the door is open but I have to slide and shimmy my way past him. "Angelo is finally sleeping but he doesn't stay sleeping. And when I came to your place I was trying to figure out how to wear this" —he grabs the carrier from the couch and throws it back down— "but I can't... I can't twist and get everything right, I don't think. And I'm not sure I've showered, or eaten, and I reek." He stops. Stares at me and I swear a pale pink rises on the tips of his ears and his nose. Scrubbing a hand down his face, he mutters, "I can't believe I'm talking about my smell." When his eyes pull back to mine, he sinks his teeth into his bottom lip and shrugs. "I need help. Can you?"

I mean... I can help him with the shower... *gladly*... but I'm certain that's not what he's asking. Which is a shame.

"I've got him." I gesture to the tiny, sleeping cutie-pie in the swing. "Go do whatever you need. Shower. Take a nap if you need it. I'll take care of everything out here."

Relief makes his shoulders fall but then his thick, blond brows pucker. "Are you sure? I haven't left him..."

We're dealing with a rather large unknown. Hannah's words come back to me. They've been difficult to forget since she said them.

"I'll stay here, in the living room. I can handle this while you do what you need to do. When has he last eaten?"

"Two." He goes to the kitchen counter. The mess I left from the diaper bag has been cleared and in its place is a notebook. I follow him while he picks it up, flashes me a page and sets it back down. "I've been keeping track. Hannah says it can help me get him on a schedule, figure out when he's hungry or tired. She bought me a book to help too, but I haven't been able to read it."

The chart he's created is intense, filled with every diaper change, a W or D circled on various ones, sometimes both and I assume they stand for wet and dirty.

He's so *sweet*.

"How are you doing?" I ask, resisting the urge to trail my finger over this chart. We did something similar at the daycare where I worked. Parents want to know *everything* about their babies when they aren't with them.

I like he wants to do it when he *is* with his baby.

"It's a lot of work." He brushes a hand down his face and sighs, shoulders slumping forward. "Would it make me a jerk if I say I understand why Angela did this? Why she didn't think she could do this?"

"No." It's the truth. I can't imagine what it's like to be a parent, but I do remember how exhausting taking care of babies is. To be thrown into it without warning or any knowledge or preparation, I imagine is terrifying. "No, I don't think it makes you a jerk or a bad person. You're over-whelmed. This *is* a lot. But you seem to be doing well."

A quick scan of his condo shows the swing and other larger items have been assembled and are set out. There is an open box of diapers in one corner along with a rolled up mat. Several blankets drape over his furniture. A large plastic container of baby wipes on his coffee table. I smile when I see the bumpers on the corners of the table and tele-vision stand.

"You look like you have everything you need. The rest will take time and practice." I flip my hands in his direction and shoo him away. "Now go, shower. Sleep if you need it. I have this and we can talk more when you're done, or we don't have to talk at all."

"Talking to you helps me feel better."

A rush of warmth like a tidal wave slams against me, covers me down to the tips of my toes. "Th... thank you. That's very sweet."

He smiles. It's timid but it changes and turns more serious, almost contemplative as his gaze slides down the length of my body. "Be back."

As soon as he's gone, I take a few minutes tidying up the living room. The blankets are folded and draped over one armrest. I gather a few diapers that have been rolled and taped close but didn't quite make it into the garbage can that's overflowing, so I dig in the cupboards in the kitchen and under the sink until I find where he keeps the extra and I change out the trash, taking the full bag to the hallway and set it outside his door. I can throw it in the dumpster receptacle at the end of the hall when I leave later.

He has a fully stocked pantry with a huge variety of healthy food. I don't understand what half of them are or what they would be used for in recipes. I do manage to find enough basic items I can use to whip together a meal for him.

My attempts at baking create cookies Mikah could probably use as hockey pucks and more than one small oven fire. I'm only slightly better at cooking, but there are a few things I can make that won't risk his physical health. Fortunately, amidst the dried seaweed, veggie chips, and quinoa, he has all the ingredients to make a homemade sauce.

I pull out the cans I need and smile when I catch the shelf to my right. It's stocked as if Angelo is going to begin eating baby food tomorrow, and I let loose a giggle. Hannah and Byron must have been balls to the walls buying Mikah everything from the store the other night. Angelo is nowhere near old enough for jarred baby food or the puff stars.

But Mikah is definitely prepared considering the half-dozen cans of formula and more bottles that are still in their packaging. There are even additional packages of just the bottle nipples in larger sizes as he grows.

I leave the walk-in pantry and check on Angelo. He's still sleeping in the swing and the *buzz click click* of it is the only sound in the room which for some reason, is rather peaceful.

Who would have thought I'd be cooking a homemade meal for a man I barely know while watching his son? Not me, that's for sure, and yet as I move around his kitchen, grabbing items and pots and pans and digging ground beef out of his freezer, I like it.

My mom worked long hours three days a week when I was really little, she sometimes wasn't home until I was already in bed. My father worked just as long hours and was often on call to help with emergency plumbing issues. It made it difficult to spend a lot of family time together, simple things like eating dinner as a family. Talking about our days. Them asking me about school. Instead, questions were usually asked in the car while they worked and hurried to get me to all the places I needed to go like dance and soccer practices, middle school dances, high school football games. Despite the rush and the usually running late, I always knew I was deeply loved.

Something that's been bothering me about what Hannah said the other night. *We're the only family he has here.* Does that mean he has family elsewhere? Or that he doesn't have any. My heart pinches every time those words come to my mind.

I didn't have a lot. But I have a home. A good family. A landing place when things in life knock me sideways. I can't imagine how I'd handle something like this without them.

I have the ground beef browning in a frying pan when Angelo lets loose a quiet cry. His mouth is doing that sucking motion again which is utterly adorable. I can't help but stop what I'm doing in the kitchen to get a closer peek at him. His tiny feet are covered in socks and he's wearing a short sleeve, long-legged outfit striped in black and blue. In white across his chest are the words "Let's Go!"

I have to cover my mouth to keep from laughing. My internet search turned up enough to show me that with Mikah's last name of Lutzgo, whenever he skates onto the ice or scores a goal, the entire crowd cheers the words covering Angelo's chest.

And he's dressed his son in it. Tiny tears form in my eyes, but I quickly blink them away. Yes. Mikah is going to be a great dad. I can imagine his nerves as he dressed Angelo in the outfit, the pride in his eyes when he saw his son wearing his fan-given nickname, and I almost melt into a puddle on his rug.

Angelo cries again and I grab a nearby pacifier before gently brushing it over his lips. According to the note, he ate an hour ago so he shouldn't be hungry. He takes the pacifier and settles back down easily, so I brush my hand over his forehead before stepping back.

This little guy. He's going to have my heart in no time. I need to be careful.

Now that he's happy, I head back to the kitchen. I finish the beef and drain it and I'm adding in cans of tomatoes and tomato paste when Mikah returns.

"It smells delicious out here," he says. His voice startles me, and I fumble with the can opener, dropping it onto the counter.

The noise bounces off the walls and my head whips in Angelo's direction. His arms are in the air, lowering slowly, so I know the noise startled him as well but he's still sleeping.

It takes me a moment to turn and face Mikah and when I do, I realize my first mistake.

I always forget how attractive he is when I'm not in the same room with him. I really need to begin preparing myself for his arrival.

He's thrown on another simple blue T-shirt, this one with a small logo of the Ice Kings on his chest and goodness graciousness, he might be trying to kill me. He's thrown on loose gray sweatpants. Cuffed at the ankles. Slung low on his hips, loose at his thighs, they're my kryptonite. It's difficult to force my gaze away from what I know is not so secretly currently hiding beneath them.

Let's just say the man has *everything* going for him.

"Sorry," I mutter and turn back to the tomato sauce. I scoop out another can of tomatoes and stir. "You startled me."

"You're cooking? I didn't expect that. And you didn't have to clean."

I give him a soft smile, at least one that I hope is soft and friendly and not showing everything I'm currently thinking. Like how much I wish he would have returned wearing nothing.

Now that's a beautiful sight.

"It's only spaghetti, and I just picked up a few things. I thought you could use a good meal. Figure you haven't had much time to sit and eat this weekend."

"Heaven," he groans and heads toward the fridge where he pulls out a bottled water. "Would you like one?"

I take it and chug almost the entire bottle. My throat is still parched. Now he's standing close, inhaling the scent of the spaghetti sauce. His blond hair is longer on top and he has a thin layer of scruff at his jaw. His eyes are blue like the brightest summer's day. So bright I might have to wear sunglasses if I were to ever look at him directly for more than a moment.

And man. *He's so sexy.* My heart jumps and leaps, does a few cartwheels and a back handspring.

"Thank you," he says, turning his head toward me.

I shrug. "It's no big deal." Inside my blood is boiling as much as the sauce. I'm not entirely sure Mikah is good for *my* physical health. Heart palpitations. Sweaty palms. Erratic thoughts. I might be having a stroke.

"It is to me. This weekend has been... painful."

I set the wooden spoon onto the counter and turn to him. "I imagine becoming a father like this isn't easy, but he's fed. You're keeping an eye on him. He's sleeping. He'll adjust."

"You keep saying that like you're so sure of yourself."

His uncertainty makes my heart ache. "Why wouldn't I be?"

CHAPTER NINE

Mikah

SHE LOOKS at me with such wide-eyed innocence it's difficult not to lean forward and kiss her. Which is not like me. I've spent so many years focused solely on hockey and not much else that the reaction I have to this girl I don't really know rattles me.

But I like the sight of her in my kitchen. Her leggings she threw on show off the curve of her hips and plump ass and the tank top does even better things to the top half of her body.

Still, she's so beautiful, and the confidence she has in me makes me never want to disappoint her.

"It's nice to hear someone so sure of themselves when I have spent days feeling not the same."

I don't like admitting to failing, especially to someone I don't know. Byron told me to be careful with her. Which I understand, but I'm ignoring his advice. He and Hannah get much more attention than I do, and he's had his name on gossip sites more than once claiming inappropriate behavior but it's all trash. I've never seen a man who loves his wife and kids more than he does.

So when he said on Friday he was going to go over and have a few words with Paisley, I stepped in and stopped him. He'd scare the girl away. When Hannah returned, she was full of uncontrollable laughter, saying I had nothing to worry about. When she repeated to us her conversation, she had tears in her eyes when she explained how confused Paisley had looked at the mention of our team name.

Not a fan of sports or hockey.

What would life be like without it? It's a concept I don't understand, but there's something appealing to that too.

Yes, I am ignoring Byron's grumpy advice.

"How is he sleeping?" She sets down the wooden spoon and rests her backside against my counter.

Shame, because I really like looking at that part of her. Fortunately for me, the front side is even more impressive. Large breasts I imagine spilling from my hands. Trim waist. Beautiful, plump and pink lips. I'm so transfixed on this beautiful creature it takes me a minute to answer. Let me just pull my tongue back into my mouth so I don't drool all over my floor first.

What'd she ask about? Sleeping. Us? Ha. No. She's talking about the baby. Right. "Four hours at a stretch at night."

"Well that's good. Really."

"It doesn't feel good. He makes these noises and I'm waking up every time."

She laughs quietly and her smile grows. "He'll grow and that will get longer and you'll get used to the noises. Is he in your room?"

"For now. Hannah and Byron ordered a bunch of furniture that will be delivered this week sometime. I have a tiny…" My brows pucker as I try to think of the word.

"Bassinet?"

"Yes, that small bed. He's in that."

I don't know what else to say. I don't want to tell her the shower she gave me time to take was my first one in days. I feel like a new man in clean clothes. I'm not used to talking about Angelo, or how much I like him and want him and how angry I am at Angela. I definitely do not want to talk about how utterly scared I am to leave him. What do I do with training? With traveling during the season?

Tomorrow, I have to call the nanny service Hannah gave me so I can start to get things figured out.

My eyes slide to Angelo, sleeping peacefully. The scent of the spaghetti sauce Paisley is cooking is incredible. For the first time in days, a tightness in my chest releases.

I like this. Her in my home, us both smiling at Angelo as he sleeps.

Before my mind can run away with stupidity, I change the subject.

"So, you know what I do. What do you do for work?"

This is a nice building. I can only afford it because of my last contract I re-negotiated and the growing interest in hockey in Charlotte. It helps we've made the playoffs the last three years in a row, and two years ago won the Stanley Cup Championship.

"I'm in graduate school getting my Master's in Education." As she speaks, she's turned, stirring the sauce and she opens a cupboard which is filled with spices. It must be woman's intuition that tells her where all of my things are because she's as comfortable as cooking in here as I am.

"Graduate school?"

My look must not hide my surprise because she laughs

again. She does it so easily. All the time. Sometimes when I laugh, I surprise myself with the sound.

She gives the sauce another quick stir before running her finger along the spoon and tasting it. I get stuck on watching her lick the taste off her finger. A low hum falls from her pink lips that shoots straight to my dick. I clear my throat and get her attention, realizing I'm only half-listening as she starts talking. I can't wipe away the vision of her lips wrapped around something else.

Damn. I've never been a guy to think with my dick as my teammates say it, but I definitely understand what it means now.

"My uncle owns my condo. He's on a three-year arrangement out of the country for his work so when he heard I was accepted into the grad school at NCU, he asked if I wanted to live in it while he's gone. That way he didn't have to worry about selling it or renting."

"You must be close with your family."

"Yeah. I don't have a lot and my parents live a couple hours away, but we're close."

She says nothing else and I have so many more questions. It's not like me to care so much or want to know so much but I'm intrigued by her. And it has more to do with her showing up at my door with a baby in her arms.

"My family is in Denmark." She hasn't asked, but I want her to know about me too. She hasn't even said anything about the team. Or what position I play. And I'm not sure if I like her disinterest or if it's killing me. There's a stigma that comes with being a professional athlete. There's the idea that all the guys only think of how often we can get our sticks wet off the ice as often as possible. In a much larger truth, the guys who play on my team and most are *good* guys. There's always an asshole or three on every team, but most of the guys I know want the wife and family. They go to church. They volunteer because they *want* to give back, not because they're forced to for their image. They are faithful. And *good*.

Paisley might not have much knowledge of sports, but I can't imagine she doesn't have some idea of what she thinks a player is.

"Are you close with them?" she asks and it's almost hesitant. Her bottle of water is gone and I almost offer her another one when she helps herself.

"No." I don't mind admitting it either. My father and I haven't spoken since the last playoff game in the spring when we lost. I missed three shots on goal and it wasn't my best game. He made sure to call to let me know he watched it and to repeat what I already knew. "My father is not a nice man, at least not to me. He pushed too hard and nothing was ever good enough. I send them money because if I don't, he will call and remind me that I wouldn't have so much if it wasn't for him."

Her lips part and her skin pales. She's tan but that vanishes as she licks her bottom lip. "That's, well, that's horrible."

"He made me the player I was, and then I became better than he ever was. I think, although he likes that I'm good enough to play in the pros here, he also hates I'm better than him. That he didn't get the chance."

Her fingers strum on the counter. I can almost see the fight in her eyes. Does she ask me about hockey or not?

"That's too bad. Parents should always support their children." She says it quietly, and I can tell it truly bothers her.

I open my mouth to reassure her I'm used to it. I've had

three years of growing up without him around. To me, my father is nothing more than a yearly bill I pay.

Before I can, Angelo lets out a loud squawk that tells me he's had it with sleeping and swinging.

We both move to him, like we're instinctively prepared to get him first, but I beat Paisley. She steps back, chuckling, and I smile at her as I bend down to undo the straps across his small chest.

"Go ahead," she says, waving her hand at Angelo and stepping back. "I should let you handle him, right?"

I take him out slowly and pick up the pacifier he spit out. He takes it again and I grab one of the blankets she threw over the couch so I can wrap him as I hold him.

"You're getting good at that." Her smile is soft and she hasn't moved far, like she wants to get her hands on him, and I like that.

She likes him.

"He likes to be held. A lot."

"Babies do." She laughs and she picks up the carrier I've completely forgotten about. It's the entire reason why I went to get her earlier. "Should we figure out how to do this?"

"Yes." As soon as I say it though, Angelo's face turns purple and his whole body tenses. I look down at him, grimacing. I've learned quickly what this means. "Maybe in a minute."

I wait until he's done filling his diaper and I'm rewarded with the stench of him and a smile that is so wide he drops his pacifier from his mouth.

Man, this kid can take a dump that'll clear the room.

"Men," she says, "you're all the same, thinking pooping is funny."

I must be smiling at him again. In addition to lack of

sleep, my cheeks hurt. I think I've smiled more this weekend than I've smiled in years. "What's not funny about it?"

She's laughing and reaching for him like she can't wait to get her hands on him. "I can change him."

"I will let you. Happily." She takes him from me and goes to the corner of the living room where I have stacked everything.

Hannah and Byron went wild on Friday night. As soon as I explained what was going on, Hannah had my laptop in her lap, Target pulled up on the screen. She clicked so fast on my keyboard I was certain smoke would come from it. She didn't stop until she snapped her fingers at me and demanded my credit card. I was in such a fog I handed it over without question.

She is a woman who knows exactly what she wants and what she's doing with babies. Who am I to question?

Two hours later, whatever she ordered was ready for pickup and Byron went to get it, leaving me with Hannah while she so gently and quietly and easily explained and taught me how to do simple things like how to change and feed Angelo.

The rocking him I picked up from Paisley although my hips don't sway as nicely as hers do. And it's amazing she does it even on the short walk to where I have his things stacked.

"Can I do anything?"

She smiles at me over her shoulder. "Stir the sauce and turn down the heat? It will have to simmer for awhile." Her brows pucker as she bends down and grabs a carton of wipes and a fresh diaper. "Is that okay? If I stay and eat, too?"

It's cute she thought of preparing an entire meal for me

and assumed herself in it without asking. "You're welcome to stay as long as you want."

Paisley's gaze softens and her lips part. I see a hint of her tongue as she runs it along her lip before she turns back to the task of cleaning up Angelo. I've surprised her. I hope she understands I mean it, and not only because I'm still scared of being around Angelo alone.

I mean it because I want to get to know Paisley more. See if there's anything between us more than me thinking she's beautiful.

CHAPTER TEN

Paisley

MY FOCUS IS LASERED in on a squirming Angelo. He kicks and wiggles while I wrestle him to get the diaper on him. Perhaps cooking a meal that will take an hour to make wasn't the smartest decision. Now I feel like a jerk, essentially inviting myself into Mikah's home.

He doesn't seem to mind, but he's probably lonely for company. It's best if I keep my head down, keep things cordial between Mikah and I, and focus on my education and degree.

Unfortunately, keeping my head down and doing the *right* or *best* thing doesn't sound like any fun. I like this guy. I like how sweet he is with Angelo and every time he smiles down at this cute little guy, my heart squeezes.

Mikah has a neon sign hanging over his head blinking DANGEROUS in all capitals.

The exact thing I'm attracted to.

Fight against it this time.

It will probably help the fight if I stop thinking about how good looking he is.

"Have you bathed him?" I ask, turning. His gaze darts from somewhere south of my waist to my eyes. Was he looking at my ass? The part of me interested in him wants to smile, maybe shake my hips a bit to check.

Not smart, girl. Not smart.

I shush my inner and silent conscience. She makes too much sense. Sometimes she also sounds like my overprotective but loving father.

"Uh." He scratches his fingers against the scruff of his jaw. "Hannah bought me a bathtub, I think it's somewhere."

"Scared to do it by yourself?"

He doesn't hesitate. "Very much so."

"I can teach you. After dinner, maybe?"

"I will take you up on all of it, the dinner and bath and teaching me how to use that thing." He points toward the carrier again and since Angelo is clean and currently happy it's a good time.

"Let's start with that." I set Angelo in the swing and strap him in.

When I'm ready, Mikah already has it in his hands. His thick blond brows are pulled close together, lips in a pout. "It doesn't look like it should be so difficult."

I take it from him and finger the straps to first make sure they're not twisted. I won't fully know until it's on him but everything looks good. The baby blue and white plaid on that thick strap that will go around his waist makes me smile. I peek up at him, stunned to find his eyes on me, intense and unwavering. Perhaps questioning what in the heck I'm doing.

"To be honest, I've never used one of these but we're both smart enough to figure it out together, right?"

"Let's hope so." He cracks a small smile.

God. He's so much more beautiful up close, it unsettles me.

"Think of it as a backward book bag. And slide your arms through this part."

I hold it up to show him and he does what I'm suggesting, wiggling his broad shoulders through the small openings. It doesn't take me long at all to figure out what is making it so difficult.

A laugh bubbles in my throat and comes out in a choking sound.

"What?" He twists, but my hands are on his shoulders. "What's so funny?"

"Hold still." I'm still laughing. The problem is he simply didn't make the shoulder straps longer and he's been trying to shove his arms through holes the size meant for arms the size of mine when his are four times larger. "Let me loosen these straps here."

"I did that."

"Not enough." I snort. It can't be helped. Does he not realize how *big* he is? And hard? And warm? Heat from him radiates through his shirt to my fingertips while I do my best to avoid touching him, but it can't be helped.

My fingers sizzle with the energy he puts off and when the clasp on the strap sticks, I press my hand to his shoulder, curve around the breadth of him and freeze.

He smells so good. Fresh like soap and a hint of cologne, most likely his body wash. I barely come up to his shoulder and when he shifts a bit, the tips of his hair brush my fingers that are doing more than sizzling.

There's a current coursing through me, straight from the apex of my thighs to my skin pressed to his.

"Are you okay?"

If by okay he means am I ready to jump him and climb him like a tree and slam my mouth to his then *yup. Totally okay.*

Another hard tug on the clasp loosens the strap that had bent but I'm able to quickly adjust his right side. I do the same to the other, this time careful not to touch him.

I might combust from heat and lust if I get my hands on him again.

"Here. Take this." My voice sounds gritty and I clear my throat. I hold out another clasp that will wrap around his waist. "I think once you get the shoulders on, you tighten this one so this big strap on your lower back evens out the weight."

"All right. So, I slide him in here."

The actual fabric that will hold Angelo is clipped together and I can see why he's confused.

"No." I slide to his front and reach up. "There are clips at the top and bottom. Undo the top ones and the holder part will fall down. Then we can slide his legs in, lift every-thing and clip it back in place."

I focus on the carrier. The reaction I'm experiencing being so close to Mikah might scare him away. Heck, it's freaking *me* out. He's everything wrong for me wrapped up in the most tempting, beautiful package. I've never excelled in self-control.

He reaches for the clips at his chest where I've indi-cated and at the last second, a blast of heat and strength is wrapped around my wrist.

"Paisley."

Oh goodness. I'm losing it and he's noticing.

"Yeah?" Even his feet are pretty. I know this because they're bare, peeking out from those sweatpants tight at his ankles. And I know this because I'm staring at them.

I think his *feet* are hot. What is wrong with me?

"Look at me."

I know what he'll see if I do. Skin flushed like I've just gone running. Eyes wide. Pupils dilated. He'll see the throb of my pulse at the base of my throat which is going erratic.

All because of being close to him. I should definitely call the doctor. Is there a hot guy syndrome with symptoms that mirror a stroke? I really need to look into it.

"I'll get Angelo. You work on those clips—"

"Look at me," he repeats himself. This time deeper. Slower. There's a rumble in his voice that forces me to comply.

"What?" I peek up and blink quickly. Perhaps it'll wash away the desire I'm one hundred percent certain is plastered on my face.

And yet... *shit.*

I see the same thing on him. His jaw is hard. Cheekbones sharp in a totally sexy way. His lips are pressed into a firm line and that beautiful nose of his that is surprisingly straight given his career, has nostrils which are flared.

His chest heaves and he swallows. I need to step back. Put space between us... between whatever *this* crazy, swirling sudden heat is. My lips part. My mouth is dry as the summer heat in Vegas and I lick my lips, seeking moisture.

His blue eyes, darkening, drop to my mouth and he heaves another thick breath. "Paisley."

I can't do this. I can't kiss him right now. Or ever. It's not smart.

I tug my hand from his grip and rub where he's branded me with my other hand. "Let's see if Angelo likes this. He'll probably love being held and it'll give you freedom to get other things done."

I'm babbling. I don't care. My voice is higher than normal and faster. It happens when I'm nervous. I unclip Angelo from his swing and am rewarded with a few kicks of his pudgy legs and a toothless big smile.

"Hey cutie," I coo. Yes. I'll focus on the baby. The dinner I must get back to.

There's a salad. Maybe garlic bread. Noodles. Maybe I should let him eat alone. I can eat that frozen meal I still have. Desperate times and all that.

"Hey sweetie. We're going to try something new, okay?" I bounce him a few times and he giggles. I smile wide. Angelo is so darn cute. He's the best distraction. "And you be happy, okay? No crying. You'll love this."

I spin to head back to Mikah, only he's moved in my attempt to flee from him. He's right *here*. The baby carrier slaps my arm holding Angelo, he's so close and my gaze jumps to him.

"Let's try this."

I focus on getting Angelo's legs through the small holes, adjusting the straps when one seems too tight for his thigh and then Mikah and I both fold up the back that will support him.

"I've got it now."

"Good." I step back, staying close in case he fumbles, but he doesn't. His large hands with veins on the back and strong fingers somehow move with ease and no visible nerves as he clips the top ones back together.

"You can adjust these straps on him as he grows to give him more room. The ones at your back were too small."

"Of course." His hand brushes the top of Angelo's head. So softly. Not at all as firm as he held me.

Like I need the reminder. I still feel him on my skin.

Yes, I've been branded by a simple touch. Not good.

I hurry to the kitchen, trying to ignore Mikah and Angelo, but the sound of Mikah murmuring to his son is too precious to block out. *His son.*

Good grief. He has a baby. For a moment my imagination runs away with me. To us on a date. Hiring babysitters. Being called back home early because Angelo is sick. A life change. A drastic one.

I still like to drink too much and stay out too late and I *like* dating.

I'm twenty-two years old. I'm not ready to settle down. Have a baby. Or be with a man with a baby.

And what happens when he travels? I imagine it being like a single parent during the season.

All the cons crush down on me, wiping out the physical desire for Mikah in an instant.

My imagination is psychotic. I have us touching and then jumping straight to life-changing drama.

Pack away your crazy, Paisley.

Friends. I can give him friends. It's all we should be.

I am actually thinking of listening to the voice of reason in my brain.

Huh. I suppose there's a first time for everything.

CHAPTER ELEVEN

Mikah

SOMETHING CHANGED. As soon as I touched her, I felt it. That connection. More intense than any spark I've ever felt unless I'm lacing up skates and going through my pre-game rituals. More fiery than the thrill of scoring a goal, beating a competitor for the puck on a breakaway.

When I touched Paisley earlier, it felt like waking up from a dream. Seeing everything for the first time.

I saw a future I want. A woman at my side. Helping me. Supporting her. I saw a woman who has such a big heart she's willing to drop her life to not only help, but cook a meal for a practical stranger. And yet it disappeared once I had Angelo in the carrier.

Angelo is getting drowsy in the carrier, his eyes slowly closing before widening. Repeat. I keep my rhythm of bounce, bounce, step until he becomes limp in the carrier. I've learned if I move him too quickly after he falls asleep he wakes right back up.

Paisley is draining the hot water from the noodles and the scent of garlic bread is coming from the oven.

My stomach rumbles and I groan at the smell.

"This is going to be the best meal I've ever had."

"You say that because you haven't eaten in two days."

She smirks at me and it's the first time since she *ran* from me in the living room she's even looked at me.

"True."

She grins before setting the strainer over the hot pot. "As soon as the bread is done, you can eat."

"We." I've been suspecting she's going to try to leave as soon as she can.

But she wants to stay. Otherwise she wouldn't have made such a huge salad and so much bread that I could feed my team.

Something is working in her eyes, but it's me who should be scared. It's me who should push her away.

I will not do that.

I like the way my body responds to her too much.

When I was with Angela that weekend, it was for experience. Sure, she's a beautiful woman and I had no problem being attracted to her. But it was mechanics. Finally having sex, learning, practice.

We both knew the score.

I've never touched a woman and had such a heat shoot straight to my groin before.

I want Paisley.

So we'll start with dinner.

"I should go." She glances at the door, and the corner of her lip disappears between her teeth. "I have class tomorrow."

"You said you'd help teach me to bathe Angelo." I'll use him if I have to. I doubt she'll say no to him.

She glances at me and I swear I hear her think. Perhaps she knows what I'm doing.

"Please," I say. I keep my distance as much as I can. "You cooked this meal. Sit with me, eat, and if you can help with Angelo I would be grateful. I like your company."

It's not much. I'm not smooth with women. Or I have never tried to be. The language difference and accent makes it difficult to *feel* smooth. I still screw up slang sometimes. Or use the wrong word. I feel more likely to be laughed at hitting on a beautiful woman I'm attracted to than getting her attention in a better way. I have not yet had those nerves with Paisley.

Her gentle presence makes it easy to be comfortable and myself.

"Okay."

Since Angelo is still asleep, I go to my room where I unclip everything the opposite way we put him in. He stays asleep when I put him in the small bed.

Success. I've done this. I'm learning quickly.

I brush my finger across his forehead and hold my breath while he squirms. He settles and at the last second, I remember to grab the baby monitor from the nightstand and turn on the one that stays on my nightstand.

Back in the kitchen, Paisley has two settings placed at the table, across from each other. I drag one of the placemats to the end of the table so I can sit closer to her and meet her at the island where all the food is set up.

My stomach rumbles again and Paisley giggles.

"My stomach already loves what you've made."

"You should be grateful. This is one of the few things I can make decently."

"You don't cook?"

"Well, I try, but let's just say I know how to confidently

use a fire extinguisher." She winks at me. She can easily make fun of herself in a way that's light and fun. Shrugging, she says, "Mostly, I think cooking for one seems like a hassle. Like there will always be leftovers for days."

"You did make enough to feed a family," I tease and I hope the tone is right.

She glances at the food spread all over my island. Her eyes turn as large as supper plates as she takes in the overflowing bowl of bread she's not only cooked but cut and set up like we're hosting a party. Or she's trying to impress.

"I guess I did." She shrugs a shoulder and slides down, filling her plate with food and a bowl for the salad. I do the same, my helpings twice as much as hers and that's only because it's all the plate can hold. I meet her at the table, aware she's scooted away from where I moved the other placemat.

It's still better than being across from her.

"Damn." I was right before. I groan as the first taste of spaghetti hits my mouth. Garlic. Spices. The sauce is thick and flavorful. "God. This is incredible."

She shoots me a glance and tucks back into her own dish. "Thank you."

I'm so hungry, I shove the food into my mouth so fast I probably look like a slob. I don't care. I'm starving and this is just what I need. Paisley doesn't seem concerned at all about the lack of conversation. She's staring out the window, eating almost as fast as me.

I imagine as soon as we're done, she will bathe Angelo and take off before I can thank her.

Only I don't have enough experience—or *game* as my teammates call it—to get her to stay.

I don't know why she moved away from me so quickly but I know she liked it when I touched her.

And almost kissed her. I bet her pink lips will be soft. They're round, her bottom more full. And I can't help but watch her swallow. The slide of her throat. Every time she wraps her lips around her fork I start thinking of other things she can do with her mouth.

If it makes me a jerk, I'm not sure I care.

As soon as I had that weekend with Angela, everything changed. I *loved* sex. Loved running my hand over a woman's breasts, the punch of heat when I brushed her slick center. Discovering how I could get nipples to harden and then what I can do with my tongue to get Angela's hips to buck against my mouth was like solving a puzzle. And all women are different. The only reason I haven't done more is because I don't want weekend hook-ups. I get enough attention walking down the sidewalk or when I'm out to eat. The gaping, wide-eyed looks. It's only cute if they're kids doing the gaping. But women?

I have never liked the attention from them. That gleam of pursuit for a goal and not a person makes my skin itch.

Yet, here I am with Paisley who didn't know who I was until a couple days ago and I can barely get her to look at me.

I'm not sure which is worse.

"HE'S SO SLIPPERY. I feel like I will drop him!"

Next to me, Paisley giggles. She pours warm water over Angelo's head as he turns toward it.

Bonus to having her teach me how to bathe him, she has to be close to me. Her arm keeps brushing mine. I want to have her always help me with bath time.

It's a weird kink, maybe. Planning a baby's bath only to

be with a woman. But I like when she's close to me, teaching me, her soft hand on my back, encouraging me. Granted, that happened once and she yanked her hand away as fast as she could, but still. After avoiding me for most of the dinner and then insisting on cleaning up while Angelo woke up mad and angry and starving, she willingly touched me.

As soon as the kitchen was cleaned, she found the baby bathtub in the hallway bathroom and set it up next to the kitchen sink with a huge pile of towels and bottle of baby wash.

"Hannah really thought of everything," she said, smiling at pale blue towels and one that looks like a monkey at one corner for Angelo's head. Who knew they made such silly things?

As I burped Angelo, she warmed the water and filled the tub with only a few inches of water. I stripped him down and as soon as I set him in the water, his entire body seemed to melt right into the chair while I held the back of his head.

Now, he's slippery as a worm and while Paisley washes and rinses his hair, I keep scooping warm water on his tummy so he doesn't get cold. His little toes look a bit blue and I realize it's the first time I've simply *stared* at him.

His rounded belly. The chunk at his thighs. I've been so scared and stressed all weekend, I've focused on keeping him alive instead of focusing on him.

And now that I can, with Paisley cooing at him and him being so much happier, something wet and burning pricks at my eyes.

"He's so perfect." I clear my throat. "Isn't he?"

I can't bring myself to look at Paisley. She's frozen, mid-pour to get the last of the soap out of his hair and then we're done.

Seeing me cry isn't going to help anything.

"Have you decided what you're going to do with him?" she asks, and her voice has gone soft. Almost worried. Possibly sad.

"I'll keep him."

"I didn't mean you wouldn't. I meant, have you thought about what happens when you go to work? Or... travel?"

She says the word like it's a bad thing. Like she doesn't *like* the fact I play hockey.

I'm not sure what to do with the tone in her voice. I could be misunderstanding.

"Hannah gave me the name of a place. Um. Like a babysitter? Au pair?"

"Nanny is more common than au pair here, but that's a good idea."

"Right. Nanny service. She said she used it when she was working when they had their first kid. I plan on calling them tomorrow."

Angelo's gummy mouth is now chattering, so Paisley reaches for the towel with the strange corner.

"Hold him up."

I do and she slides the corner over his head. It falls down over his eyes and I'm holding him with my arms out, his legs kicking and he gets more unhappy by the second until she wraps the towel around him and then another.

"There you go."

I kiss his cheek and hold him tight to me. I need to change my clothes again. So does Paisley. We've both been splashed and have spilled water on ourselves, but I did it.

With help, but it doesn't seem too hard by myself, either.

"There." She slides her hand down Angelo's back, smiling at him. She must love babies because she always gets this soft and sappy tone in her voice when she looks at him. "I can change him?"

"I'll clean up." She takes him from me, but for the first time, I'm almost reluctant to let him go. But it's Paisley, it's not like she doesn't know what she's doing.

But still. I have a few days off Coach insisted I take, but now I have to consider leaving him for hours at a time? With a stranger?

My teeth grind together while I clean out the bathtub and put the unused towels and baby soap away. By the time I'm done, Paisley has Angelo dressed in what I now know is called a sleeper. He's sucking on his pacifier and he looks perfect in her arms, beneath a thicker blanket, tucked close to her boob.

"So, you'll hire a nanny?"

I don't know if she realizes she always does that swaying bounce move when she holds him, but I like seeing it every time.

"I think so." I brush my hand through my hair. Everything on me is wet, but if I leave to change, I have a feeling I'll come out to a missing Paisley. "It's probably best. I have room for someone to sleep in and stay here when I travel. And I'll have long days, a weird schedule during the season."

"Having him be here in his own home will be good for him."

"Yes? You think?" I think so too. It's nice to confirm I'm doing something right. "Good. This week I have to call them. My lawyer is figuring out when I can take a blood test. And then we'll have to find his mom."

My jaw is in danger of snapping. Every time I think of

Angela and everything she kept from me, I want to punch a wall. But I need good hands for my season.

"Do you... do you have doubts?"

Doubts? I have too many to list. The top of which is if I'm capable of this. I'm twenty-three years old. An adult in the eyes of the world and a star in the hockey world.

But I still like to hang out alone and stay up too late playing my Playstation that sometimes it also feels like I'm only pretending to be grown up.

And now to be in charge of a baby? Yes, I have too many doubts.

But is Angela a *liar?*

"I don't think so. Angela, his mom, well, some guys on the team know her. I do not think she'd make this up. And..." I swallow my thoughts. Do I want her to know she's the only woman I've been with?

A snickering sound comes from her and she looks like she's holding back a laugh.

"What?"

"Nothing." She waves her hand in the air but she seems to be laughing harder. "It's just... well, your names and his. I mean, it sort of pisses me off she clearly named her son after her and then left him. But you two... together..."

"Me and Angela?"

"No. You and Angelo. The names fit."

"I don't... I don't understand."

Her smile grows as she notices my confusion and she lets out a giggle. "Well, your names. They sound like they go together. Like the artist. The painter? Michelangelo? That's you two when you put them together. Mikah-Angelo."

She laughs softly again and the sweet sound is contagious because I find myself laughing as well. "I hadn't thought of that."

"It's cute." She presses her hand gently to the side of Angelo's face, running a finger along his brow. I've seen her do this before. She's very tender. "I like it. And him."

She doesn't mention me. But her eyes flutter to me and she quickly looks away.

I want her to know even if she thinks it's strange.

"Angela is the only woman I've been with, um... have had sex with."

It's a bomb she doesn't see coming and her green eyes flash.

"My birthday last year." I clear my throat again. It's suddenly gone dry and the longer she goes without saying anything, the more heat creeps up my neck.

"Well, wow. I suppose then from your side that would take away any doubts about him being yours."

"He's mine."

Somehow, I know it. I might not be bonded to him yet and he is still a stranger. But I see me in him and in the blond fuzz on his head.

"My life has been hockey," I tell her, because I want her to get it. I want her to know everything. "I worked hard all my life to get to the NHL in America. It was my father's goal for me before it was ever mine and I never had time for anything else, or maybe it's more correct to say I wasn't given time for anything else."

Her eyes soften and everything about her looks sad.

"Have you told your parents yet?"

"No. My father will be angry and my mom will take his side. I'll let them know eventually. But not until everything else is settled." I haven't seen them since I moved here. I've had no desire to return to Denmark and I have not offered to fly them out. They could come if they wanted to with the money I send them, but they won't.

In my arms, Angelo has fallen asleep. My clothes are still damp but I don't want this to end.

"I should get going. I have early class tomorrow."

It's an excuse. I don't know if I've scared her away by telling her I don't have much experience, but I hope not.

She moves to step around me and there isn't much space between her and the counter. I slide out my arm, stopping her, and my hand settles on her hip.

I have to look down at her, she's so much shorter than me, and her head tilts back, eyes meeting mine. She doesn't have the look of someone turned off by what I've said to her. She's guarded, but her cheeks are pink.

Yes. I think she likes it when I touch her as much as I do.

"Thank you, for dinner and your company and your help. It's your company I like the most, though. Please, come over anytime."

Her body relaxes, leans into me. And it's the same sensation I felt earlier when I held her. Heat swirls and pulses and even though there's a baby in my arms I still want to pull her to me and do *more*.

"Mikah," she whispers my name like a warning. "This... I don't know... I think friends is good for us. You know? With you... Angelo... we're both busy."

"We can start with friends."

But I'll push for more. Another night. Soon.

CHAPTER TWELVE

Paisley

"HEY MAGGIE? YOU LIKE SPORTS, RIGHT?"

I can't believe I'm asking this. I can't get Mikah out of my mind. It's Wednesday and Maggie and I are in a study in the room in the library. We're supposed to be focused on researching teaching techniques for children who have been diagnosed with disorders such as ADHD and ADD and the differences of what will help both learn most effectively.

We've been friends since our first year in college. Her attire when she isn't being a teacher assistant is usually leggings or shorts and a wide variety of tank tops and sweat-shirts showing off sports teams like the Raleigh Rough Riders, the professional football team in North Carolina.

But she's also talked about going to basketball games and she's excited about the new professional soccer franchise coming soon to Charlotte.

I know all this because Maggie talks. A lot.

"What? You know I do. Why?" Her question is barely a mumble and she doesn't bother looking up from her computer screen. Something I should be more focused on.

I shouldn't have started this conversation, but I can't stop thinking about it.

About Mikah.

About one of the last things he said to me. *We can start with friends.*

Like he wants more. I flew out of his condo so quickly it's a wonder I didn't slam through the wall on my way out, leaving a hole in the shape of my body.

He's clearly not thinking straight what with the lack of sleep and major life shift he's experiencing. We barely know each other!

But his touch.

I shiver at the memory of his arm across my stomach, hand falling to my hip, his thumb that brushed against my side through my shirt.

"No reason," I mutter. I need to kick him out of my mind. It's best for everyone.

"Oh, no no no." She swivels her chair and rolls it toward me, feet pushing her forward. She looks ridiculous and every time she jolts forward in her chair, her dark brown hair wrapped in a thick messy bun on the top of her head wobbles. "You're asking for a reason and you've *never* asked about sports. We're talking about this. What's going on?"

She's never mentioned hockey. Maybe she doesn't like it. Maybe she doesn't know anything.

"Do you like hockey?"

My mouth needs to sync up with my brain. Stat. Why am I continuing this? I have work to do. So does she.

"I mean, it's okay. I *love* it during the playoffs when it's really intense, and I like watching it live. Asher gets tickets through his company a few times a year and we can watch from a suite which makes it that much cooler. And when they fight on the ice? That's so sexy."

"They fight?" I try to imagine Mikah throwing a punch. I can't do it. He's so quiet and sweet. Sexy and built, sure, but his personality doesn't seem like someone who can lose their cool.

Now, the guy... Byron who came to his house last Friday? Him I can see fighting for fun.

"Yes. And it's *awesome*." Maggie is nuts. She has to be. "But for the most part, I spend most of the fall watching football. Once that's done though, I follow hockey. Why?"

"I finally met my neighbor."

"The hot one?" She leans forward, hands curl around the edge of the chair like she's about ready to jump out of it.

It's possible I've mentioned my obsession with Mikah a time or twenty, and now I'm wishing I hadn't because understanding dawns in her dark brown eyes.

"Are you telling me your hottie neighbor is a *hockey* player? For who?"

"Ice Kings," I mutter. Now I wish I wouldn't have brought it up. I can't tell her *how* I met Mikah. I promised I wouldn't say anything and even if I trust Maggie, I don't like hiding information.

I've teased her before that she should have had a career in journalism with as much as she loves to dig into other people's business.

Case and point... she's already jumped out of her chair and she's at my desk.

"Who. Who is he? I don't follow it closely enough to know the names or anything, well, except for the Taylors but everyone in hockey knows Jude and Jason and their brothers. Their family is a legend in the game."

I'm lost as she babbles. I have no clue who she's talking about, but she shoves me out of the way and wiggles my mouse hooked up to my laptop.

"Who's the guy?"

"Mikah Lutzgo." I'm still mumbling and strangely warm. It's the sun outside burning me up. It has to be.

"Oh, I've heard that name. He's good. Young, right?"

"Our age."

"Wow." Her eyes pop open and she types in his name and then she falls silent.

She Googles his name and clicks on the images tab and suddenly my screen is filled with images of the guy I've spent *days* thinking about. Blond hair. Strong chin and cheekbones. Eyes narrowed in concentration through the face mask. My mouth waters. He looks larger in his gear, but I've seen him without anything on at all.

Stop thinking about Mikah naked!

It's pointless to yell at myself. I can't stop picturing that first glance of him. Or how he looks in gray sweats after they're wet from giving Angelo a bath.

"Holy cow. You weren't kidding, he's hot." She grins down at me and I swear she's blushing. "Like mega hot. And this is your neighbor? Did you finally get the guts to go say hi or something?"

Something like that.

"We met in the hall. Said hello, started talking."

"You *talked* to him?"

"A little. Over the weekend." And then cooked him dinner, had a drink, fantasized about him, dreamt of him... wanted to go say hello a dozen other times. It's possible my stalker status should be upgraded to obsession.

"And you haven't said anything until now?" Her voice is pitching higher and then she frowns. "Listen, Paisley. This is serious girl code you're breaking here. You meet the hot guy you've gaped over for months and you call your friend." She shoves her thumb into her own chest and continues. "You *talk* to the hottie, you call your friend. You find out he's a professional athlete.. you call. Your. Friend. Capiche?"

She's leaning close to me, serious as stone. It's too bad she's so cute with her squished up faux-angry face. It's difficult not to laugh at her.

"Step back. I don't need to smell your lunch."

She huffs but listens. "So tell me everything. Every single thing."

She's a dog with a bone and won't stop so I tell her about meeting him in the hall on Friday and stopping by his place on Sunday. I don't like lying, or hiding information, so there isn't much I say just that we hung out for a little bit and talked.

She squeals with glee, insists he's interested in me, and I don't know how she gathers that since I didn't tell Maggie anything about what he actually said to me.

By the time I enter my building later, my carryout dinner from Chipotle I stopped and grabbed on the way in my hand, I'm halfway through talking myself out of stopping by his place.

And the reasons why I should stay away are fleeting.

THE ELEVATOR DOORS start to close and then a hand is right there, stopping them. To my surprise, Hannah scoots around the corner, two kids in tow, and Byron follows.

"Paisley!" She smiles but it falls relatively quickly. Perhaps because I'm the unknown who might try to make a few bucks selling what I know of Mikah to some asshole on Twitter. As if. "How are you? Having a good week?"

"Um. Yes. It's okay. How are y'all?"

She grins down at her kids, placing a hand on the top of each one, a boy and a girl. "Crazy as always. These are my hooligans, Silas and Samantha, but we call her Sammy."

"Hey guys." Two little blond-haired, blue-eyed beauties grin shyly up at me before looking to their dad.

"Dad! I want to hold the baby," Sammy shouts.

"No! I get to. I'm older." Silas makes an angry face and throws his arms across his chest.

"Wait your turn or you won't get to hold him at all. You know your mom will hog him all night."

I'm smiling at their conversation and Hannah shrugs. "What can I say? Babies just do something to me."

Byron grumbles something I don't understand but Hannah slaps his chest. "Like you mind."

Based on the look he gives her, something that heats me straight to my toes, regardless I didn't hear what he said, I have a very clear understanding of what *babies* do to Hannah.

Which means I'm changing the subject. Pronto. "Y'all here to see Mikah and Angelo I take it?"

"Yep. Word has gotten out to the team, so the girlfriends and I decided we're bombarding his place to get our snuggles in. Guys are coming, too. You should stop by. Mikah would probably love to see you again."

She gives me a look that makes me fight against fidgeting and pummeling her with curiosity.

Did he tell her about Sunday?

"Calm down, babe. You're scaring the girl." Byron's not wrong.

Hannah's sweet but I can already tell her personality is like a powerful tornado, whipping everyone up in her orbit.

"It's okay," I say. "And that's sweet of you to offer, but I need to eat dinner and get some work done."

"Oh that's okay." She reaches down and whisks my Chipotle bag out of my grip. Chips crunch from her grip that has me cringing.

Chipotle chips are *life*.

"Mikah said he's ordering pizza and wings for everyone. You can come eat with us. At least stay for awhile, maybe a drink and then you can get to work. We'll probably be too loud anyway for you to get much done."

Since she's holding my dinner hostage, I don't really suppose I can argue with her.

I'm still not sure I can keep up with her. We didn't exactly part as new best friends last weekend.

"Um."

"Better drop it," Byron says. He shakes his head like he's annoyed with his wife, but his smile says he's anything but. "She'll get her way eventually. Usually does."

I hold up my lunch bag and messenger bag. "Can I at least drop this off at my place first?"

Hannah nods, all serious. "I'll allow it."

"Kind of you."

She laughs and tosses an arm around me. "It'll be fun. And you'll get to see Angelo again."

She's tempting me, and teasing. It's weird how she can do both so easily like we've known each other longer than a five-minute interaction in which she essentially stopped by to see if I would sell gossip to blogs or whatnot. But when she's not staring me down like there's a possibility I could be chewed gum on the bottom of her shoe, she seems likable. In the same way Maggie is crazy and my other friend Pippa is loyal and nutty.

"Will I get to hold him?"

She shrugs shamelessly. "Maybe."

CHAPTER THIRTEEN

Mikah

MY CONDO IS PACKED with teammates. Sebastian Hendrix and his wife are here. Jude and Jason Taylor are here with Kate, Jude's fiancée. She's currently holding and bouncing Angelo, talking animatedly with Regan. She's the wife of Duke Fletcher, one of our defenseman, almost as big of a guy as Byron, who I'm still waiting to arrive with Hannah and their children. My large sectional couch is heaving from the weight of the rest of my team, all settled back, watching ESPN, talking about the upcoming season with beers in their hands.

It's a night to celebrate.

After calling the nanny service company Hannah recommended last week, my next and first stop was to head to the team's medical clinic. It took me about an hour to figure out how to get Angelo ready to leave the apartment, but I was feeling pretty confident.

Until I got to my Land Rover in the underground

garage and realized the car seat Hannah ordered for me was still in its box upstairs and I remembered her saying something about how to the car seat chair clicks into a base, which I didn't have for the seat Angela left at my door.

I trekked back upstairs and stared at the new car seat still in its box, trying to figure out how in the hell I was going to get everything back downstairs, with Angelo, and not lose my mind.

More than once my gaze flickered to Paisley's apartment, but she'd told me she had school early in the morning, so I doubted she was home.

And I couldn't rely on her for everything. I wanted to get to know her—not treat her like help.

By the time I dug out the car seat and base, shoved straps into the right places on the chair, and re-situated Angelo, he decided that was the perfect time to fill his diaper.

Sweating and frustrated, I'm still pretty sure I wasn't very nice as I grumbled and changed him. Remembered I hadn't grabbed a diaper bag so I did that, and fortunately Hannah had said she'd pre-stocked it with everything but bottles and formula.

So I did that.

And holy crap, if parenting is always this hard I wasn't sure I was capable of any of it.

Still, I forced myself to power through when all I wanted to do was call the team doctor, tell him I'd be in another day. But I really wanted to get the blood test going so I could get my name added to Angelo's birth certificate.

By the time I got the base secured in the car, hopefully doing it correctly, Angelo clicked in and the diaper bag ready to go, he was a screaming, unhappy mess and he cried the entire twenty minutes to the team's practice and medical facility.

Where I'd missed morning workout but arrived at the exact right time for the team to be done.

They lost their minds when I explained what happened. Some died of laughter. Some looked ready to pummel Angela on my behalf, for reasons they didn't explain but I can imagine.

And the others, they looked so damn scared they stepped back five feet as if me simply holding Angelo in their presence was contagious.

It was surprisingly Hendrix who stepped forward and took Angelo's car seat from my arm, telling me he'd watch him while I saw the doctor. He's a good guy, so it didn't surprise me that he offered, but because he doesn't have kids. Still, he unclipped Angelo like he'd done it a thousand times before. He held him with the ease I hold my hockey stick, shooing me into the office.

Overall, my first outing with a baby wasn't the success I hoped for, but we survived.

And I only needed one beer when I got home to wash away the nerves and stress of it all.

Tonight we're celebrating. The girls insisted they had to come see Angelo and my teammates are with them, even the single ones, because as of four o'clock this afternoon, it's official.

I am, with ninety-nine point nine percent certainty, Angelo's father.

I'm not sure how to feel about that except I know when I got the phone call the first thing I wanted to do was go across the hall and tell Paisley.

It's hours later and I *still* want to tell her.

So it's a huge shock to my system, but a complete

welcome surprise, when Hannah and Byron come through my door, Silas and Sammy jumping and shouting with their usual ear-piercing volume leading the way, and Paisley trailing behind them, looking completely uncertain and pale behind them.

"Hey." I go to her first and ignore the choking sound Byron makes as I slap his arm and pass him. "How are you?"

"Um. Well, Hannah stole my dinner in the elevator and insisted I come over tonight."

"She did what?"

"See?" Hannah shoves a bag from Chipotle into my chest and I'm forced to grab it before it falls to the floor. "What luck, huh? We ran into Paisley in the elevator and insisted she has to come and hang out tonight. I said you ordered dinner and she's free to eat hers here. Good idea, right?"

"Um. I don't have to."

Paisley is eyeing the bag in my hands like she's desperate to bolt. I drop it to my side and out of her reach. If she can grab it, she might vanish. I want her here.

"It's a good idea. Come on in." Since I haven't lost all manners, I squeeze Hannah with my other arm. "Good to see you, too."

"Mm-hmm. Congratulations by the way."

"Thank you." My grin is so big it almost splits in two. It's been five days since Angelo appeared and the bonding thing, I worried about over the weekend? That's disappearing.

Now I can't imagine leaving him. Impressively, we've gone for two morning walks and he didn't scream or poop, once. In fact, he seems to love being pushed in the stroller. It's not the kind of exercise I'm used to, but it feels good to know I'm no longer trapped in my home.

I guide Paisley farther inside since her feet are still right in the entryway, keeping her on the far side from her dinner.

"Congratulations?" she asks so quietly I can barely hear her over the noise. Everyone is excited to see Byron apparently. More than a few curious gazes are on Paisley. I ignore them all.

"Yes." I set her takeout dinner onto my kitchen counter, away from the pizza so no one else thinks to eat it. "I had my blood tests done on Monday and results came in today. He's mine."

My chest aches as I say it and my grin is huge. I can feel it hurt my cheeks.

"Wow." Her eyes sparkle and before I can blink, her arms are around me. "That's wonderful. Right? I mean, at least to *know*."

She's hugging me. Silly, how good it makes me feel. I hold her tighter. "I didn't need the test. But it's... well, yes. It's good."

She pulls back but I put pressure on my arm at her lower back, stopping her. "We went for walks this week. And I took him to the team's practice building."

"You did?"

Her pride for me sears a heat to my chest. I like that I can impress her. Perhaps I should be embarrassed but I'm needy for her affection. Her belief and confidence in me. I've never needed it from anyone before. Outside hockey teams, I've never had it before, either.

"That's great, Mikah. Really. And the nanny company?"

"They're coming tomorrow. They want to see my place, meet Angelo and talk to me so they can find the right person. I think, though, that I don't want anyone *living* here."

"They offer that?"

"Yeah. But that seems, weird." I said *no* immediately when they offered that option. Me living alone with a nanny? Awkward. "But I will need someone who can stay when I travel. Or have night games. It's not... the easiest schedule."

"I'm sure they're used to that."

"Let's Go!" I'm jolted out of my focus on Paisley as it sounds like my entire team has shouted the stupid nickname the crowds cheer for me. It makes sense, given my last name. I do not laugh as I look up to find all the men on my team who are here, ten of them, standing by the couch, beers raised.

They do this to me all the time.

Now *this*, this embarrasses me.

"Hey *Let's Go!* When are you going to introduce us all?"

"Never. You are all animals!"

In front of me, Paisley giggles. She flashes me a wink which I return easily.

They throw their heads back and laugh, clink their beers together and I cringe at the thought of the glass cracking and small pieces falling into my rug. Angelo plays there.

"Ignore them," I say to Paisley but she's laughing.

"I think that's impossible. I can handle anything they throw my way, but I think I'll start with saying hello to Angelo." She scans the room and shocker, finds him in Hannah's arms. She takes a step away from me and then, to my surprise, her hand falls to my bicep. "I'm happy for you, Mikah. Make sure no one eats my dinner."

"I will guard it like I guard the puck."

"I have no idea what that means."

She releases her hold on my arm and steps away but before she can get too far, I call to her. "I'll teach you."

She shakes her head, smiling, and I don't know what that means. If she thinks it's ridiculous I would offer, or that I think she might care. My gaze stays on her as she heads toward Hannah. Regan and Katie are still close by and Hannah introduces them to her.

Unsurprisingly, Sebastian's wife, Madison is nowhere near Angelo.

I've long since stopped wondering why the two of them are together. Or at least... why she stays, unless it's because of the money. Sebastian Hendrix is one of the nicest guys I've ever met, and I don't think Madison has a kind bone in her entire body.

At least, I've never seen it.

Not my problem though, and since he loves her, the team doesn't talk about it around him. But in the last few months especially, she seems even meaner, less patient.

I push his problems out of my mind. I have enough of my own to handle.

And yet, I still smile when I see Hannah hand Angelo over to Paisley and as soon as she has him, she sends me a smile from across the room.

Warmth slams into my gut like I've been checked into the boards.

All over a smile.

Fatherhood must be turning me into an emotional sap.

I grab a beer from the fridge and rejoin my team in the living room.

"Who's the pretty girl?" Jason asks. He and his brother Jude are our starting wingers. Their father used to play for the New York Rangers and their older brother did as well until he retired. Jason is almost ten years older than me and a veteran on the team. At thirty-two, he's almost a dinosaur in a game that keeps calling up younger athletes and drafting us before we finish college or recruiting us from the European leagues like they did me.

He is also one of the guys who enjoys attention of puck bunnies, always having fun on and off the road. He's one of the best men I've ever met.

He's still not getting anywhere near Paisley if I can help it.

"Neighbor, and that is all you need to know."

He throws back his head, laughing. "Calm man, I don't steal what's already taken. She's the one who found Angelo?"

I've told them all the entire story although Byron spilled most of it. I don't mind. There are usually no secrets on our team. We're a family, and the Ice Kings are a much better family than my blood one.

"Yes. Paisley. She goes to school here."

"She's sweet. She know you're interested?"

"I think given the way we met that she might be scared of me."

"Nah. She's got baby-lover written all over her. Look."

As if I've stopped looking at her. I understand what he means. She holds Angelo so naturally, he could be hers. She's doing her hip sway bounce move, smiling at some-thing Katie is saying to her. They both laugh, looking down at Angelo sleeping in her arms.

It's a pretty sight, her holding my son so nice.

"I'm not sure how to make a move," I admit and it burns in my throat.

"Oh, Lutzgo." Jason slaps my shoulder, shoving me

forward. At six-one, I'm a tall guy. Jason's bigger and stronger too. He might be a dinosaur in the league, but he still has the strength and speed to beat anyone. "Young grasshopper. Let me teach you everything I know."

"What do grasshoppers have to do with anything?"

CHAPTER FOURTEEN

Paisley

I CAN'T BELIEVE it's ten o'clock and I'm still in Mikah's apartment. At this point, I'm not sure wild horses could ever drag me away from another meeting with his teammates, especially their wives and girlfriends. I've met so many people tonight that most of the guy's names have blended together, but the few women who are here have been fun.

There's Debbie, who arrived later, with her husband whose name I forgot as soon as I met him. And Regan and Katie. Another woman, Madison, I think, convinced her husband to leave shortly after I arrived but I was only introduced to her on their way out. She didn't talk to any of the women for long and I don't think anyone was sad to see her go.

She's apparently not very nice. Not that anyone said much, but what they implied was enough. I get the sense they're being cautious around me, still treating me like someone on the outer edge.

It shouldn't bother me so much especially given I understand. They're not going to gossip about the guys on the team or the women involved with them until they know me.

Hannah and Byron took off with their kids a couple hours ago claiming they had to get the little ones to bed so they weren't too tired for school in the morning.

The longer I stay here, the harder it is to remember why I shouldn't be.

I *like* Mikah. I like the way the tips of his ears turn pink every time the guys scream his nickname. I like how even when he's not holding Angelo, he always seems to have one eye on him. He might have doubts about how he's doing but you can see how much he loves him already.

There are still a half-dozen people left, the beer mostly gone, or the players have switched to water. I haven't had a thing to drink and I'm craving a snack since it seems like yesterday when I finally managed to eat my burrito bowl, talking with Katie about her job as a physical therapist in between bites.

She moved down here last Christmas from Chicago and moved in with Jude right away.

He's barely left her side all night, constantly checking to see if she needs anything. Kissing her. Touching her. Patting her ass a couple times and making her jump and swear at him.

I like them.

But it's late, and I really need to head home. I still have work to do and it's best I get on it before I fall asleep.

"I should go." I nudge Mikah's leg with my finger where he's sitting next to me on the couch. He forced Katie to move down from her spot next to me after he put Angelo down to sleep earlier. The baby monitor sits on the table in front of us. "I have work to do."

"I'll walk you out."

"That's not necessary," I say, but he's already standing and holding out his hand for me to take.

I slide mine into his without thinking, like it's the most natural thing to do, and when I do, Katie winks at me.

They're being silly. Treating me like we're together instead of neighbors slash mostly strangers slash almost sort of friends. I roll my eyes at her and squeeze her hand as I pass by.

"We'll do that shopping trip soon?"

"I'd love to. I'll show you all the cute places in the burbs."

"As long as it includes a stop at the ice cream place you mentioned you have a deal."

We talked quite a bit about all the second-hand vintage boutiques, and she claims there's a small town near her with an adorable downtown area that has three vintage markets she adores. Bonus, one of them is right next to what she swears is the best ice cream parlor she's ever been to.

I can't wait. I have no plans to redecorate my uncle's place so I'm in no position to do purchasing, but I love getting ideas and gathering small items that help make his place feel more like my home.

"Shopping?" Mikah asks as we round the couch.

I wave and say goodbye to the others who still linger. Jason, one of the brothers I think, tips his chin and lifts his beer. I swear he winks at Mikah as we pass him.

We're at his door, his hand still holding mine when I answer his question. "Katie suggested a place near her she wants us to check out someday and I told her about other stores near Uptown. I said I'd help her with their house."

From what I learned, they became engaged earlier this summer, but Katie moved in with Jude last Christmas. She's been slowly making the home he owns south of Charlotte into theirs, and it sounds like a big job. Partly because the home sounds enormous. Partly because according to her, Jude had nothing but couches and televisions and a couple of beds, so she's working with a blank canvas.

"So you like her."

"She's sweet."

He opens the door and then we're in the hallway where it's quiet and it's only a few steps to my own apartment. My keys are in my hand, my phone in my back pocket. I don't exactly need his help getting home, but I'm reluctant to let go of his hand.

I *like* this guy. It's more than his looks or the fact he has a baby. If anything, that's still scaring the crap out of me. But Mikah is pretty irresistible and he has such great friends. None of them come across as millionaires or guys who are cocky and arrogant due to their success.

They're *people*. Sexy, loud, people.

I jiggle the keys in my hand. "I think I've got it from here."

In answer, Mikah squeezes my hand harder and takes the dozen steps to my door. Before I can put the key in my lock, Mikah has my keys in his hand and he's doing it for me.

"Mikah—"

He grins at me, and then he's pushing open my door, pulling me in behind him like I'm entering his home and not mine.

"I'm glad you came over tonight. I'm happy you met my friends."

He tugs me toward him and there's a breath of space

between us. It swirls with heat and anticipation and *please dear Jesus, do not let me be misinterpreting this.*

"I like you in my home," he says and his voice is deeper. Smoky with an edge to it.

I swallow the bundle of nerves growing in my throat. "What's... what's going on?"

"I like *you*, Paisley."

My jaw unhinges. I'm not expecting it and before I fully process what he's said, his hand is at my jaw, thumb brushing along my cheek, his rich blue eyes so intense and stealing anything thought I have.

I dig deep, find the remains of my voice. "I like you too, but—"

"No buts. Nothing good comes after a but."

And then his mouth lowers, dances across mine in the softest brush. It's all I need before I forget my issues with him. The negatives of me falling for a guy like him.

"Oh," I breathe out on a whisper as a shiver rolls through me. His lips are warm. Soft. Gentle.

He tastes like the smallest hint of beer and the lingering woodsy scent of his cologne.

He kisses me again, and this time, I don't hesitate. I lean toward him, press my hand to his side and hold on for dear life as he deepens the kiss, slips his tongue over mine and then into my mouth.

And oh sweet goodness, he can *kiss*.

I'm lost in it, the warmth of his body, the strength of him. I can tell he's holding back, but I imagine what will happen when he loses that control. How much power he possesses in his tall and muscular but still lean frame.

"Oh," I gasp against him and take what he's giving me, falling into him as he steps toward me until my back is at my door. My whole body is *alive*.

With a kiss. A tame one, at that.

He pulls back slowly, ending the kiss. With his hand now at my hip and his other at my jaw, he tilts my chin up. He's so much taller than me. His blue eyes have deepened and his blond hair is messed.

I want to dig my fingers in it and muss it up more.

"I want to see you. Alone. And soon."

I blink at him. Once. Twice. "A date?"

"Yes."

"But... you have Angelo."

"Then we spend time together when he's sleeping. Or I have the nanny come over."

"Mikah..." He has *so* much to deal with. "I'm not sure now's the time."

"I will figure it out."

He kisses me again, firm, hard, and I barely remember him telling me Angelo's mom is the only woman he's been with. He certainly doesn't have an inexperienced feel to him. He's confident. So certain of his decisions.

I'm not there.

"We'll talk," I say instead. Because inside I want to scream *yes*, but my ridiculous conscience is warning me to slow down.

He just found out he's a father, for goodness' sake.

"We will."

He reaches around me and grins as I stumble away from him. As he steps through the doorway, I hold the door open and he drops another sweet kiss to my cheek that shoots a flame of heat down to my core.

A cheek kiss. What is wrong with me?

"Goodnight, Paisley. Sleep well," he murmurs as he pulls away.

I stay in the doorway as he heads back to his place. And dang... he looks good walking away.

"'Night, Mikah," I say.

He lifts his hand, opens his door, and a rumbling, loud echo of his teammates shouting, "Let's Go!" bursts through the doorway.

He blushes and shakes his head, grin stretches ear-to-ear. "Goodnight. Again."

"Bye." I go back to my condo, doing the exact same.

Yeah, Mikah is dangerous.

In more ways than one.

"YOU KISSED HIM?"

"Shh." I reach for Maggie with my hand outstretched to cover her mouth. I made the mistake of mentioning I saw Mikah again last night with some of his teammates and the girl lost her mind, peppering me for every single detail and because I can't get the kiss out of my head.

Hours later, I woke up to thinking about it, showered and got ready for school thinking about it, when she asked, I couldn't lie.

She really has to be quiet before Ms. Felarky overhears and scolds us for not getting to work.

Like I've been able to work or focus on anything all day. I spent the morning doing my TA office hours and I'm not sure I helped a single undergrad who came in for help with their senior student planning projects. The elementary school majors need to focus on lesson plans, filling out an entire school year of tests and projects and the timing before they can do their student teaching and graduate. I'm still not sure if I listened to anything they said or just approved it because my head's in the clouds.

And working on that paper Maggie and I are supposed to be doing? Not happening.

My mind is clouded with the memories of a sexy, single dad hockey player who kisses like he has more experience than he's alluded to.

If he's that good at kissing... what else does he excel at?

The part of me that's been neglected since earlier this summer is *aching* to find out.

"I mean it," she says, voice full of glee and body bouncing like she's on a pogo stick. "He's a professional athlete, Paisley. And do you know how much money he makes? The guy is *loaded* and young and has his entire career ahead of him. It's *crazy*."

"You... you know how much money he makes?"

"Well yeah, that's all public information. A quick Google search and Wikipedia page will tell you everything."

My eyes almost bug out of my head. "And you looked into him?"

It feels... wrong.

Maggie opens her mouth, but I don't want to know. "Don't. Don't tell me. If anything happens with us, I want it to come from him."

"But—"

"No." My fingertips are burning to do my own looking. Yeah, I've scanned pictures of him. But his *salary*? That's crossing a line and despite being curious, because how much do hockey players actually make... a slimy, icky, feeling slides through me.

No. I won't check that out. I know enough to know the condo he lives in cost almost a million dollars if it was priced near Trent's when he purchased it. That's enough to give me a clue as to how successful he is.

"Paisley—"

"No. I can't."

She huffs back in her chair and pouts. "Fine. But we're going out for drinks tonight and you're not getting out of it."

"You're not coming to my place to stalk him." I'm already guilty of doing the same. He doesn't need my friends drooling over him, too.

"Well, no. But we can stop by and say hi?"

"You're incorrigible." Fortunately for her, I've already texted my friend Pippa and said I needed advice. "But Pippa and I are having dinner and drinks tonight at Nuvolé 22 if you want to join us."

Nuvolé 22 is one of my favorite rooftop bars in the area. Bonus for me, it's within walking distance from my place. Plus, since it's over twenty stories high, there's usually a nice breeze so even though it's scorching hot outside, by the time the sun falls later, it should be a great night.

Plus, once I texted Pippa this morning declaring I'm having *boy issues*, she demanded a girl's night to discuss.

Not that I'm complaining.

My head is completely twisted up with hockey players and babies, plus there's the not so difficult reality of what that means for me with my family.

Outside of utter and complete disappointment.

Sigh.

"We're meeting at seven-thirty," I tell Maggie.

"I'll be there."

"Good. Now let's get to work."

"Right, like I'll be able to concentrate now."

You and me both, sweetheart. I spin my chair back

toward my desk and awaken my laptop screen. "Try your hardest."

Surprisingly, I spend the rest of the afternoon diving into research articles, getting lost in the fascination of the science behind the disabilities I'm studying and how it relates to *how* students with them can learn most effectively.

By the time I get back to my condo, I'm regretting texting Pippa and telling Maggie anything.

I'm exhausted. For a moment I consider texting the girls and having them come here instead.

But... the food.

I have yet to go grocery shopping and replenish my freezer selection meals.

I'm still unpacking my work bag and my lunch tote when a knock comes from my door.

Frowning, I head toward it and as I peek out the peephole, a spike of adrenaline and excitement races through me.

I open the door and Mikah is there, one hand on the doorframe, head peering down at me. He looks as tired as I feel.

"Hey—"

I barely get it all out before his hands are at my cheeks, and his lips are on mine.

He's kissing me and oh sweet Jesus, it's as beautiful as I remember. Possibly more. Because he's said nothing but stopped over to kiss me and *well, holy goodness gracious.*

He pulls back abruptly, and I have to stop myself from falling into him. "I've thought about nothing but that all day and had to see if it's as good as I thought it was last night."

"Better, I think," I say without thinking.

I'm rewarded with a dazzling smile and humor in his eyes. It's possible he gets better looking every time I see him.

"Come have dinner with me?"

If it leads to more kisses like that? *Yes*. I'm about ready to speak when I remember. "I can't."

"Oh."

"I want to." I reach for him. My hand curls around his bicep and *wowzers*. He's so built, it's crazy. "I have plans with some friends tonight."

"Tomorrow."

This feels suddenly like it's moving so fast. It's still not been a week since the first time I talked to him. And there's so much involved in this guy.

Still... those kisses.

"Tomorrow," I agree and am rewarded with another smile. He's so much more confident. Perhaps he always is. Perhaps it's Angelo that makes him uncertain but even with that, he seems to be rocking it. And speaking of... "Where's Angelo?"

Mikah unclips the monitor at his belt I didn't notice before and holds it up. "Sleeping. I've been reading the book Hannah gave me. I'm working on the schedules it mentions. He seems to like it. Or, well, he sleeps better at night anyway. Six hours last night."

He says it with pride in his tone and a smile on his face. I'm pleased for him. "Good. That's good."

"Okay. I will let you get ready and go. But there's one more thing I want from you?"

I assume it's a kiss, which I'm more than willing to help him with, so I'm surprised when he pulls out his phone. "I need your number."

Need.

Not want.

Not asking.

Yeah, I have a feeling I'm only beginning to understand Mikah and how confident he can truly be.

It's such a turn on. I type it in and send myself a text so I have his number, too.

As I hand the phone back to Mikah, he wraps his hand around my wrist, lowers his head and then he's kissing me again and it's so good, so slow and tempting I think again of canceling girl's night... but not to stay home alone... but to do something much more... um, physical, with the boy across the hall.

CHAPTER FIFTEEN

Mikah

THE NANNY SERVICE SENDS LEAH.

She's young. My age. And she has barely looked at Angelo since she stepped foot into my home.

As soon as I opened the door, she blushed from her cheeks to her breasts, because she's wearing a shirt that barely hides them, and breathed my name.

Yes. It came out in a breath, "Mikah."

I wanted to immediately take a shower with the way she raked her gaze over my body. I was holding Angelo, and I don't think she saw him. I'm not certain she saw me.

I'm pretty sure she only sees Mikah Lutzgo, the *hockey player*.

I have not been nice to her, but the service insisted she's worked with many families with difficult schedules like mine and is very professional.

I try to ask her questions, but she dismisses me. Runs

her hand along the kitchen countertop and if she's trying to be sexy while she does it, it doesn't work.

My skin itches with the need to get her out of my home but I'm currently on the couch, feeding Angelo. I have worked all week long to get him on a schedule. Sometimes he seems fussy, so I add a couple more ounces. Then he's happy. Keep him awake for a couple hours, having him sleep for two. Sometimes it works. Sometimes it doesn't. But sleeping for five or six hours at night has been beautiful.

I'm getting the hang of parenting him. I even gave him a bath myself. Although I think maybe I ended up with more water on me than he did.

I check the clock again. It's almost five. Paisley should be home soon. I want Angelo sleeping later so we can spend more time together.

Kissing.

On my couch.

With her beneath me.

Perhaps with her mouth tasting of sweet white wine like the kind I bought earlier and put in my fridge.

On the coffee table in front of me are a list of questions Hannah emailed me to ask the nannies who come to talk to me.

"Leah." I call her name because she's still in my kitchen. I am certain she is imagining me screwing her on the countertop with the way she looks at it and then me. I might not have experience with women, but I have been hit on plenty. The look in her eyes makes my skin crawl.

Like I am the prey.

Please. That's ridiculous. Young and inexperienced does not equal naive and stupid.

"Yes, Mikah." She's breathing my name again. It's weird. I'm not sure I've heard her real voice.

Since I can't kick her out until Angelo is done feeding and burped because I've learned when he's interrupted from either he gets cranky, I am stuck with her.

I might as well practice the questions.

"Tell me your typical day with a baby. Do you leave the house? Find activities to do with them?"

"Oh yes," she says and for a moment, she looks happy. "But mostly I enjoy preparing delicious meals for you... or the families I work for... to come home and enjoy."

I don't need a cook.

"With Angelo," I say. Leah will definitely *not* be my nanny. "What will you do with him? Go for walks?"

"Oh, sure. We can do that. I like being outside and staying active."

She pushes out her hip and drifts her hand down the length of her body. She is pretty. With big breasts and a small waist.

Paisley is prettier. And doesn't wear the face of someone willing to drop their knees if asked.

As if thinking of her conjures her, my phone buzzes next to me and her name pops up on the screen.

"Excuse me," I say to Leah. Her face is pinched up. Possibly mad I haven't hit on her yet. I have no plans to. She needs to go. "I need to answer this."

I open her text and smile. *Yes.*

Paisley: Are we still on for tonight?

Yes. Absolutely. We can get to that later.

I grab my phone and send her a text, amazed I've been able to figure out how to do all this with only one hand.

Me: Interviewing a nanny and she's giving me crazy eyes. Come help.

I'm not sure if that will get her running, but I left the door unlocked. As soon as Leah stepped inside earlier and looked at me, I didn't want us locked in together. It feels weird having another woman in my home.

This whole thing is strange and so far I don't have the highest opinion of this service. I'm supposed to trust someone like Leah with Angelo while I'm gone? And staying in my home while I travel?

What if she really is the best option they have? I'm more concerned she'll dig through my personal things or take photos of herself naked in my bed or something.

The idea sends a cold shiver down my spine.

No wonder why most of my teammates' wives' stay home once they start having families. It makes sense.

I'm halfway to a panic attack when the door opens, and I instantly turn toward it.

Paisley is there, hair piled on top of her head, cheeks flushed. She wears a cute skirt and peach blouse, tucked in at the waist and slightly wrinkled. The blouse is loose and flows beautifully over breasts I want my hands on.

"Hey honey," she says. "How's the sweet little guy doing today?" She swishes and sways toward me, and I notice she hasn't taken her eyes off me before she's in front of me.

Her hands are at my cheeks and then her lips are on mine.

She's kissing me, and I only have a vague recollection of Leah in my home and how much I need her to go when Paisley pulls back and winks.

"Think that'll do it," she whispers and kisses me again.

"What?"

A strange sound comes from behind me and Paisley pops up, brushing a finger to Angelo's cheek in my arms. She grins widely. "Hi, I'm Paisley. Mikah's girlfriend, are you the nanny?"

"Girlfriend?"

I cringe at the tone in her voice. She doesn't sound disappointed or surprised, but angry.

"Yes, and I'm sorry, but I've been running late, and we have dinner plans this evening." Paisley smiles down at me. "Have you asked all the questions?"

"Yup."

"Great." She claps her hands together and swings her arm out toward the door. "I'm sure he'll call you later, or the service will to discuss plans to move forward. But we should get going."

I have to fight back a grin. I should have been able to do this myself, but I swear taking care of Angelo and losing sleep has stolen brain cells. I've read mom-brain is a thing. But I haven't heard of dad-brain yet. I'm certain I have it, though.

Perhaps I should have been ruder to Leah, but I don't want her saying any negative about me to the service yet. Not until I give them a chance for someone else that won't drool over me.

Plus, this hasn't been all bad. I now know that when Paisley is bossy, especially dressed in that tight skirt and silky blouse, she's one hundred and ten percent sexy.

"Mikah?" Leah asks, and her smile is no longer trying to be seductive. It's tight and makes her face looks pinched.

"Thank you for coming, Leah. The service will let you know what I decide." I focus on Angelo, hoping she gets the clue I'm dismissing her.

After Paisley says goodbye as well and the door closes, I breathe a full breath for the first time since she arrived.

"Thank you. That shouldn't have been so hard, but she wasn't getting my hints."

"I think she's got a head full of NHL hockey stars." Paisley giggles.

In my arms, Angelo pushes the bottle's nipple out of his mouth and grunts.

She holds out her hands. "Can I take him?"

I love that she always seems to want her hands on him. Since I've been thrown up on twice today, the decision is easy.

"He's all yours." I hand her a burp cloth first. Once she has it draped over her shoulder, I hand him to her.

"And you? Do you have a head full of NHL hockey stars?"

"No." She kisses Angelo's cheek and smiles at me. "But I've had a head full of *you* all afternoon."

"Yeah? Want to tell me about it?"

She playfully covers one of Angelo's ears with her hand and winks. "Maybe later."

"I can't wait." I lean in and kiss her. She tastes like mint and everything fresh and beautiful. *Skønhed.*

Angelo lets out a burp that can rival any one of my teammates and Paisley pulls back, laughing.

"I think I've done my job."

She jiggles him with a soft, gentle bounce and he burps again. Sometimes I'm still scared of how small he is. I have an appointment on Monday morning with a pediatrician I found earlier this week. Angela's letter didn't say anything about doctors, so I have no idea of knowing if he's been seen and whether he's had any shots.

Paisley readjusts Angelo, smiling sweetly at him before turning that smile to me. It's blinding how gorgeous she is and how much I like looking at her while she holds my son.

"I should go," she says. Her smile slips before she kisses

Angelo's temple and hands him over to me. "I have a few things I need to do before I was supposed to be here later."

"Thanks for bailing me out."

"Anytime. I'll come back in a couple of hours?"

"Yes." I walk her to the door, kissing her one more time. I need time to get ready too. I want to cook us dinner after Angelo's in bed so we can actually enjoy time together, just the two of us. And I might need to schedule a quick Instacart food delivery.

She hums softly when I pull back from the kiss, licking her lips like she doesn't want it to be over.

I know the feeling.

"Paisley," I whisper, and wait for her to open her eyes. "When you come back tonight."

"Yes? Is there something I can bring?"

"No. Just you... but wear the skirt."

CHAPTER SIXTEEN

Paisley

WEAR THE SKIRT.

I fully intended to come home from work, shower and change and dress somewhat nicely for a night in with Mikah but his parting words to me from earlier have given me a much better idea.

His intentions for the evening were clear in the way his gaze caressed me like a lover's touch. I can still feel his hand on my hip, the warmth and fullness of his lips on my skin.

I originally planned to come home, get some work done, shower and clean up, but all thoughts of work flew out the window with his command.

Wear the skirt.

Please. Like it's the most seductive thing in my closet. Boy is he way off base.

So now, I've spent hours prepping, eating a quick snack because I'm always starving after school and work, and while I wish I could take the time for a quick workout to de-stress, something tells me I'll be having one later.

With my hair curled, makeup freshly applied, casual and light, I'm not wearing the skirt Mikah requested.

I'm wearing one of my favorite summer dresses. It's a mint green color and shows off my tan. The front drapes low and loose, dipping down in the center to show off a small amount of cleavage. The waist is skintight down to my mid-thigh. It hugs my bottom half perfectly. The top is held up by two thin straps at my shoulders and where the front drapes loosely in a seductive but modest way, the back is nonexistent.

Which means Mikah will be able to tell that not only can I not wear a bra with the dress, but there's a very high probability I might not be able to wear underwear either.

I am, of course, but my thong is minuscule.

If he thought I looked good before, I can't wait to see the way he looks at me now. Hair curled, draping low and pulled back into a loose ponytail at the nape of my neck, the rest of it drapes over one shoulder. I've left off accessories, only because I don't want them getting in the way later.

I grab my keys and purse and slide into a pair of flat gold sandals. They don't go great with the dress but they're comfortable and I'm only walking across the hall anyway. After double-checking to ensure I've locked my door, which seems silly since we're the only two condos on this floor, I lift my hand and knock on Mikah's.

To my surprise, he opens immediately, and the look of shock on his face is exactly what I've been hoping to see when he catches me in my outfit.

"I didn't wear the skirt," I say, jauntily. It gives me great satisfaction to watch his gaze dip and stall at my chest, and then further down.

He slides his gaze up, still silent, but I catch the way he's clenching his door, unmoving, frozen in place.

I like that I've stunned him.

"No. This is better. Much better." Before I can react, he reaches out with his other hand, and his arm wraps around my waist. His hand is at my lower back, hot skin of his burning palm to my cool skin and then he's slamming me against him. Kissing me. Hot, insistent lips on mine.

I open for him and follow him as he steps back into his home. The door closes behind me right before the cold wood is pressed to my back and the strength of Mikah's warm frame is at my front.

"Oh," I gasp into his mouth.

The sensations are overpowering, warring with each other. My hands have minds of their own because I shove my hands to his hips, yank up the shirt he's wearing. I don't notice the color, just that it's in my way.

He takes my mouth with confidence and strength and a skill I'm surprised by given his confession at inexperience. My body seeks his, presses against him and I hitch my leg over his thigh. I'm desperate to know what other areas he's talented in.

My hands find his hips, the muscled strength in his lower back and I hold him against me as he presses his weight into me. I'm pinned between the door and Mikah and I've forgotten everything else until he groans into my throat.

"Food. I wanted to feed you first."

I huff a sound as he slows the kiss, pulls back, teases my mouth, my chin, my jaw. He brushes his lips over my cheek, hands at my neck, thumbs creating a stir of sensation from the gentle swipes beneath my jaw.

He's grinning down at me. My body is throbbing for

something that definitely isn't food. It takes me a moment to settle myself.

"Hey," I say, lips lifting into a smile. I slide one hand from beneath his shirt and press it to his cheek. He has only the smallest hint of stubble and it scratches my fingers, but I like it. It will feel delicious scraping other areas when we get to that.

I can't wait for it.

Behind him, a familiar and grumpy squawking sound interrupts the moment. I roll to my toes to see Angelo. He's on the floor, on a thick mat beneath two overhead arches where toys dangle. His little legs are flopping up and down and he reaches relentlessly for a set of hanging rings. His movements are jerky and rough and every time his hand falls to the floor, he lets out an irritated sound.

"Angelo," I whisper, smiling at Mikah.

He kisses my cheek. "Angelo. We'll pick this up later. And if you missed it, I really, really love the dress you have on."

I step around him, feeling sassier than usual, but I'm pretty confident I know exactly where we'll pick up later.

Dropping my purse to a side table by the couches, I wink at Mikah. "If you like what you see, try imagining what you can't."

His jaw falls right before a rough growl sound echoes in the room. Pointing a finger at me, he scowls. "That is not nice. Not nice at all when Angelo is still awake."

"Early bedtime tonight then?"

"For him. Yes. You? Absolutely not."

A delightful shiver of anticipation rolls through me. *Yippee.*

I do my best to brush it off while I sit next to Angelo on the floor. He's so damn irresistible.

Careful of the short dress, I fall to one hip, tucking my legs up and to the side beside me. I hold out my hand and wiggle my fingers, letting Angelo easily latch on to one with his tiny but strong fist.

"Do you need help with dinner?"

I look up at Mikah, only to find him watching me with an intense expression, his eyes focused on where Angelo holds my hand.

"No." He slides his gaze to me. "You look perfect right where you are."

He spins and heads toward the kitchen. I shake Angelo's little fist still gripping me and I'm rewarded with one of his large, toothless smiles. I can't be so close to him and not love on him, so I scoop him up and manage to get to my feet where I carry him into the kitchen.

Mikah might like watching me with his son, but I'm pretty sure watching Mikah cook will be even better.

CHAPTER SEVENTEEN

Mikah

IT'S OFFICIAL. I'm being cock-blocked by my own infant son. He's done so well this week, sleeping when I want him, stretching it out for longer periods of time, I was beginning to get cocky with my parenting skills.

Now? Not so much. Which is a shame considering I *really* want to pick up where Paisley and I left off earlier when she was grinding up against me, and I had her pressed against the wall.

Angelo has been crying since the middle of dinner. I bounced him on my knee while Paisley ate, and when she was done, she took over with him. We fed him, changed him, and I can't for the life of me figure out what is making him so unhappy.

Paisley is now in the kitchen washing the dishes, wiping off the countertops and her look of concern matches mine completely. I was hoping he would've been sleeping for most of the time she was over so she and I could have some time alone, but that looks like it's not happening, delete.

All I can think about is the feel of her body against mine earlier and the way she succumbed to my kiss like she wanted it maybe more than I wanted to give her one. She's sexy and more beautiful than ever in the dress she's wearing. Now all I want to do is figure out how to get the little stinker in my arms to stop fussing and lay back down so she and I can resume what we were doing before.

My eardrum is in danger of shattering with his loud screams and even though he might only way twelve pounds, after holding him I'm concerned my arms might fall off.

"Any ideas?" I ask Paisley. I bounce him like she usually does but he doesn't want his pacifier and I swear he's getting angrier by the second.

"I can take him if you need a break."

A break? I need to go back to last fall and make different choices. Guilt curdles in my stomach like it does every time I have these thoughts. Normally when I realize how much Angelo's arrival is truly changing my life. Not that I'm not starting to love the little guy screaming like a banshee in my arms, but this is not the way I ever envisioned becoming a father.

It's very rare I wish I had a better relationship with mine, or my mom for that matter. If I did, I would fly them in to help me get on my feet. Maybe give me a night where I can forget what my life has become.

Yeah, I need a break. A long one, but for now I'll take what's offered.

"Please."

She slides him out of my arms, wincing at the harsh sound of his scream. Then she grins up at me and somehow that screaming becomes a distant hum.

"He's going to be a loudmouth when he grows up."

I swipe a hand down my face and fight a yawn. It's after nine and I was so sure he'd be sleeping, but since I'm juggling a thousand more pucks in the air than I'm used to, I'm so damn exhausted.

"Let's hope not. I am not used to this yet."

Defeat and stress knot my shoulders. I not only hate I'm feeling this way I hate more I'm letting Paisley see it.

Her smile dims at my admission.

"Go." Paisley juts up her chin. "Go sit. You look like you're dead on your feet."

Another yawn builds in my throat and I fight it back. More than dead on my feet, I'm frustrated tonight isn't going how I want it to.

"Fine."

"It's okay to ask for help you know."

"I wanted to have a night with you, looking like you do, kissing how you do." I'm trying to lighten the mood and it must work because Paisley blushes, shakes her head like she can't believe I've said all that. I can't either, not with Angelo still screaming in her arms.

"We'll have others. Go sit. I'm going to take him to his room. Maybe rocking him will help. Actually, have you by any chance bought a humidifier or diffuser?"

"I have one."

"Okay. I'm going to take him to my place and grab something. I'll be right back. Will you get the humidifier ready with some water?"

"What are you doing?"

"Grabbing lavender. I'll be back." She comes to me and kisses me, lips lingering on mine in a way I'll currently do anything to help calm him down. "We'll get him sleeping and then we can be alone."

"Sounds like a good plan."

She winks and steps back. "I have them occasionally."

A weird, heavy quiet descends as soon as she's gone, and it takes me a moment to remember what I'm supposed to do. I'd blame the dress she's wearing again, but this time I'm pretty sure it has everything to do with the fact I can barely keep my eyes open.

Hell. What is wrong with me that I can't stand the screaming and constant noise Angelo makes when he's upset, but as soon as he's gone it feels like a part of me is missing?

They'll be back any minute though, so I go to his closet in his room and dig out the humidifier. It's in a box Hannah bought that first night. She said it helps with stuffy noses and cold, and the hum of the machine sometimes helps her kids sleep better.

I toss the box in my hands gently and shake my head. "I should have thought of this. Hopefully it works."

The slow crescendo of Angelo's healthy lungs returns so I rip open the flaps and put the few pieces together. His bedroom has a connected bathroom, so I fill up the basin.

I'm trying to find a place to set it up when Paisley walks into the room.

"Good job, Dad."

It takes me a second to realize she actually means me. "Thank you. You have lavender?"

She shakes a tiny bottle in her hand. "Yep. I'll add it to the water and then we can get everything going again. Then I want you to go sit and chill."

Oddly, I want to stay and watch her. She moves so confidently and easily. Not only do I like looking at her, now that Angelo's back in the room, I want to make sure he's okay.

But Paisley has this and sitting down for a few minutes sounds like a great idea.

I wait until she's changed him again, tried the pacifier and been denied and she looks up at me from her place in the rocking chair, feet kicked up on the ottoman, and laughs. "Go Mikah. Or once he's down, you're not going to get more kisses."

She's teasing. I like the way it looks on her.

"I'll get more kisses either way." I leave the room quickly, just in case she's serious.

Back in the living room, I collapse into the couch and throw my feet up on the coffee table. My head falls back to the couch cushions and while I can still hear Angelo crying, it's muted.

She must have gotten up and closed the door after I left.

Nice of her.

It's the last thing I think before my eyes close and I fall asleep.

CHAPTER EIGHTEEN

Paisley

HE'S ADORABLE, sleeping on the couch. His head has fallen to the side, lips parted. His lashes are long, brushing against the top of his cheekbones and every once in awhile, a low, brief snore comes out.

He'd dressed up for tonight, at least nicer than the athletic pants and T-shirts I usually see him in, but not to the extreme of the suits I've also spied him in. He's wearing jeans, frayed at the knee and hemmed at his ankles. The pale blue shirt he has on is also faded and with his arms propped along the back of the couch, a hint of his abs and a soft line of hair peeks out from the space between.

It's taken me almost an hour to finally get Angelo settled down and sleeping. And I can imagine with how tired Mikah looked before he's been asleep for nearly as long. My chest constricts as I stand there, staring at him like I'm still the stalker I was from behind a closed door over a week ago, but I'm not sure what to do now.

Leave? Give him a night of peace and quiet?

Or do what I really want and wake him up, see if I can rouse him for at least a kiss before I take off.

Let him sleep. My subconscious that loves caring for people wins out. For now.

Instead of leaving or curling up next to him on the couch and throwing myself at him, I head to the kitchen and fill a glass of white wine. Since Angelo cried while we ate, neither of us drank it but Mikah already had it open so I quickly fill a glass.

I can use it after spending an hour with a baby who pretty much screamed in my face.

Man. That was rough.

With a glass of wine in one hand, I grab my phone and tuck my feet under me on a chair that has a view of the city. Not that there's much to see since it's dark except the streetlights and car lights, but it's still peaceful.

I'll read a book on my Kindle app, sip my wine, and I'll ensure Angelo is going to stay asleep before I head out.

And if Mikah wakes before then... well... we'll see.

I pull up a book I bought last weekend and still haven't had time to read, one of my favorite romance tropes about a Hollywood star who meets a small-town girl and falls in love with her while working on her farm.

A quiet snort escapes me, and I quickly cover my mouth, peeking at Mikah. There's definitely a slight similarity to my current situation. Still, I'm riveted by the story, falling in love with the couple while they repair sheds and outbuildings after a tornado rips through their Kansas town.

My wine is gone, and I'm still reading, when movement followed by a groan surprises me and makes me jump.

Nothing to see here, just a psycho watching a hottie sleep.

I snort again and Mikah's eyes slide open, followed by another groan and a swipe of his hand up his back and back through his hair.

"What..." He glances at me and closes his eyes and then they pop back open and he seems wide awake and alert. "Angelo?"

He shoves to standing, almost panicked. I'd laugh except *wow, I'm totally falling for the way this guy is falling in love with his son.*

"He's fine." I climb out of the chair and place my hands on his forearm. "He's good, Mikah. Sleeping. You were out so I thought I'd stay for a bit in case he woke up."

"How long have I been out?" He glances at the watch he wears on his wrist, thick black and something that screams *athlete.* "It's almost eleven. Hours?"

I've lost track of time while reading. "It took about an hour to get him down. I thought I'd stay so you could sleep and started reading. I guess I lost track of time too."

"Shit. I didn't realize I was that tired." He slides his hand to my neck, pressing his fingers at the back and dips his head. "Thank you."

He kisses me softly, slowly, and I melt into him because when it comes to kissing Mikah, I can't do anything but. The wine has relaxed me and I'm a whole lot turned on when he pulls back, glancing over my shoulder.

"I should go check on him."

Of course. And it's late. "I should get going."

"Stay." He shakes his head. "Stay with me. Have another drink, we can watch a movie or something. Tonight didn't go the way I wanted, but I don't want it to end."

And how am I supposed to say no that? "Okay. Let me run home and change then. Out of this dress."

His gaze dips to my dress, now probably wrinkled and

crinkled from sitting in it so long and he frowns. "I have clothes you can wear."

He's several inches taller than me and a whole lot bigger. I doubt he has clothes that will fit. But the idea of snuggling up with Mikah and watching a movie while wearing his clothes is too good to pass up. Plus, I like he doesn't want me to go home yet.

"That'd be great."

"Come on." He grabs my hand and pulls me down the hall until we reach his bedroom. It's an exact mirror of mine except lacking the expensive and over-sized, manly furniture my uncle has.

Instead, it's all black and utilitarian, looking like something he could have bought and assembled himself from IKEA. A thick, light gray cover is on his bed, neatly made, which is more of a surprise than anything. And his room is completely picked up and tidied.

It makes me wonder if he cleaned for me or if he's always this neat.

"Closet," he says and leads me there, opening the door and flipping on the light switch.

Yeah, there's no way he cleaned for me. Every single one of his shirts and suits are neatly ordered, hangers I swear spaced perfectly two inches apart. If I'm not mistaken, they're color-coded, going from light to dark. My closet looks like a bomb exploded all over it and then was hit with a hurricane before recovery was started.

He pulls open a set of built-in drawers on one side of the large closet, completely filled whereas my clothes take up about a quarter of the large space in mine. I'm not at all surprised when he has drawers of perfectly folded flannel pants and another drawer of T-shirts.

The blue Carolina Ice Kings logo stretches across the

front of the black T-shirt.

"Thank you."

He holds them out, a sheepish look on his face. "They'll probably be too big."

"But comfortable and perfect." I take them into my hands and then we stand there, saying nothing.

Until Mikah's expression darkens.

"I hope you know I want nothing more than to stay in here and watch you strip out of that dress and into my clothes."

"I imagine someday you might have that opportunity."

Lust flashes in his eyes. I slap him playfully with the clothes in my hand.

"Go. Check on Angelo. Give me privacy and then we can chill out."

WE'RE on the couch where I'm wearing Mikah pants that are three sizes too large for me, a shirt I'm swimming in, and a bottled water in my hand. The glass of wine I sipped earlier has made me sleepy and if we're trying to salvage this night, drooling on his shoulder while I fall asleep isn't the way that will happen.

He's next to me and we're scrolling through his plethora of movie apps trying to decide what to watch but in reality, we keep getting distracted by our conversations.

He started it by asking me if I wanted to watch a thriller movie to which he received a very loud and enthusiastic hell no from me.

I've just suggested an old slapstick humor movie and he declined. "Sometimes the American slang loses something in translation, so I don't find them funny."

I'm so curious to know anything and everything about him, I lose all interest in finding a movie to watch.

"Have you always studied English?"

"We begin studying it in primary school. Early. But it's still different to speak it every day here. The first year I lived here was rough. I barely got jokes, cuss words." He shrugs like it's no big deal, but he's so young. And I imagine not knowing the language of your teammates would make connecting difficult.

"How long have you lived here then?"

He gives me a sly smile I feel down to my toes.

"What?" I ask

"You haven't looked into it?"

I jolt from my spot on the couch. "What?"

Mikah's hand slides through my hair. The gesture should be calming but I'm so confused by what he's asked I'm anything but calm.

"Online," he murmurs. His attention is solely focused on my hair, his hand playing with it. Perhaps he's spotted the small but raised mole at the side of my neck. Yeah, Mikah can be intense. "You haven't looked me up."

Oh. That's what he's talking about.

His hand is still in my hair, distracting me. His blue eyes seemed to have darkened.

As much as I want to know everything about him, I want him to know everything about me.

"Only pictures," I admit. "After that first night Hannah came over and told me who you were I did, but then it felt wrong, so I stopped." The memory of Maggie in our office last week sparks something in my mind. "My friend Maggie on the other hand... she did, but then I didn't let her say anything."

As I'm talking, his hand on me has stopped moving, his

focus not solely on me.

"I find it odd you don't know or care about sports," he says and it's in such a strange tone I tense. "But I like it too."

A soft laugh falls from me. "You're not answering my question."

"Because I care more about learning about you than talking about me." He's smooth. Perhaps it's his accent that makes every word he says sound like sex—the rough and gritty kind of sex. "I was drafted when I was eighteen. But they didn't call me up and move me here until I was twenty."

"You moved here when you were twenty? How old are you now?"

It's strange, I don't even know this about him.

He laughs. "Twenty-three."

"That couldn't have been easy," I mutter. It's crazy to think he's only been in our country for three years.

"The guys on the team made it easy. There are a few from other countries. It is not as uncommon as other sports."

"I like the guys on your team. But how was it getting connected? A new language and country to navigate doesn't seem easy."

"That first week or two, I thought I was going to get sent home. Everything was hard. The guys were older. I had to prove I was good enough to be here. Coach yelled at me. Maddox kept looking at me like he wanted to rip my face off."

I laugh. Byron is large and scary, and if I was twenty, facing against him, I'd be petrified.

"Yet you're so close to him now."

"He has a heart as big as his body, he is just careful who he lets see it. After a few weeks, things improved. I found my feet, so to speak, and then my age or the language didn't matter. Then, the guys became friends. And now, they're family. I don't know what I would do without them. Especially with Angelo. They've all been... so great."

He has a soft smile on his face. I don't know if it's for Angelo or his teammates. But it does remind me of earlier.

"Were you able to call the service? About finding someone new?"

The panic in the tone of his text had scared me until one glance at the girl in his condo showed she had *fuck me* eyes stamped all over her. I had hoped I wasn't overstepping boundaries when I ran in and went straight to him.

"I said she wouldn't work out. Then I changed what I require to make the nanny older. That girl..." He shakes his head, the tops of his chiseled cheekbones turn a light shade of pink. I brush my thumb over one, feeling his heat. He turns, nips at the tip of my thumb and grins. "That girl was not what I wanted, especially when I consider that she has to stay here when I'm out of town. They say they have someone else. I meet her Tuesday."

"I hope it goes better."

"Me too." His hand threads through my hair and slides to the back of my neck. "I want to know more about you—about where you come from and your schooling and everything else. I also very much want to kiss you. I'll be honest. I'm not sure which to do first."

"We can talk later."

It's easier to choose the kiss.

There's not much to tell him. I'm from a simple family in a small town and from what he's experienced, I feel like I haven't lived at all. Our lives are vastly different and even though I've stopped that difference from getting to know him, I still don't know if that's enough.

CHAPTER NINETEEN

Mikah

I'M WIDE AWAKE NOW, thankful for the nap Paisley let me have earlier and I'm more thankful she stayed.

She stayed to see me, gave me time to rest when she could have easily gone home and called the night a loss. But now she's here, on my couch, smelling like vanilla and sweet white wine and my body craves to get to know every part of her.

We can talk later.

I smile at that and lean in, pressing my fingers to the back of her neck. We can definitely talk later. I want to hear what she has to say when I can finally get my hands on her the way I've been wanting.

"Come here." I pull her toward me, and she comes easily, pressing her soft, warm lips to mine and that's all she gets before I take over. My other hand slides to her waist and I pull her with me, shifting back so I'm on the couch and she's straddling me.

Too bad she's not still in the dress. I would give anything to see her thighs spread over mine, her dress riding up to obscene heights while I can run my hands down her smooth flesh. I'll settle for the visual of her wearing my clothes. It's permanently burned into the back of my brain anyway.

She's damn cute, whimpering when I press her against me. My dick is hard. Hot. Pressing against my jeans and demanding release, on his own mission to find what I know will feel *so damn good*.

"You're good at this," she hums against my lips.

I wish I could say something smooth like *I've had lots of practice.*

What comes out instead is, "I must be a natural."

She huffs a warm puff of breath against my lips and then I fuse our mouths together, seeking the hot cavern of her mouth with my tongue, tangling it with hers. It's only a prelude to the other parts of her I want to know even more.

My hand at her hip, presses against her, lifts my shirt that hides her delicious body. She tenses when my thumb brushes against her hip, the tender skin above it.

"Is this okay?"

"Yes. It tickles." She pulls back, lips wet from our kiss and my gaze zeroes in on her tongue as she runs it over her bottom lip, tasting me on her.

Damn. I might not last long. I was not nervous with Angela. My first time. But this... this, I do not want to screw up.

"I can stop." But please, I hope she doesn't want that.

"Don't even consider it. You can touch me wherever you want, Mikah."

Consent. Her need and desire pulses at the base of her throat and I pull her back to me, avoiding her mouth and kissing her throat, finding the spot that makes her shiver in my hold and her hips buck against me.

"Oh."

"Yeah." It's a rumble from deep in my chest. My body feels like it's on fire.

We kiss and move, bodies pressed together. My hand dives further beneath the shirt, across her stomach, up to her chest where *yes. Himmel.* Heaven. She's not wearing a bra.

"Can I take off your shirt?"

"It's yours." She laughs, breathless. Because of *me. My touch. My hands.* Turning her on feels like a victory all on its own. "You can do whatever you want with it."

I didn't know sex... making out... I didn't know it could be so fun. I like her confidence. The way she urges me on. Her playfulness.

I push up the shirt, groaning and pressing my hips into her when her breasts fall free. Larger than a handful. Gorgeous and full, her light brown nipples are hardened points and my mouth waters.

"Vidunderlig. So very gorgeous."

I take one in my mouth, sliding my tongue around one nipple while I massage her other breast. I could spend hours learning the feel of her, the weight of her breasts and I like mostly how every time I bite down a little bit harder, suck one into my mouth with a bit of pressure, her breath hitches. Fingers dig into my hair, pushing me against her.

"Yes." She gasps as I pinch her other nipple. Everything she likes and reacts to I file away. I will learn everything she loves about the way I touch her. "Please. Touch me."

Her hips roll, press against my dick that is screaming, aching, for relief. I will deny Paisley nothing.

With my mouth still tasting her breasts, sucking on her

flesh, biting her nipples, I run my other down the contour of her smooth stomach to the waistband of the pants.

Ugly things. Too big for her. They're the smallest pair I own. Shrunk and too short for me. They swim on her.

She's perfect in them.

I press my hand beneath the waistband, reveling in the hitch of her hips, every roll, every whimper she shoots down my throat until I'm the one groaning at the feel of her.

Silky. Smooth. Hot. *So damn hot.* And wet.

"Shit," I pant. "I might embarrass myself here."

"I can help you."

"No." If she touches me, frees me in any way I'm done for. I at least want to please her first. Give before I take. "Later. If you want."

"Oh." She rolls her hips that presses right against me. "I'll want later. Trust me."

This time I'm the one laughing into her mouth, smiling as I kiss her. It quickly dies as I find her center. She's swollen and burning up. So damn hot it feels like warmth and wetness and everything beautiful. And then I find her bundle of nerves. It pulses against my fingertip and I seek further.

Good Lord in heaven. She's so tight and I press a finger inside of her.

She gasps into my mouth, whispers a *yes*, grinds against me and *yeah. I've got this.*

I find the rhythm that works for her, pressing and rolling and sliding my thumb over her clit, and pull back from kissing her.

I want to see what I'm doing to her. Watch how she reacts. Her head falls, and we both watch my hand, shoved down to her pants, but I can see where my fingers disappear into her.

Hear the slick sounds.

Her gasps and whimpers turn to groans and her hips buck faster against my hand. Against my dick.

"Oh God. Mikah." She still has fingers digging into my scalp. Pain and pleasure. It mixes together and I dip my head, suck her nipple into my mouth while I keep watching my hand. Watching Paisley come apart. "So close. More."

She's reduced to words and not sentences. Sounds with only vowels.

I'm not sure if she means harder or faster or keep going, but I take a risk and add another finger and she throws her head back, hair falling all over the place and the scent of vanilla hits my nose.

She's close. So close. I can feel her throb around my fingers and her hips lose control.

I rub her harder. Faster. Twisting my fingers to find that rigid space of flesh inside and when I suck her nipple into my mouth one last time, she falls apart.

She bites down on her lip. It doesn't hide the noises she makes. They're glorious.

I've made her come apart. I've never seen anything more sexy, watching her buck against my hand, rubbing my dick through my jeans and I bite down on my own lip so I don't come in my jeans.

"Vidunderlig."

She collapses to my shoulders and laughs. "What does that mean?"

"Gorgeous. Although I think the word in English might be prettier."

"I like when you speak Danish."

I usually only do it when I'm by myself, working out problems in my head, talking to myself. There are four different languages teammates can speak on the team but the only one we all know is English. I rarely speak in my native language anymore and yet I realize I do it plenty around Paisley. It comes without thought.

"Come here." I slide my hand out of her pants and wrap my arms around her. Her breasts press to my chest and her fingers finally release from my scalp.

I would tease her for hurting me, but I like it and I want her to do it more.

Next time.

When I've had the patience to get her to a bed, but I hadn't expected our kiss to turn into this.

Not that I'm complaining. Nope. No complaints here except my dick is still hard and wanting attention.

As if she knows, or understands, her hand slides between us and presses against my bulge. "It's later," she whispers, kissing the column of my throat. Her lips press against a vein there and *yes*. I like this idea very much.

Her lips are curled into a smile, I can feel it, hear the whisper of her quiet laugh.

"You don't have to." But God, I definitely *want*.

If she stays, we'll do this again, in my bed. Naked. I want her more than I can remember wanting anything other than hockey.

Paisley's hand goes to the button of my jeans and her fingers work quickly. Frantically. It's almost like she wants my dick in her hands more than I do. She leans back to her knees, breasts swinging in a tantalizing way so close to my face and grinning at my still covered dick like it's dessert.

The zipper goes down.

And *yes. I most definitely want.*

"Can I?" she asks, hand sliding to my waistband. She's wiggled back on my lap to give herself more room.

Oh yes. She can. I will let her do whatever she desires.

Until a piercing cry comes from the hallway.

"No," I moan and close my eyes, cringing.

"Angelo," she whispers. Her head has turned and she's looking in the direction of the hallway, his bedroom, to where he sounds very unhappy.

"I should go get him." But it will take me a second to move. I don't tell her that. Instead, I kiss her quickly, brush the hair off her cheek and slide her off my lap. I grab her shirt and hand it to her. "You get dressed. We'll be right back."

ANGELO IS NOT happy when I enter his room. He's kicked his legs so much he's no longer swaddled in that weird way where his arms and legs are so tight only his face shows through the blanket. I'm more than a little frustrated he's cock-blocked me once again, but somehow, as soon as I have him in my arms, that frustration melts away.

He has the strangest effect on me. Making me feel bigger and stronger than I already am in the weirdest, most indescribable way.

I dig through his crib for his pacifier and come up empty, so I grab another one from the changing table. The furniture was delivered and installed earlier this week and my condo is quickly being overtaken by baby things. Baby things are everywhere.

I like cleanliness. Order. Rules and priorities where I can make lists and ensure everything runs like a well-oiled ship.

Angelo undoes all of that in the span of twenty minutes and my home has never been more disorderly since Angela dropped him at my door. And yet, I'm not irritated by that either.

He rejects the pacifier, head whipping back and forth and pinched up in the way he does when he's really angry about something.

And still, I smile at him. "I should probably thank you. Or maybe your mom." Although I do not want to thank Angela for anything yet, except for maybe giving him to me. "Without you, I might not have just had my hand down my neighbor's pants."

A snort comes from behind me and I turn. Paisley is in the doorway, holding a bottle, shaking her head and laughing at me. "I don't think you should let him know what we just did."

"He doesn't understand. And besides, I think he likes it." He's quieted down.

Perhaps he smells his formula. Perhaps he likes Paisley more than he likes me.

I will take the credit for it this time though. I bounce him in my arms and reach out for the bottle. "Thank you."

I don't remember the last time he ate and I'm not sure what time it is now except that it's late and he only slept for a couple of hours. Maybe if I can figure out how to get him happy now, he'll sleep until morning. Hopefully it's not wishful thinking.

Angelo takes the bottle and begins chugging like I haven't fed him in days, except for only a few hours. "I wonder if he's having a growth spurt. The book says they can eat a lot more and be unhappy."

"If he finishes that and gets fussy, we can give him more."

"Would you mind grabbing a diaper and his wipes?" I've taken to keeping most of them in his room.

"No problem." Paisley sashays by me and I'm drawn to the swish of my shirt and my pants on her body. Especially now that I know how good everything beneath it feels in my hands. She grabs what I'll need, and I gesture with my head for her to head back to the living room first.

"I'll feed him out there. Change him. See if I can get him back down."

"Also, you want to check out my ass when I'm in front of you, don't you?"

"Yes." There's no point in lying.

Paisley laughs and as she passes us, her hand presses to my cheek. I turn and kiss her palm. "It's getting late. I should go... unless, do you want me to stay?"

"The night. Yes. I want that." Even if it takes a while to get Angelo back to sleep, I still want to climb into my bed with Paisley. I want to hold her and sleep with her and wake up next to her even if sleep is all we do.

"Okay then." She winks at me. "Enjoy the show then."

She puts extra sway to her walk, and I grin, following her. In my arms, Angelo is still chugging his bottle. His eyes drift close as he does, and his body relaxes in my arms.

Good. Hopefully when he's full, I can change his diaper without rousing him too much.

And then I can get Paisley back in my arms. Her body pressed to mine.

Yes, that is definitely how I want to end this night.

CHAPTER TWENTY

Paisley

THE ROOM IS dark when I blink my eyes open. It takes me but a brief moment to remember where I am, whose bed I fell asleep in. Mostly because I'm still laying with my head pressed to Mikah's bare chest, his hand wrapped around me and resting on my lower back.

It's been a long time since I've woken up pressed to someone and yet this is exactly how he wanted it last night. I'm more surprised I haven't moved. I usually enjoy my space in a bed, but perhaps that's because most men I've slept with haven't meant as much to me as Mikah does even in the short time I've known him.

And he wanted me here. Like I was going to say no to him.

"Stay," he'd said again after he fed and changed Angelo and put him back to bed in his crib. "Stay the night with me."

I hadn't expected anything else to happen. I was exhausted, from the late hour and the orgasm and goodness gracious. For a man with little experience, Mikah knows exactly how to work a woman's body. The memory alone of how quickly and confidently he learned what I liked, watched my responses and brought me to an orgasm that had me fighting a scream makes my body flush with heat down to my toes that are pressed against his ankle.

Angelo is quiet based on the sounds, or lack of sounds, coming from the monitor on Mikah's nightstand. The clock says it's almost seven, which means Angelo has slept for over six hours.

Thank goodness. With how unhappy he was last night, I'm glad he's sleeping. I would think if he was sick, he wouldn't have slept so well overnight.

As much as I want to stay curled up next to Mikah, or perhaps wake him doing more enjoyable things—after all, I still owe him an orgasm—there are other things I need to do today.

Work. I'm behind on my research. I wasn't lying when I said I had a head full of him. He's consumed all of my thoughts since we officially met, and I've been slacking on things that must be done. I don't have time to waste today.

Beneath my hand, Mikah's chest rises and falls, deeper and then shallow, becoming unsteady. I feel his head turn. His lips press to my head.

"You're still here."

"Just woke up."

He squeezes me tightly to him and groans. "Spend the day with me. Just like this."

"You're still dreaming if you think Angelo will allow that."

"Perhaps I should have hired Leah." I snort at that the thought. "Then I could have you alone all day."

I press up on his chest so I can smile down at him. He's sleepy and disheveled and frustration lines his brow. "I'll give that to you anytime you want it, but to be honest, I have to get to campus this morning and get work done. I'm behind on my thesis research and I have a check-in later this week."

He groans again, wipes a hand across his face and then shoves back his hair. "It's early. Stay with me just a while. Like this. Possibly with less clothes on."

Beneath the sheets draped across his hips, he only has on a pair of black boxers. I slept in the shirt last night. "We're practically naked already."

"Practically naked. Not naked."

He rolls quickly, so fast, I squeal as his body is suddenly on top of mine and his elbows are by my shoulders. He keeps his weight off me, but his fingers slide to my head and then my scalp where he threads his fingers through my hair. I tip my chin up so I can look him in the eye.

"You make a valid argument. But I really do have to work." At the thought, my lip curls.

"You don't like your work?"

"Oh, no. I mean, I don't really like school. But I've always wanted to be a teacher. I think I'm just ready to be done." The last thing I want to do is lay here beneath him and think of anything else.

I press my hand to his cheek and lift my head, kissing his chin. It's all I can reach.

"Maybe, if you let me up now, I can bust my ass on campus this morning. Then we can have the afternoon and evening together?"

"I think that sounds perfect. On one condition."

He leans forward and keeps coming until I'm forced to fall to my back. He *still* keeps moving until his lower half is pressed to mine. *Wow* and *oh dear sweet heavenly Jesus.* He's hard. And so big.

"What's the condition?" I ask, losing my breath to this man.

"Kiss me."

"That's it?"

"Two conditions then. Kiss me. And on Monday, come to Jude's Labor Day party with the team. All families are invited."

"Okay." That's easy. I like his teammates. And the girl-friends and wives I've met. Plus Katie, Jude's fiancée and I totally hit it off last week.

"Good." He grins and drops his head. "Now, about that other condition."

How can I not give in? I lean forward and press my lips to his. True to form, Mikah allows me to lead it for a moment before taking over.

And I love that about him, too.

***

AFTER I TEXTED Mikah to let him know I was on my way home from school, he met me in our hallway. Angelo was in the stroller, strapped into his car seat and facing Mikah, happily sucking on a pacifier, feet moving back and forth on the seat like he was excited to see me.

He's probably too young for that, but I like imagining it. Mikah insisted they were ready to go so I let them in for a few minutes to change my clothes and throw my hair up. It's cloudy with rain forecasted for later in the evening, making it a good afternoon to be outside with Angelo. It's not too hot or sunny for him.

We're now walking through Charlotte, headed to one of the city parks while devouring lobster tacos from a food truck we stopped at.

"What's it like? College? Graduate school?"

He tilts his head and presses his overflowing lobster taco closed at the top. I'm not sure how it's possible a man can look so sexy chomping down on a taco. Mikah pulls it off so well it takes me a moment to process what he asked.

And then why—he never got to go to college. Or maybe he didn't want to.

"It was fun." I try to remember my undergrad years but they're a blur of a lot of beer, a handful of frat boys, and late-night Jimmy John's sub sandwich deliveries. "A lot of work, a lot of studying. Classrooms that looked like auditoriums and sat hundreds. But there were weekend parties. Fraternity and sorority parties and get-togethers. Football games. Basketball games."

"And you went to those?"

I bump my hip into him. "Purely for the social aspect, I promise."

"Of course." He eats the rest of his taco and balls up the wrapper, pressing it into the cup holder of Angelo's stroller. "And graduate school? It's different?"

"It is. A lot of classes can be taken online and there are a lot of programs that are for those already working so it's mostly night classes. I'm lucky Charlotte has the full-time day program. I wouldn't want to work full-time and then go to classes all night."

"What do you want to teach?"

"Ah. That's the million-dollar question, isn't it?"

His eyes widen, as if I've surprised him. It's more

surprising to me that I know so much about the kind of man he is but know so little about him. "You don't know?"

"I always wanted to teach high school. But when I did my student teaching, I started thinking about middle school. And while I can teach English, I also keep debating about Social Studies. I want to take a subject kids usually find boring and make it more interesting for them. So, I guess, now, I don't really know. I have more time to figure it out, though."

In front of us, Angelo makes an unhappy sound and Mikah pulls back the cover to check on him. He's spit out his pacifier so Mikah pops it back. As he does, Angelo gives a full body shiver on his tiny little frame and sighs happily.

"He's so sweet." I can't believe how much I love this little guy. "I like him."

"I do too." Mikah leaves the cover open and starts walking again. "I also like you."

We dodge a couple boys racing down the sidewalk with a mom hurrying behind them. She gives us a harried expression and a quick I'm sorry before yelling their names as she passes us.

"Imagine that in a few years," I tease Mikah, laughing at the small boys who look to be around six or so.

Mikah's face pales and his eyes widen. He looks back at them, at Angelo and shakes his head. "Sometimes it is hard to think of more than a day. Years... that's... that seems like a lot."

I love how he can seem so confident, adjust so easily to becoming a dad and so easily unsettled.

"Have you told your parents about him yet?"

"No. They'll find out eventually. I thought of calling my mom and letting her know. But, no good will come from it, I do not think. And right now, I do not want someone telling me I cannot handle this."

"That sucks. I can't believe your dad is so harsh."

"Harsher than you can think of." We walk a little bit more and he turns to me, blond brow arched, head tilted in a way he seems to do whenever he's curious. "Your dad. What would he say?"

"If I showed up at home pregnant or with a baby?" I laugh at the thought. "He'd probably first get his shotgun and go hunting for the guy who knocked me up."

Mikah's already pale face turns whiter. I laugh, shoving his shoulder playfully.

"I'm kidding, but he's a small-town guy with small-town morals, you know? He thinks there's a way to do things and getting pregnant outside of marriage wouldn't be one of them. But I don't know..." I trail off, considering. I can see my father's disappointment in his eyes, my mom's fear. And then I see their hugs and feel their warmth and my eyes burn from it.

"They'd be shocked and disappointed," I admit. "I think all parents would. But they're good people and they love me. As soon as the news settled, they'd hug me and help me in any way they could."

"You come from good people."

"You might not think you do, but you're one of the best I've met, Mikah. Not many men would take a baby into their home, trusting it's theirs and doing everything you've done to give him a stable and loving home."

"I want to be better than my own father."

"You will." I have no doubts.

I cover his hand with mine on the stroller and we keep walking, connected and close. I never would have imagined being my age, so young, and dating a man with a child, but there's something so beautiful and right about every moment I've had with Mikah and Angelo, I stop questioning it.

I like this guy a lot. And I'll do whatever I need to help him find his footing, as well as grow closer to him.

CHAPTER TWENTY-ONE

Paisley

KATIE WASN'T JOKING when she said Jude lived in an enormous palace. No wonder why she knows where all the best antique and home furnishings stores are. She has to have been decorating the inside since she moved in last winter.

The home is massive, the gate at the neighborhood was my first clue but I'm still surprised by the elegance and size of Jude's home as Mikah pulls his car into the long drive that has a turnaround near the front door. It's currently lined and packed with vehicles for manufacturers I can only ever dream of affording. I'm not even sure why this money surprises me. They're professional athletes, after all. But there's something different about knowing they have money and *seeing* it.

It's so far outside what I'm used to nerves assault me.

Next to me, there's a man holding my hand, squeezing it

gently and behind me, there's a beautiful, little boy, babbling happily in his car seat.

And how did showing up like a happy little family become my life? And is it stranger that bothers me less than all this money?

"This is pretty much the perfect place to hold a team party." There has to be thirty cars out front and there's still space for more. The yard is massive, and I haven't seen the backyard.

"Pool and ball courts in the back. We can all show up and be big kids. Plus the kids can run wild, too."

"Does the whole team usually come?"

"Not all, but most. Some of the single guys miss because, well, it's family friendly. I didn't come last year, I don't think."

For a brief second I consider asking him why this year, but I'm not sure that's needed. Angelo in the back seat makes this more of Mikah's speed these days and I'm sure once we step through those doors, someone will swoop in and grab him and Mikah will get a break from daddy-duty for a few hours. Something he probably needs.

We've spent most of the weekend together when I haven't been on campus or at my place catching up on laundry and cleaning. But those times have mostly revolved around Angelo, and it should. I'm not complaining.

But we also haven't had any "alone" time like we did on Friday and even in the times where we could, Mikah didn't press for anything after the make-out session on Saturday morning in his bed. I'm not pushing for it. I'm not certain if he needs or wants more time before taking things further, and I don't need more affection to know he likes me.

He's teased and implied he wants more, but he hasn't taken us there. Unless he's waiting for a clue from me.

He pulls his SUV to a stop, sparkling black Land Rover that's so clean inside and out and still has a lingering smell of *eau de new vehicle* scent, it makes me curious how old it is. I've learned Mikah is particularly clean and neat, so perhaps he's had it for years and it still smells new.

Whichever. I open my door and climb out, then open the back door on the passenger side so I can grab Angelo's car seat from his base. It's easier to grab him than wait for Mikah and by the time he reaches us, Angelo is in his car seat, the plastic handle over my forearm and I have his diaper bag, something that's possibly four sizes too large and stuffed full like we're on a weekend getaway over my shoulder.

"I'll take him," Mikah says, reaching out.

"I don't mind." I already have him.

"You do too much already." He divests me of the car seat and the diaper bag with ease and for a moment, he looks so damn sexy holding his baby with the diaper bag on his shoulder, I gape at him.

"You're really hot." Yep. I say it. Who knows what happens to my filter sometimes around him.

He gives me a look part amused, perhaps slightly turned on. "I could say the same about you."

He looks down at my feet, toes freshly painted in a bright turquoise color that matches the swimsuit I have on beneath my coverup with a bright floral pattern all over. The coverup is modest, the bikini beneath is absolutely not, and I almost feel bad knowing I'm going to end up spending the next several hours teasing Mikah relentlessly with my sexy swimsuit.

Perhaps it'll be the jump he needs to move things *forward* between us.

A girl can hope. Or at least, this girl can.

As for Mikah, he's dressed in bright blue swim trunks with large and hideous bright green flowers on them. He looks ridiculous, and yet sexy, because he's clearly bought them for the fun of it. On his top, he has a plain white T-shirt on and as soon as I saw him my first thought, "I hope there's a wet t-shirt contest later today."

Boys only, of course.

And really, it would be a good idea. Perhaps the team could do it for a fundraiser of sorts. All the hot hockey players hosing down their shirts to the pleasure of women. So much more fun that watching women do it.

At least for me, but I suppose to each their own with what view they'd find more gorgeous.

"You ready?"

While I've been ogling him, he's stepped to my side, draped his arm behind me and placed his hand at my back.

"As I'll ever be." I'm thankful I met his teammates before otherwise this would be incredibly intimidating. As it is, Katie's already texted me letting me know she's excited to see me and I know Hannah will be here too.

Before we reach the elegant double-door front entry surrounded by luscious plants blooming brightly, and bushes looking perfectly trimmed, the raucous sound of children and men and families inside filters out.

There are a lot of people here. Most of whom I haven't met, and they will all know me as Mikah's date.

I don't want to disappoint him or make a bad impression.

Perhaps my sexy and strappy bikini meant to titillate Mikah is too much. The last thing I want people thinking is I'm some puck bunny. And women can sometimes be worse than men in their judgments. My steps falter on the brick stairs we're headed up and Mikah stops, juggles Angelo in his car seat.

"What is it?"

"Nothing." I'm staring at the door. Nerves are making my stomach roll. I'm being silly. Who cares what people think.

But oh God. What if this gets out on social media?

Yeah, the bikini might be too much. It's not the most risqué thing in the world, but definitely sassier than I usually wear.

"Um. I think I'm nervous."

Mikah's hand is still at my back, fingers digging in, calloused finger pads that feel delicious on my skin scraping along the cover up.

"What are you nervous about?"

"Well, besides wanting your friends to like me, I think maybe I should have chosen a different suit."

At my shoulder I have a swim bag packed with our towels and sunscreen and a few bottles of water. I also have an outfit to change into later. Maybe I'll just throw them on now and forgo the bikini altogether.

"Why?"

His brows are pulled in, lines dig into his forehead between them.

"Um. Nothing." I'll simply go use the restroom when I get inside. Change my outfit and stay out of the pool. Who cares that it's going to be well over a hundred degrees today and there's no end to the summer heat in sight yet. "Never mind."

I take a step toward the door and he grabs my hand, tugging on me so I have to spin around or lose my balance.

"What is it?"

"Nothing, it's just... my suit is well, sexy, and I want to make a good impression on your friends."

To my utter and complete shock, he sets down Angelo's car seat, double-checks to make sure the sun isn't in his face and still pulls the visor on the car seat down further. Then he drops the diaper bag.

He crosses his arms over his chest. "Show me."

"What?" My eyes dart toward the house. The blinds are closed, but anyone could leave. Or arrive. And he wants me to do what? Rip off my cover-up?

"Show me the swimsuit. I've been thinking of this since Saturday when you said you'd come. I want to see you in a bikini." His lips twitch. Those Caribbean blue eyes of his smolder. "Mostly I want to see you in nothing, but the bikini will work."

Oh. Well. *Wow.* He's so sweet and kind. His bossy sexiness always throws me. Comes out of nowhere. And now there's an area of my bikini bottoms growing warm. Wet.

Great.

"Mikah."

"Let me see, Paisley. If you won't show the rest of them, do not deprive it from me."

And well, hey. I mean, I wore it for him anyway. Slowly, I lift my cover-up. It's loose and comes to my knees with a deep V-neck and wide, loose arms. It fits like the softest and lightest robe, almost a Mumu. I still love it.

"Tell me if I should change, okay? And be honest."

His gaze is fixed on my stomach area, stormy eyes holding the area and I see a flash of something darker, something that makes me hotter and it's not the obscene heat it's the obscene look on his face as I lift the cover-up and pull it over my head. My braid that's been draped over my shoulder flips to the back and itches my spine as it falls.

I barely notice.

Mikah's hands now dig into his hips. His jaw clenched tight. Gaze slowly but so intently roaming over my body, I feel it like a scrape against my sensitive skin.

"Mikah—"

I can barely breathe his name. The way he's looking at me is so... much.

"Later," he says, and his voice has gone low, difficult to understand with the accent and the look on his face. "Later when I take you to bed, we will start with you in that and then I will enjoy stripping it off you."

My knees shake. "It's too much."

"It is perfect. And sexy. And I will feel much honor if you wear that with me next to you." He finally meets my gaze again and that twinkle in his eye I love so much returns. "I will feel other things too, but perhaps we can finally take care of that tonight, too."

"Oh." He means *him*. Every time I've gone to touch him, he's stopped me. Said *later*. "Does this mean it's time for *later*?" I ask, lingering on the word, letting him know what I'm implying.

"Yes. Tonight is later."

Yippee. "And the suit?" It's a bikini but not. Dozens of thin turquoise straps criss-cross over and across my stomach and my back. The sides are open, almost making it look like I'm tied and strapped inside silk and satin. It's evocative.

It reminded me of Mikah's eyes when I saw it online and rush shipped it.

"Everything you wear is perfect. Sexy. I like it." He bends down and grabs the car seat. "Are you ready now?"

I mean, it's possible I'm ready to ditch the party all together and get to *later* now, but I'm pretty certain that's not what he means.

"Sure, Mikah." I throw on the cover-up, wait while he grabs the diaper bag. I pick up the bag with our towels and outside supplies and he throws the door open.

As soon as we step inside, his teammates who I swear huddle together in anticipation of Mikah preparing to enter the room, all throw their heads back, and shout, "Let's Go!"

Mikah grins down at me, pink hitting the tops of his ears. "I really hate that."

I laugh, shake my head, and shove him inside with my hand now at his back. "I don't think you mean that, superstar."

CHAPTER TWENTY-TWO

Mikah

"YOUR GIRL IS SOMETHING ELSE."

My girl. I like the way that every man here knows Paisley came with me. She isn't stealing the show, putting on an act, but she still seems to draw people to her with a natural grace I have been almost drooling over since the day I met her.

Jason, my teammate currently grinning at her, is the one who I owe a lot of it to.

I clink my glass of water to his. "Thanks for your help."

"No problem. Anytime you need help from the master come to me."

I grin into my glass of water, forcing myself to tear my eyes from Paisley. As soon as we entered, the women swooped in and took Angelo from me, fawning over him like so many women tend to do. Paisley was swept up with them and even though I wanted to see *more* of her bikini, and more of her out of it, I drifted off to the guys.

I have barely spoken more than four words to her since we arrived hours ago, but there will be time for that later.

"What are you losers sitting out here talking about?" Jude asks, sauntering up to us and slapping his brother on the shoulder. Their family is the best. Both guys are cool to hang out with. I went a little starstruck when I met their dad, John Senior, former New York hockey player, a man I grew up idolizing and wanting to be like.

When I first was drafted to the Ice Kings, I was sure his sons would be full of ego and arrogance, but they are good guys.

"Paisley," I admit, and I do not care. "And I was thanking Jason for helping me get her."

Jude's brows jump. "You took my brother's advice? And it worked?"

"Shove off baby Jude. I have mad game."

"Yeah with girls for a night or two, not long-lasting ones."

Jason makes a face that says he wants to punch his brother, but he is full of crap. The guys never fight. Not in any way that says they mean it. They're too close for that.

"His advice worked for me."

Which is stupid I needed it, but the night Paisley was at my place and Jason pulled me aside, he said one thing that stuck with me. That gave me the confidence to go after what I wanted, finally, going after something I want off the ice.

Girls like boldness and confidence. Say what you feel. Tell her what you think. But make sure it's honest. That's all you have to do.

For a man who seems to know women so well, I'm surprised he doesn't seem to care about anything more than short-term flings.

"Katie really likes her. She seems sweet. How's everything going with Angelo?"

I haven't had time to tell anyone about the nanny company, although I dealt with them immediately Friday night. They have someone new coming tomorrow. Time is ticking down.

We start training camp soon and exhibition games shortly after. Then the season begins.

If I'm going to be able to focus on my game this season, I need to know Angelo is taken care of while I am gone.

"Good. I guess." I take a sip of my water and shake my head. "That is not true. I think I fail at everything and every time I think of Angela, I want to punch someone. Not her," I say quickly. The guys know me, but that doesn't mean I want them thinking I'd hit a woman.

Never. But if I would... Angela would be at the top of my list.

"Have you talked to her at all? Ask her what the hell she was thinking?"

"I'm leaving that to my lawyer." My jaw tics as I think about Luke tracking her down. For someone who claims to be easy to find she doesn't seem interested in speaking with him now, and even though he tells me not to be concerned, I can't help it.

Today is not that day to be angry thinking about her, though.

"Where is Hendrix?" I scan the crowd. The entire team isn't here, but most are and it's not like Hendrix to miss out on a party. Plus, I want the change of subject.

"Madison is probably demanding attention," Jason says, seething behind his bottle of beer. "I'm sure he'll show later."

"I wouldn't count on it," Jude says. "The man's been in a crap mood all week."

"Because of Madison?" I have never understood the two of them. She acts like she hates all of us and the team and yet she has no problem enjoying the money.

"Who knows." Jason shrugs and he lifts his hand toward Chauncy across the patio. "And who cares. If he knows what's good for him, he'll kick her to the curb. I've gotta talk to Sawyer."

He takes off, heading toward Sawyer who has a girl at his side, someone I recognize. "What is Sawyer's sister doing in town?"

From what I can recall, she still lives in Toronto, Ontario where Sawyer is from. She usually comes to one or two games a year, but usually only around the holidays.

"You didn't hear?" At the quick shake of my head, Jude's jaw drops. "Dude. Sawyer's pissed. Her fiancé has been treating her like crap, so he offered to fly her down for the weekend. But apparently when she got back from work the other day before her flight to grab her bag, her entire apartment she shared with him was cleaned out. Everything but her clothes and shit plus the account they shared was empty."

"No shit?" I'd be pissed I didn't hear about this, but I haven't been hanging out in the locker rooms after practice or weight training. I throw on my clothes and hurry out of there so I'm sure I've missed a lot.

Sawyer is protective, no doubt, and with the way he stays close to his sister, his girlfriend Debbie too, I feel bad for her. No one deserves someone in their life who doesn't make them feel like the most important person. I watched enough women being treated like they don't matter to have learned exactly how *not* to treat someone you claim you care about.

Which really makes me hope I don't screw things up with Paisley. It's not like I've had the best role model.

"Damn. That seriously sucks. Anyone know where he went?"

"Sawyer's making calls. She's supposed to be here only for the weekend, but I think Sawyer's trying to get her to stay longer."

"Good. Good for her." At least, I think it is until I see Jason approach her on the other side of the pool. She straightens her spine and narrows her eyes at him. Whatever Jason says to her, smiling like the happy-go-lucky guy he usually is makes her scoff.

"What's going on there?" I tip my beer in their direction.

Jude shrugs. "Fuck if I know. He and Sawyer went to college together. He's known him for years, so I figure he knows Tessa."

"Doesn't look like she likes him."

As I say it, her cheeks burn bright and she spins, stomping away from Jason. She heads straight to the bar and slams down her beer.

Jason, on the other hand, shoves his hand to his hips, glaring daggers at her I can feel from a dozen yards away before he tips his head back to the sky.

"He's probably just pissed about her shit. When he and Chauncy met, she would have been like, sixteen or something. Like a little sister."

Yeah... no. That is not a little sister vibe I have from the pissed off Jason. He's too laid back for that. Whatever. It's none of my business.

I punch Jude in the shoulder. "I'm going to go check on Angelo."

I haven't seen him in an hour. Some of the men who have teenage children hired their kids to watch the younger ones. I'm not used to Angelo being away from me. I thought it would be easy, but other than Paisley, he's the only one I keep thinking about.

"See you later?" Jude asks.

"Probably."

Or not. I still keep thinking of Paisley in her swimsuit. And how I want to take it off her. She hasn't ditched the cover-up since we arrived, and I give her a small, brief wave on my way inside. There is a room on the main living area that I think is supposed to be a library, but based on the lack of books, I don't think Jude has ever used it. It's where the kids were supposed to play inside.

Soft, childlike laughter guides me down the hall and I'm almost to the room when a warm hand wraps around my wrist and tugs.

"Hey you."

It's Paisley. My chest squeezes at the sight of her. Now that I know what's beneath the baggy but soft cover-up, it's all I can see when I look at her. Her head is tilted to one side, green eyes sparkling with mischief. Her cheeks are pink, perhaps from the scorching heat outside. Her blonde hair, spun like gold, flops over one shoulder with the end of it brushing over her breast.

It's her lips that grab and hold my attention. They're pressed into a smile. One that hints of teasing to come, or better yet... something else.

"What is it? You okay?"

"Doing great, Lutzgo. Come here for a minute."

Before I can ask where, she's dragging me down, past

the library, around a corner and into a room I haven't been yet.

It has a bed, simple white, fluffy cover, no headboard, and one dresser. The room is plain as can be and I assume it's a guest room. I'm really not thinking of Jude's guests in his house when Paisley places her hand on my chest and pushes me backward.

"What are you doing?"

"I keep thinking of *later* and I can't concentrate on anything else."

Oh. Yeah, I like where this is going. My eyes go to the door behind her. It's shut. And locked.

How did she do that so quickly and quietly?

"You are?"

Her hand on my chest runs down to the edge of my shirt, and then her palm is at my stomach, sliding to the back. She moves closer until her breasts are pressed to my chest and a heat hotter than the hundred-degree temperature outside floods my system.

"What are you—"

"Shh. I'm sorry, Mikah. But I don't think I can wait until later anymore."

As she speaks, she's rolling to her toes, pressing her lips to mine. I do not want to wait anymore either. And I forget all the reasons why I was waiting, which was mainly so we weren't distracted by Angelo in the middle of anything important, when her hand at my stomach moves to the center of my abs.

And then *down*.

My dick is semi-hard, getting harder by the moment and when her fingertips press over my growing bulge, all my muscles constrict.

Right. There was another reason why I wanted to wait.

Because the last thing I want is for this to be over too soon, for me to embarrass myself. To make Paisley think I'm not good at this.

"Paisley." My hand covers hers, and together we put pressure to my now, fully hard cock beneath my swim trucks.

Good Lord, I do not want to be interrupted.

And I most definitely do not want to blow too soon.

"I know you don't have much experience," she whispers, and this time, my muscles harden for an entirely different reason.

Embarrassment. I might have implied it, but who would have...

"Paisley." My voice is rough. Thick with lust but shaking with nerves.

"I figure," she keeps whispering like I'm not trying to stop this. We should talk first.

I should explain.

"I figure, if I take care of you now, it will be better for both of us later." Her hand at my dick presses, slides along my covered shaft. My hips buck into her hold. They now have a mind of their own, my hips, my need. All rational, careful thought has fled my brain.

"You don't have to." But God, please, if you're there, help her stay on this path.

My embarrassment recedes, quickly taken over the desire to have her.

To have her *want* this. And me. Not just my dick.

But *me.*

"Oh. I might not have to, but tasting you has been all I can think about. It keeps me awake at night. I think of you, inside of me, before I fall asleep. Trust me, Mikah. I want this."

She squeezes again, firmly, not too hard. The perfect amount of pressure along my length to pull a groan from my throat.

And then she surprises the hell out of me, dropping to her knees, curling her hands around the waistband of my swim trunks and tugging them with her.

"Shit," I gasp at the sight of her. The top of her head, blonde and highlighted in my view and eyelashes fluttering along the top of her cheeks as her focus is on my dick. Hard and erect.

Aching.

Burning with the thought of what she's about to do.

My hand goes to her hair and I run a finger over her head, behind her ear, getting her attention until she tilts her chin up at me.

She has her hand on my dick. Slowly stroking. It's painful and incredible and my jaw may break from trying to hold on.

I will not go too soon, but hell, I could give it all to her right now.

"Take off your cover," I grunt. I do not think I'm being nice.

Paisley does not seem to care.

She grins at me, lets go of my dick, and she wiggles on her knees until she's pulled the cover-up over her head and tosses it on the floor next to her. It pools like silk and my shirt joins it after. My swim trunks that I kick off to free them from my ankles are next.

I'm naked and staring, speechless, at her on the carpeted floor. The strings of that swimsuit. The brightness of it.

It looks like a puzzle, a maze, something I will have to solve to take off her later.

But more than that, it's Paisley—

On her knees. To *please me.*

God. If there has ever been anything more beautiful, I would be surprised.

My balls are full and pulled tight and she just looks at me, smiling.

"I knew you'd be gorgeous everywhere." Her voice is a whisper. Pleased.

And for some damn reason, I *like* that she likes looking at my dick.

"Please." I am begging. Her hand is firm but small. Her nail polish is bright white. And her strokes are short, and then long. Teasing. At risk of taking me to the end before I feel the warmth of her mouth.

"Suck me." No woman has done this to me. I have fantasized about me, jerked off to the idea of it. But now I feel like I'm being a jerk and I don't want that. Not for Paisley.

"Mikah," she whispers and she leans forward, slides out her tongue and takes one slow stroke around the tip of me. "I like it when you're bossy. It makes me wet. So stop thinking, start enjoying, and say or do whatever you want."

She might kill me. There goes my season. This woman might bring me to my knees right here.

"Pais—"

And it's all I get out before she puts her mouth back on me, but it's not just her tongue, it's her whole mouth, sucking deep, taking me in until her lips meet the curve of her fingers.

And oh holy shit, I will most definitely not survive this. It's so warm. Wet.

My hands go to her head mostly to keep myself from falling over but also because if she likes it when I boss her, there are other things I want to.

Like have control.

It might be the only want I have.

I am careful with her, not pressing her hard, and I let her work her magic while I mumble curses and grit my teeth.

There are people in this house, I'm vaguely aware of the voices and the activity and the memory that I have a *kid* who is not too far away.

But Angelo, for the first time in weeks, is the very *last thing* on my mind as Paisley keeps sucking me. And then her hand drifts down to my balls and—

"Holy shit," I bite out. "Do that. More."

My orgasm is close. But I want this. Her squeezing my balls, sucking them. It is dirty and so damn sexy that she seems to get so into this.

My teammates have said there are two kinds of women.

Women who love the power and control of a blow job, of giving and having that power over a man.

And women who dole them out as chores on birthdays and anniversaries.

Thank you to the God in Heaven if he exists that Paisley seems to be the first.

"Yeah," I groan, and she takes me deep. She has one hand on my hip, the other on my balls. She gags when she takes me deep and I can't help it.

I really like that, too. Her eyes water as she peers up at me, and I do what feels right. I hold her there for a minute, watch her green eyes darken from her tears before pulling her back.

"Do it," she whispers. Her cheeks are flushed. "Do what feels good, Mikah."

It sounds like a dare. Perhaps she's as desperate for me as I am her.

"You look sexy down there. I want to do to your mouth what I want really want to do to your body later."

She pumps my dick and licks off the glistening liquid that is there. "Show me."

Goodness. This woman.

She keeps getting more perfect for me.

I take her again, pumping my hips into her throat. I like the way she moans when I hit the back of her throat, the way she hums around my tip when I pull out. Her suction is divine. It only makes me think of how tight she'll be when I finally get her to a bed.

And that's all it takes. The thought of my dick in her. How wet will she be?

How tight?

"Paisley," I grunt. "I'm going to—"

As if she knows, she moves both of her hands to my hips. She pulls me toward her, takes me all the way until I feel my dick down deep in her throat.

She swallows and it's so damn good I come. My orgasm lights up my veins like a wildfire and my fingers dig into her scalp.

"Yes," I groan, as I empty myself, my dick throbbing, my balls feel like they're exploding, and Paisley takes it.

She takes it all, gasping and swallowing and making it all feel like the best present in the world. And when I am done, she eases off, circles my head with her tongue and smiles up at me.

"I take it you liked it?"

CHAPTER TWENTY-THREE

Paisley

I'M FILLED with a sudden rush of feminine euphoria at what just happened.

I can't believe I just gave Mikah a blow job in Jude's guest bedroom.

It's not me. I don't mind being bold, but I'm definitely not a take charge and drive the men crazy kind of girl. I blame Mikah and his *show me* attitude earlier with his arms crossed, dropping his gaze to my swimsuit and my breasts in such a way that hours later I still feel his eyes on me.

I blame him for driving me so crazy lately with the desire to have all of him, I can't stop thinking about what it will be like.

I blame him for looking at me with such intensity all afternoon. The only thing I've been able to think of is *later* and what exactly that means.

Mostly, I blame his genetics and even his jerk of a father

for blessing Mikah with such glorious DNA that it's impossible to not want to do what I've done for him.

And I'm still on my knees, going from bossy vixen to teasing temptress in a matter of moments.

Yeah. I like this guy. A whole lot.

I hand him his shirt and swim trunks, but he ignores them as he takes my wrist, gently pulling me to my feet.

"I am blown away by how beautiful you are," he says. His heart is racing. I can see it in his pulse at his throat and the way his chest heaves and another powerful rush floods my system.

I can bring this hockey playing star to this trembling mess. It's good for my own ego and confidence.

"You did not have to do that, but I am so, so very glad you did." His finger trails down my cheek. My hair must be completely messy from his fingers digging into it. I reach up and pat it down.

"I wanted to."

He swallows slowly, his gaze taking in my flushed and heated skin, swollen lips, the tremor of my own rapid pulse.

"I wish I had a sitter for Angelo. I want time, alone with you."

"About that." I'm suddenly nervous and clasp my hands together. It's not my place and it most definitely wasn't earlier, but when Hannah saw me watching him earlier, she brought it up. "I sort of lined one up for you... or us... maybe?"

His blue eyes narrow and he pushes his lips out. He looks stern. Possibly annoyed. Who can blame him? I definitely overstepped.

"Hannah saw me staring at you earlier and she teased me about what you're like in bed. I told her I didn't know yet and she said she'd watch Angelo after the party today."

"She what?" I've ruffled him. He runs his hand through his hair, shakes it before it falls to his hip. And yeah, I'm staring. I mean, he's still naked. And totally unconcerned.

And I might have already seen him naked, but him naked and *hard?* Well... Mikah is glorious. Every single inch —and there's a lot of them.

"She—"

"Let's go." He grabs my hand and yanks me toward the door.

"Mikah!"

"What? If she's offering, I'm taking her up on it. I want you. Alone."

"And I love that." I gesture to his lower half and I can't help but laugh. "But maybe we should get our clothes back on first?"

Mikah glances at the clothes still strewn on the floor and curses. "I lose my mind around you. Forget everything." He yanks on his shorts and tosses me my cover-up. "Do not think you'll be wearing that long, but no one is seeing that suit besides me."

His bossiness is a side of him I didn't expect. Especially not when he grabbed my hair earlier, held me against him... the memory makes me flush and I lick my lips.

"If you keep looking at me like that our first time will be in Jude's house and that is not what I want for you."

"Okay, okay. Keep your pants on." I throw on my cover-up and when I look at Mikah again, his brow is puckered. "What?"

"My pants are on. I just put them on."

I laugh again. "It's an expression. It means be patient."

I slide up to him and he wraps his arm around my lower back. "I think we have waited enough, yes?"

IT TAKES MUCH LONGER than I'd like to say our good-byes. Then we have to find Hannah in the swarm of teammates, find Byron to get his keys to the SUV so we can transfer the car seat base to their car. Hannah assures Mikah almost a thousand times when he keeps repeating Angelo's schedule that she's got this under control. Thankfully, when he packs the diaper bag, he packs it like he's going to be out of town for the weekend so I'm certain Angelo has plenty of food, pacifiers, and diapers for a few hours.

Hannah and Byron promise to bring him back to Mikah's later tonight, which gives us *hours* alone. No one pushed for an overnight babysitting job, so I kept my mouth shut.

I planned enough I probably shouldn't have, but when Hannah teased me earlier about having sex with Mikah, and I admitted we hadn't yet, I mentioned Angelo... and it all went from there.

Hannah and I might have started a bit rocky a couple of weeks ago, but I'm starting to completely love this woman.

We're now in the car on the way back to our building, Mikah taking corners in his SUV like he's being chased by men with guns, zipping through the streets of Charlotte. His hand is on my thigh, mine covers his, and we've barely spoken until when he whips his SUV through the underground parking garage, yanking the steering wheel one last time into his spot.

Mikah turns off the ignition and turns to me. "Are you hungry? We can order something to eat if you would like."

I had a burger, potato salad, regular salad, not to mention the regular snacks and chips and vegetables with dip. Plus, I couldn't pass by the dessert area and not snag a few cookies.

Twice.

In my defense, they were small.

Also, I like cookies and all things sweet and I have no regrets.

"I had plenty of food at the party."

"Good. That is good then." He shoots me a look, but it's not the same intense one I'm expecting and then I realize…

He's nervous.

I open my door and flash him a wink. "So, your place or mine, superstar?"

I do what I usually do when I see it on him and make it fun.

Because sex is *fun*. I mean, once you get past the head bonking, teeth-banging, knee burns and awkward positions or falling off beds, which really makes it all that much more fun.

But that's the point of some of the mishaps, sex is always better when you're comfortable with your partner when those happen, when you can laugh, or snort, and get back to the groove enjoying yourself.

I'm at the back of his SUV before him, but barely, and his hand takes mine.

"Should we get our bag?" I have the tote with our towels and things in the back seat.

Mikah shakes his head. "I will come get it later tonight. Or tomorrow. Or… when I remember. I do not care about beach towels or sunscreen right now."

"Oh?" We're in the parking garage lobby which is much more utilitarian than the main lobby and we have to use our keys to enter the elevator so while we wait, I rest a shoulder against the wall. "In a hurry for something?"

"You tease me, and you make everything fun. I keep thinking what else you can make fun."

His hand's still in mine, thumb brushing along my inner wrist. "Mikah. It's okay to be nervous."

"I don't think that is the right word. More... anxious? Perhaps that is right?"

Possibly. But I don't need him *worrying* about anything either.

"There's no need. Trust me, with everything we've done so far, I will have no complaints."

"You will if I come in my pants like I'm fourteen and Ms. Halderslug bent over to lift a folder off the floor."

His description is, well... perfect.

"Mikah." I laugh, shaking my head and pull him toward me until he collides with my shoulder and then my chest as I adjust. "That was disturbingly visual and even if you do happen to have a fantasy of your high school teacher while you're with me and come too soon, we'll figure it out. That's part of the nerves everyone has with a new partner. We're all different. We like different things."

"I know. And so far, I like all the things you like."

This *guy*. I can easily fall for him and all my reservations weeks ago when I found out who he is have vanished. Well, they're there, shoved to a back corner where I place unimportant matters like remembering to water the two houseplants I have, but I manage to do a decent job silencing them.

The elevator door dings and opens and Mikah ushers us, keeping us close, chest to chest, his chin tipped down, mine tilted up.

And then he kisses me. And I hope with the way I respond I melt away all his anxious thoughts, giving him the confidence I know he wants like he has on the ice.

CHAPTER TWENTY-FOUR

Mikah

SHE MAKES me feel too much. Too many good things. Something deeper than the love I have for hockey. The thought alone should make me terrified.

Hockey is all I've ever had.

But now I have more.

I have a son. I have a family made and built on my own from the love of a game we all adore, and I have a woman who constantly builds me up, looks at me like I can *do this* and sometimes, that emotion is overwhelming.

It's currently overwhelming me, the heady need to strip her out of her cover-up and swimsuit again, to figure out how to get those straps off her and to return to her what she did to me earlier.

We kiss until the elevator stops at our floor and then we stumble out of it, my back hitting the wall before I change our positions, my hand on the wall above her head on the wall.

Thank goodness we're the only two homes up here. As we kiss and stumble down the hall, we are making way too much noise.

"Paisley," I grunt and fumble with the keys from my pocket and fumble even more to get my door unlocked. I have never been so clumsy with my hands before.

Once my door is unlocked, I pull back. I need to get my bearings and slow things down before my worries in the elevator come to fruition sooner than I could have ever imagined. My dick is impossibly hard, rubbing against her heat.

At least she has no worries of Mrs. Halderslug. There isn't a single thought in my brain except for pleasing her.

And even then, I'm pretty certain ninety percent of my brain is in my dick.

"Inside. Now."

She drags her lips off my throat, and I feel the loss of her straight in my balls. I can still feel her lips around my dick. Her mouth on me, taking every inch and deep in her throat.

Paisley winks at me, sashaying her sweet ass into my home and as soon as we're both in, I lock the door. As soon as we're alone, she turns to me.

Her blonde hair is wild, coming undone from the braid and the first thing I want to do is undo it completely, wrap it around my fist. Take her from behind. Watch her ride me.

So many things I want to do with her. To her.

She doesn't give me a chance because her hands fall to the hem of the baggy dress thing she has on and she lifts it... stealing my breath and the remainder of my thoughts as she exposes her swimsuit again to me.

"Bed." I bark it out. She's reduced me to an animal. Incapable of politeness.

Winking again, she walks backward down the short

hall, toward my room. Her fingers trail along the walls, arms out, and I watch every movement. I follow her, waiting for my moment to attack. I'll let her think she's in control. I'll even allow her to have it for a bit, too.

She moves into my room and I'm right there with her, flipping on the lights despite it still being afternoon. I can see plenty, but there's no way I'm missing a moment of this. I want to catalog and learn every curve of her. Every freckle.

Paisley stops at the end of the bed, knees to it and before she falls back, I shake my head.

"Stop." I'm right here, curling my hand to her shoulder, running it down her arm. Goosebumps follow in my wake. Turning this woman on is thrilling.

My hand trembles as I settle it on her hip, my fingers slide under two of the straps there and my other hand goes to the side of her neck.

"This suit. It's a maze I want to solve and tear to pieces at the same time."

"Please don't." She laughs. "It was really expensive."

"You'll never wear it without me." Apparently, I'm possessive. She laughs again, but I'm not joking. There's a pool on the roof of the building's sixth floor. There's a whole outdoor park up there, and I don't even want her wearing the suit there.

I meet her gaze, let her see how serious I am. Her laughter dies instantly.

"Mikah—"

"You're stunning. So beautiful. Like a pink sunset. My favorites. I don't want other men looking at you or admiring it."

She shakes her head. If I've made her mad, we'll fight about it later. But there will be people who discover she's connected to me. They will want her to get to me. I'll explain it all later when rationality has returned to my brain.

"There's a clasp at the back."

My hands are exploring her wound body, giving me too many other ideas. I find the clasp at the back she mentions and then ignore it. Instead, I grab her hips and lift her easily.

She lets out a laugh and shoves her face into my shoulder, clinging to me. "Mikah!"

"Hold on to me." I put a knee to the bed and crawl up it, easily holding her until I can bend forward and settle her on my pillows.

She's been here before, even spending the night. But I have never wanted her like this so badly.

As soon as her back hits the bed, she loosens her grip on my shoulders but keeps her ankles locked at my lower back. I push up to my knees, staring down at this gorgeous, effervescent woman. So small. So sweet.

Becoming so much more to me than I could have imagined weeks ago.

"I don't know where to start." I whisper it, afraid of being too loud. I do not want to break this moment.

She runs her hands down my arms to my waist and pushes up my shirt. I tear it off my head, remembering how I did this less than an hour ago. And then her hands are pressed to my hot flesh, the ridges of my abs.

I have never in my life, remembered, *needing* someone as much as I need her. It's not about her being *a* woman.

It's about her being Paisley—*the* woman.

"Mikah," she gasps as I brush my fingers to the small patch of fabric at her center. It's so small, barely covers her sex before two straps crisscross over her hipbones and then back over her stomach. Her belly button is on display, and her abs constrict with every panted breath. When I brush along her sex again, her abs tighten and her chin tips up.

I bend down and kiss her, moving the strap of greenish-blue fabric to the side and then I'm there. Right there. She's soaking wet.

"Mikah." Her hand curls around my wrist. "More," she gasps. "Please."

I tease her slit, gritting my teeth. "Are you sure?"

She shoves her head deeper into my pillow and groans. "I told you. Anything you want to do to me, I'll want. Whenever you want."

I will hold her to that. "Can you come like this? With just my fingers, teasing your clit?"

"Possibly." Her legs tighten around my hips. There's no possibly about it, but it's not how I want her to come. Gently, I unwrap her legs, pulling back from her so I can run my hands up and down the soft creamy flesh of her inner thighs. The even softer skin behind her knee. I lift one of her legs, kissing her there and she squirms.

"Perfect. And you taste delicious."

I set her leg on the bed, spread wide. Her hands are curled into the bed covering beneath her. If only I had a camera to capture this moment. When Paisley becomes *mine*.

It's that thought that snaps my control and I move down the bed further, pulling to the side the center of her suit. Our eyes meet and I keep my focus on her, as I press my mouth to her clit for the first time. As soon as I do, her hips buck and a hissed *yes* falls from her round, pink and swollen lips.

Her grip tightens on the coverings. My dick, hard as stone, punches into the bed as I taste her, suck her clit into my mouth. I add a finger. Then two. Looking at her for consent as I do, but she just opens her mouth and lets loose a sound that tells me she enjoys everything, absolutely everything I'm doing to her.

It's the encouragement I need to keep going and I fuck her slowly with my fingers, my mouth on her clit. She's drenched. Whimpering.

"Mikah. So good." She threads her fingers into my hair, nails dig into my scalp.

Yes. "Hurt me. Show me how much you love what I can do for you."

"So close. Please, please..."

I lick her clit again, press my fingers into her hard, adding a third and relish in the sound she makes as I stretch her. I curl them, find the ridge inside of her and her legs press against my head as her orgasm hits her. Her core, swollen and drenched, clamps around my fingers and I ride her through her climax, pressing one hand to her thigh to keep her held open until she breathes out, shivering from the pleasure.

And me? I could be a God and not feel as powerful as I do at this moment. She's unraveled, eyes glazed, wisps of her highlighted hair clings to her forehead and she's slow to open her open.

"You... you are good at that. A natural."

I slowly drag my fingers out of her, kiss her inner thigh before resettling her swimsuit.

I am also still hard as a rock and need to be inside of her.

Shoving to my knees, I slide a hand beneath her back and pull her up with me. "Let's get this off of you, shall we?"

"Please." She's breathless. A surge of power thunders through me. I've done this. Made her languid and relaxed and almost sleepy. Her head flops to my shoulder as I find the clasp and undo it. I start with the straps at her shoulders and help her wiggle out of her suit.

It's easier than it looks to get her out of it and soon she's fully naked. "Exquisite. Every inch." I trail a finger down her cheek, brushing away her hair. She turns and nips at my finger, grinning. "You're only being sweet because you want to fuck me."

"I do but you're exquisite anyway." To prove how much I want her, I shove down my swim trunks.

Thank God. I've been dying to get out of the fabric and my dick juts straight toward her as I reach for the nightstand. The box is still sealed from when I bought them months ago. I rip the plastic off with my teeth and then tear off a strip of condoms, throwing the ones I'll save for later to the bed next to Paisley.

She holds them up in the air. "You think we'll need all of these? We only have a couple of hours."

I take them from her and silence her with a kiss. "I guess we'll have to see."

Ripping open the first packet, I keep my focus on Paisley, kissing her while I slide back over her and roll the condom on. I am the master of multitasking and right now there are too many things I want to do. To taste. To memorize.

Thank God she took care of me earlier or I would have already blown in my pants.

"Ready?" I ask. I wish I could be smoother. My demand for her is too great. "I'll go slow next time. Or last longer. Or..."

"I want you, Mikah." She slides her tongue into my mouth, kissing me like she isn't the one who just orgasmed. I grip my dick, settling it at her opening.

She spreads her legs wider, planting her feet into the bed, and then I'm there, pressing in.

And sweet holy Mary Mother of God. I'm not even Catholic. At least not since I was ten, but thank God for the Virgin Mother.

Paisley is swollen and so hot. She's tight and I move slowly, watching her expressions as I push in, pull out.

"Yes," she gasps and kisses me harder. Her hands go to my ass, my back, my thighs until I'm fully seated in her, and if my Catholic upbringing tells me I'm going to hell for this... I am one hundred percent okay with it.

There is nothing better than the heat and slickness of Paisley, tight around me, whimpering into my mouth as I move slowly.

It's killing me to do so. My balls are pulled tight. Full. My skin is burning, and the base of my spine is on fire.

"More," she groans into my throat and I feel it hit my balls. My God. I only have one sliver of a thread of control left and every time she tells me to do something it severs.

Her hands grip the back of my thighs, pulling me deeper into her body and showing me how she likes it.

I press a hand to her chest and lean back. "Hard?"

"As hard as you can."

I smile at that. Her sass. Her confidence.

And then I give my girl exactly what she's asking for. I take her hands, entwine them in one of mine and press them into the bed above her head. She's confined, and based on the sounds she makes, she loves every thrust as my hips slam against her.

I do it again. And again. I take her mouth and kiss her with the same intensity as I thrust into her and soon her fingers are digging into my hand, stabbing pain into the back of mine that drives me insane.

The noises she makes drive me on.

Every clench of her pussy around my dick brings me closer to my orgasm, but I hold off, wanting more than anything for her to come again.

She lets loose, clinging to me and throws her head back, mouth open, screaming my name on her release and I slam into her again, harder. Faster. Repeatedly until I've followed her over the edge.

"Fucking hell," I grit out through my clenched teeth as I come, slamming my mouth to hers and kissing away her cries as we ride out our orgasms together.

It's the most incredible moment of my life and I never want it to end.

Not with Paisley. Not ever.

CHAPTER TWENTY-FIVE

Mikah

"LUTZGO! LUTZGO!" My name is shouted by fans of all ages. My teammates and I have our own, small crowds of fans gathered around the edges of the board, slamming their signs and their memorabilia to the glass which separates us.

It's the first day of training camp and I'm surprised at the crowd who have come out. As soon as we finish our practice we're currently warming up for, there will be an hour where we do nothing except skate around on the rink with the kids, signing whatever they've brought for us.

Every year, the crowd and fan base in Charlotte grows, which is impressive. Hockey is more popular in the northern states, but with our success over the years coupled with Charlotte's growth from people originally from New England, our team is becoming more popular.

Hockey is becoming more popular.

It's finally here. The season. The thing I live and breathe for every year. This first day we step on the ice not only to practice and prepare, but to show our fans how we've improved and what they can expect of us for the next six months.

It's a week of celebrating while season planning is thrown into hyper-drive. It's four long days of practices and open skate times and events for the fans as well as families.

For the first time I have my own small cheering section. Paisley is here, taking the day off from school even though I insisted she didn't have to.

She's several rows up, center ice, standing with Katie. But the best thing about having Paisley here is my new nanny Viola who I hired earlier last week. She's perfect. She's more of a mother figure than a babysitter. She's forty-five, divorced, never able to have children of her own. When her husband left her, she decided she'd rather devote her life to helping children than spend her days being an accountant like she was doing previously. She explained this to me within the first few minutes of coming to my home and I already knew then I was going to hire. So far, she's been the sort of mother figure I always wished I had—was always jealous my friends did have.

She came with Paisley this morning because after the open skate, Paisley and I are going over to Coach Woods's house for a dinner with the rest of the team while Viola takes Angelo home. Currently, Paisley is standing, bouncing Angelo in one arm with the largest and most ridiculous pair of noise-canceling headphones over his ears I've seen. He's bundled so warmly I can't even see his face, but still...

My son is here. With a girl that I am quickly falling for. In the last few weeks, her constant energy and kindness and faith in me has grown to levels so deep I sometimes don't know what to do with them. And that doesn't count the depth of what I feel for Angelo.

It's amazing two weeks ago I was worried about not bonding with him enough. Not loving him *enough*. But somehow, in the last week or so, he's become everything to me.

He wakes me at night once or twice. He still has screaming fits, I don't know what to do with it sometimes. He's also started smiling. And when he's on his back, he rolls to his side like he's trying to roll over. When I tickle his belly, I can pull the biggest laughs from him. I now have a hundred videos of his giggles on my phone. And almost every night, Paisley and I put him to bed together, she quietly teases me in her loving way of how overprotective I am becoming of him.

A far cry from a man who only weeks ago laughed at the thought of putting bumpers on the corner of my tables. I now have every outlet blocked, every cabinet door and drawer locked even though he still won't crawl for months.

Emotions threaten to overwhelm as I take the ice, smiling at them cheering me on. Paisley grabs one of Angelo's furry covered fists—she insisted on dressing him like a teddy bear—and waves it in the air.

The practice is tough, but like always, Jude and Jason and I fall into our forward line like the trio we usually are. Jason misses a pass or two, which causes me to check on him once the second line takes over. We're scrimmaging, with the first line playing the back-ups and the second and third lines backing up each other, against us. The line that takes over us are usually bench players, some who are only fortunate to travel with the team once or twice a year. Then there's Klaus Newman, the right-winger who was switched from second line to first last season when Jude was hurt.

He's incredible. I can see Coach watching him with intense focus. A ball grows in my throat at that. Any of us can lose our line. We can be switched up and sometimes are, but the Taylors and I have had great success when together. But that doesn't mean Jude isn't worried about Newman taking his. Last season, when Newman played with us, we gelled quickly and powerfully. We were practically unstoppable, winning eight games on a ten-day away road stretch.

Jason spent most of it worried on Jude's behalf, but now, he's the one I'm more worried about. He's skating like he's angry at the team, slap shots coming too quick, wrist shots weak. He should have been put in the sin bin for a tripping call against Duke Fletcher, one of our team's defensemen, and I'm pretty sure he's ready to rip off his gloves and have a go at Hendrix.

Which makes no sense. We're on the same team and Hendrix is one of his closest friends.

I squirt the bottle in the holder in front of our bench into my mouth and tap his stick. "What's going on? Pissed at something?"

He sucks back at his own water, his gaze on the ice. Jaw hard, Eyes narrowed. "Nope."

From anyone else, I would believe them. But Jason likes to talk and joke. He's loud and boisterous and even though he takes his career seriously, he usually treats hockey like one big, fun game.

"How's Sawyer and Tessa? They find her ex yet?"

"Yeah. They found him. He's in Nova Scotia."

He shoves to his feet, apparently done with my questioning. He and Sawyer went to college together. Were roommates for three years before Sawyer graduated a year before him. After Jude, Sawyer is probably like a brother to him so it's understandable he's pissed about Tessa.

But there has to be something else. Jason rarely lets *anything* get to him outside an opponent in the rink.

The whistle is called, and he and I jump the boards, quickly skating to take the puck from Hendrix and getting back to it. For the next hour, everything else is pushed out of my mind. My focus and life is zoned in on a three-inch rubber disc. And when practice is done, I glance to the end of the rink where the free skaters are lined up, anxiously stepping in their rented skates to come out with us. Before I meet them though, I skate to Paisley. She's standing with Angelo at the home team bench. Ice flies up in the air as I pull to a stop. I pull Angelo from her arms while planting a kiss on her lips.

"So, we're here. Wanna tell us why?" She's taller than me since she's standing in the raised bench area and smiling down at me.

"Yeah. I believe it's time I go public with this little guy." I've planned this but didn't tell her. I don't want Paisley to be aware of cameras or press or nervous about it and once she said she was skipping class to come, I made sure the sports reporters who would be here would make time for me first.

"What?"

I gesture toward the guy coming our way, cameramen behind him. When I turn back to Paisley, her blue eyes are as large as the hockey puck and her skin the color of ice. "You... you want me here? For this?"

"Off camera," I assure her. It's not like she's his mom, although I definitely like the sound and thought of it. "I wanted you close."

"Okay. Yeah. Sure. I'm here for you. Always." Her smile is shaky, and she reaches out, brushes a hand over the teddy bear hat on Angelo's head.

She straightens it and takes the headphones from him. "We should probably make him look cute, then."

The reporter, Niklas Karlsson, is a former professional hockey player. He now works for the major hockey network and is most known for his on-ice interviews immediately following the games.

"Mikah Lutzgo." He stops his skate at my side, shock apparent on his features as he takes in Angelo. "Long time no see apparently."

"Lots has changed," I agree. "Which is why I wanted to talk to you today. Niklas, I'd like you to meet my son, Angelo."

It grates on me he still has Angela's last name. For three weeks my lawyer has tried to get in contact with her and she hasn't once answered. For someone who originally claims to be easy to find, Luke is now talking about hiring a private investigator. At some point, we might have to go backward and bring the police in. I probably should have it done the correct way from the first night, but I didn't want everything to go public. Plus, I was the fool who trusted her.

Now Angela has me worried. If she was so anxious to get rid of him, why is she hiding or dragging her feet on fully letting him go?

That is a worry for another day, and fortunately for me, Niklas doesn't ask his last name. Instead, he has the camera on, his back to Paisley so she doesn't have to worry about being on camera, although I don't care.

He welcomes Angelo into the Ice Kings family and we joke about baby spit-up and sleepless nights. It takes a few minutes, but it's done.

Hockey fans across the world will now know I'm a father...even my own.

When Niklas leaves, I hand Angelo back to Paisley. She

leans down and brushes her lips across mine. Hers are freezing. Mine are still hot from practice. I'm learning Paisley is always cold. Even when it's ninety outside, she can have cold toes.

"You look so sexy in all your gear and holding Angelo, talking about how much you love him."

"You look sexy all the time. But mostly when you have nothing on."

Her cheeks turn bright pink, nothing to do with the cold and she shakes her head. "Go play with the kids. I'll get him to Viola and meet you outside the locker room later."

"Deal."

I kiss her again and I'm bumped into the boards when Hendrix skates by. "Oh. Sorry."

He winks. He's not sorry. He's skating backward, holding onto a small boy who looks part terrified and part ecstatic to be on the ice with him.

"On it."

I skate away from Paisley only to reach the end of the rink when Jude skates up next to me. "Let's go, slowpoke."

Slowpoke my ass. I'll show him.

I grab one of the older boys and narrow my eyes, pointing at him. "We will race this fool and win, right?"

The kid's ankles shake in his skates. "Uh. Yeah. Yeah, definitely."

I elbow Jude so hard he almost falls to the ice, pull the kid onto the ice and shout, "Let's go!"

CHAPTER TWENTY-SIX

Paisley

I CANNOT BELIEVE the day I'm having. Skipping a day of classes has never been so much fun, not even in undergrad. Those days of missed classes were usually due to hangovers where I spent the day on the couch, chugging water, and prepping for the next night of partying ahead.

Today has been for hockey. It might be a sport I still know absolutely nothing about, despite Mikah's attempts to teach me, but I cannot deny the appeal after watching him practice all morning.

The way they glide across the ice so fast like they're flying, and then can come to such a quick stop without falling on their ass, sending ice into the air. Every time a stick met the puck, the sound of wood on rubber *slapped* into the air like a fist through a wall.

And yeah, they're covered under so much padding and protection it's not like you can check out their backsides like in other sports, but to me, it only adds to the attractiveness of Mikah. He hides so much muscle and power and control beneath his gear, and I'm one of the very few who have seen it fully unleashed.

Needless to say by the time I see him take the ice of open skate with dozens of kids and parents, I'm not only turned on, but I'm seeing an entirely different side of him as he laughs and plays with the kids. He dishes out high-fives and fist bumps and words of encouragement so easily it makes me wonder how he's ever doubted himself when it comes to Angelo.

He's a natural. On the ice. With kids. In bed.

I'm beginning to think there's absolutely nothing Mikah can't excel at when given the opportunity to flourish.

An arm lands on my shoulder and I'm pulled toward Katie and out of my moment of drooling over Mikah.

"Hey you. Like hockey yet?"

I smile at her. "It's growing on me, definitely. How's Jude doing?"

I know he was injured last season and was unable to play for most of it. He's been on the ice all spring and summer, practicing for this return.

"Nervous, but that's only mentally. Physically he's stronger than ever."

"Probably because he had a good therapist."

"Please." She laughs and drops her arm from me. "Like he listens to me. Every time I try to help him with his stretches it leads to something unconducive to his healing, so I stopped."

A very unfeminine snort comes from me, and I shake my head. Katie's hilarious. "His parents aren't here, are they? I thought they were coming."

"Oh. They'll be here. And trust me, you'll have to sit close to us at the first game. John Senior, his dad and his mom Sonya are something else. The first time I watched a game with them I almost peed my pants laughing so hard at him." Her gaze lands on Jude on the ice, smiling and waving as he slides a young girl on skates through his legs and back to her feet. "They're at Joey's training camp early this week out in Vegas, though. They travel a lot during the season, trying to catch as many games from all their boys as they can. This year was actually supposed to be Joey's for them to be at for the first game, but they wanted to be here for Jude."

A flash of something appears in her eyes and they narrow.

"You're worried."

"Nerves, like Jude, probably. We'll shake it off. As soon as the first game is over, everything will be fine. You are coming though, right?"

I've considered it, although Mikah hasn't said anything about me coming, but after today I'm not sure I want to miss it. Jude and Jason's parents seem entertaining alone at least. Plus, I hear they sometimes bring out puppies on the ice during one of the breaks.

Puppies on ice? How can I miss it?

"Probably."

"Good. I'll make sure Mikah gets you seats near us. Now come on, the guys will be out here for a while and then need to clean up. And I'm starving. I hear the team has food we can eat in one of the suites. You in?"

Happily. I'm all in. With hockey. With Mikah. With Angelo. Crazy how a few weeks ago I was drudging through my building, exhausted, and I have an entirely different life that leaves little time for any moping or exhaustion.

"Yeah. I'm in." I grab her hand and squeeze. "Show me

the way. And maybe... maybe teach me something about hockey while we're at it."

She pulls me along right after it. "Anything you need, girl, I'm here."

MY HAND IS FISTED along the line of buttons on Mikah's dress shirt. I'm pulling him down the hallway to my door, avoiding going back to his place quite yet. We still have time before he sends Viola home for the night so I'm taking a short detour to my couch. Or my bed.

Wherever we land.

Mikah is smiling down at me, part playful, part heady with desire. We have definitely found our rhythm together over the last week. I take, he gives. He gives and I take. I am fortunate he appears to enjoy giving more than taking. I've dated the reverse in the past and it doesn't end well—usually with him satisfied, and me still wanting. Sometimes he lets be in charge, but it's never for long. It's more the illusion of control, anyway, like right now. He's willingly allowing me to pretend I can actually move him with force.

"Do you know what I've been thinking of all day?"

He bites his bottom lip, glances at my fist, wrinkling his perfectly pressed light blue dress shirt. "Ruining my clothes?"

"No." I yank him to me, thrilled when he stumbles from the surprise and kiss him. "I've been thinking of how hot you look in your uniform, how it hides all your muscles and your sexy body. And I love that that's all for me—"

"It is. All of it."

"And it's a total turn-on I'm one of the few women to see it. All those women who follow you on social media.

Who freak out with hearts in their eyes emojis with every picture you post, and I'm one of the few who know how completely amazing you are." I take my other hand holding my keys and clutch and press it to his chest. "All of you. Inside and out."

Without a word, he slides my keys from my grip and skates his arm around me, unlocking my door and guiding us in. "You say things I don't know how to handle."

I drop my clutch and kick the door closed as we turn sideways to get through the doorway. "I can think of a few ways you can handle me?"

"Yeah?" He kisses my cheek, the hinge of my jaw.

As he does, he undoes the knot at my waist of my gray wrap dress, an outfit I changed into after Katie and I grabbed food. The wives and girlfriends were allowed the visiting team's locker rooms to change if we wanted so I took up the opportunity to slide out of my jeans and winter coat I'd worn for the practice and into a casual and comfortable dress with flutter sleeves at the shoulders and a straight neckline. The skirt flutters and moves, thanks mostly to the way it wraps and ties at my waist and brushes and floats along the tops of my knees when I move. I have on a pair of strappy, red sandals with a two-inch heel, but even with the help of height I still have to hold on to his shoulders to be tall enough to kiss him back.

Our mouths press together and like every time he kisses me, my body warms to the tips of my toes and fingertips. Everything about being with Mikah is effortless. From the way our bodies work together to the way we seem to be in sync with what we want out of life.

He wants a family.

I want to help him with his, and then someday create

one of our own. It should scare me. We're still getting to know each other.

I also know my father took one look at my mom when they were nineteen, freshmen on the community college campus they were attending and knew without a doubt he was going to marry her. It took her one week to agree she would someday marry him. Two years later, they made it happen.

As crazy as it sounds, I feel the same way about Mikah. I'm falling for him, quickly, and I don't care I don't have a parachute attached to guarantee my safety.

I unbutton his shirt, barely noticing he's moving us backward, into the living room until my knees hit the armrest of my couch.

Mikah unwraps my dress and growls down my throat as his hand meets my heated skin, presses them to the back until he's cupping my backside. I'm wearing a thong, and when his calloused fingers meet the sensitive flesh of my ass, I roll my hips into him, yanking his shirt from the waist of his khaki shorts.

God, he feels so good. All the time. I have a running list of what he looks best in. It changes with every new outfit he puts on.

He's hard behind his shorts and my hands dive to his waistband to free him. In outfits. In his black boxer briefs. Possibly his white ones. Everything he's in is a turn on to me, and I hurry to see all of him. His hair below his navel is coarse, perfect, not too thick but teases to the glorious gift of all of him, and I shove my hands there, fingers into his waistband of both shorts and briefs where he's warm.

Hard.

Long.

He throbs in my hand as I find him and squeeze.

A curse is swallowed into my throat.

"This what you wanted when you yanked me down the hall?" he teases, thrusting into my grip.

"Yes." I meet his gaze, no shame in my admission, only pure need hopefully showing in my eyes.

Mikah shoves down his shorts and stands in front of me, all six feet one inch of him, lean but muscled. A bit of weight on his abs that don't show bricks but make his strength clear.

"Turn around and I'll give it to you, then."

Oh goodness. A ripple of pleasure pulses at my sex. Bossy Mikah is sexier than any of the rest of him. I love when he gets like this, commanding, but waiting for my consent.

I give it freely.

Turning around, I tease him, knowing he likes it. I let my dress fall from shoulders, shaking my hips as it brushes my ass on the way to the floor. I'm still in my heels, so I'm careful as I step away from the dress and reach behind my back to the band of my bra. It's red, to match my shoes as well as my thong. Lace. It's a sexy, glamorous set and based on the heat burning my flesh from his look alone, he enjoys it more.

Which is what I hoped for.

I undo my bra, gather my hair and drape it over a shoulder so he has a complete, unfettered view of my back and then slip my fingers into the lace of my thong at my hips. I shimmy them down slowly, turning to watch him over my shoulder, but he doesn't notice me looking at him.

His gaze is settled at my hands, my ass, watching the movement of the lace deliciously scrape down my thighs. Once I've kicked them from my ankle where they land on top of the rest of our discarded clothing, his gaze whips up to meet mine.

"Bend over." His hand presses to my shoulder and he doesn't shove gently, but firmly.

I fall forward in surprise until my hips hit the armrest and then I'm angled, ass up in the air, fingers digging into the couch to cushion my fall and brace.

When he gets bossy like this, he doesn't go slow.

I love him furious and fast.

He barely takes a breath before his fingers are at my slit, rubbing, tasting and teasing. There's no need. I was wet and ready for him before we stepped off the elevator. I mewl into the couch cushions, sounds of pleasure pulled from my throat as he works me quickly, dragging the pleasure from my body so easily.

My legs are trembling, ankles shaking in my heels and it takes effort to keep them from slipping on the wood floor, but I stay still for him.

I feel the weight of his chest as he bends over and then his mouth is at my ear, hand brushing hair out of my way.

"You like this?"

I arch into him, grind my backside against his hard dick. "Yesss."

"More?"

"Always. Always more."

"Good. Come for me and then you'll get it."

I feel it barrel down, spikes of pleasure starting at my thighs and spreading outward, down my legs, up my spine and I clamp around his fingers, screaming his name and slamming my eyes shut. I buck against the armrest, find him behind me and he's *there*, where I've never had a man go. As I hit the tip of them *there*, animalistic sounds tear from my throat. He's not even trying, but he's just found a way to make my orgasm stronger. Louder. And I come on his fingers while pressing against him, my body quaking from the force of it until it starts to leave me, and he lifts off my back.

The vague sound of foil tearing filters into my mind but I'm still lost... falling... *needing* him to put me back together to barely registers before his hands are at my hips, pulling back.

"Brace yourself, *skat*." My eyes flicker open at the word. One I don't know, but it's said with such emotion I *feel* it. And then he's there, the thick head of his cock pushing into me, slowly but in one long thrust and I crush the cushions beneath me in my fist. "Damn. Du er så smuk."

I listen to the parts of his guttural language I understand and obey, bracing myself while he seats himself so deep inside of me it borders on painful.

And then he lets go, and I hold on for every glorious moment.

CHAPTER TWENTY-SEVEN

Mikah

A MONTH AGO, I came home from training, exhausted, muscles aching. I planned on another workout, a shower, and then to head to George's with the guys for a quiet night with a few drinks.

It was only a month ago when Paisley knocked on my door, a baby in her arms, and me... completely clueless as to how to even hold said baby.

The same baby who now rests comfortably in my one arm. I have him facing out, hand at his crotch so he can kick and babble his way through our morning ritual of where I wake when he does, some days at six, some days, like today, at the bright burning time of five-thirty.

Awesome.

I'm exhausted after last night's home pre-season game. I didn't get back here until well after ten, my body bruised and battered after a tough win against Edmonton. We play them one more time tomorrow night and all I wanted to do this morning was sleep in, hold Paisley in my arms where she still sleeps in my bed, go get coffee with Angelo in the stroller.

Instead, he woke up wet and dirty, fussing while I changed him and now that I have him dressed in clothes for the day, I'm mixing his bottle while a pot of coffee brews in my Ninja coffee machine. I can brew a full pot of strong black coffee for me and make Paisley a cappuccino as soon as I have time to wake her.

She's been at every home game so far, even though they're only pre-season games and every time I slip onto the ice, I do a slow, warm-up skate around the rink until I find her, usually mid ice or behind home bench, always in the lowest section where she's easy to notice. It's the first time since moving to America where I've known without a doubt that there is someone there for me. Not the player. *Me.* I'm playing so much better and so thankful she's there even when I know she's sacrificing her time and school-work. I spent hours last night showing her my appreciation.

It's no wonder my legs hurt today. My abs and thighs. Hell, even my ass muscles are sore and I'm pretty sure that's from when I took her hard, her knees in the bed, hands wrapped around my pillow where she shoved her face when she came.

Loudly.

So loudly I'm thinking Angelo might have to start wearing his noise-canceling headphones to bed instead of just to the games.

"La-leesh-da."

He babbles, a mouth full of bubbles spits to my counter and I laugh.

"You like that idea?" I set down his bottle and turn him.

Like I always do, as soon as I see his face, I kiss him. His nose. His forehead.

This daddy gig hasn't been easy, but it's now been over a month. I'm settling in. I have an incredible nanny with Viola. She even cleaned my home even better than I do when I was in Washington for an away game earlier this week.

And even better, my lawyer Luke has said they've finally found Angela and he's working on getting in contact with her. Apparently after she dropped Angelo off, she took a trip to the Caribbean where she's been lounging on beaches, possibly drinking her way through coconut rum and beach bums. Luke has also officially filed a petition for me to be added to the birth certificate, something we have to wait on while the proper state departments work their way through it.

It's taking longer than I want.

Until she legally signs away her rights, I will also be on tenterhooks, waiting for her to show up and take him back.

It will never happen.

"It won't," I tell Angelo. "She will never have you. Not after what she's done."

He grins at me, toothless as always but he's growing more active during the day and sleeping better now that I feed him six ounces instead of four at every feeding. Viola gave him a bath last night so he smells like his soap with a hint of spit-up.

It's the strangest combination and the best I've ever smelt.

I hold him close and grab his bottle. It's easier to feed him when I'm sitting, but I can do it all one-handed in a pinch, which I do now, filling my mug of coffee while he starts to take his. I'm careful to keep my hot coffee out of his flailing arms and legs and move us into the living room. One of my modern, black leather and black metal chairs has been moved to my guest bedroom so Viola has a place to sit and two weeks ago I went out and bought a recliner chair. It looks like a spaceship with wide arms, a table I can put up on the side and cup holders on both armrests. I pull up the side table now and set down my coffee.

I've fallen asleep in this chair almost every day since I've had it.

If I was single, I would probably live in it.

Fortunately for me, I have Paisley and a reason to use and sleep in my king-sized bed.

"We like her, do we not?" I ask Angelo. I like his early morning feedings even when I hate being awake so early. It's quiet outside, the city not yet fully awake and bustling. I can take an hour if I need to, to hang out with nothing to do but spend time with Angelo. I usually read to him, place him on the playmate near my feet while I catch up on news and sports games from the night before, scroll through social media.

Ever since camp when I did the quick interview with Niklas, my accounts have gone wild with women, fawning over the photo I posted of me holding Angelo. Behind my shoulder, there's a hint of Paisley in her winter coat.

It's my favorite part of the picture.

The comments about her, though, are not kind, but there's nothing I can do about that.

Someday down the road, after Paisley is done with school, when she's settled and teaching, I will make it more permanent. As is, I already want her to move in with me. It seems silly to have separate rooms divided by a hallway. She spends almost all of her time here and I love it.

"You like Paisley, right?" I brush my finger over his

cheek. My son is a fast eater. He gulps his food down in minutes and then usually rips a burp that can rival Maddox's.

I'm rewarded with a quick smile around the bottle's nipple and then his brows push together as he concentrates on his food.

"Well, I like her," I whisper to him. I sip my coffee. That's not right. I more than like her. I think I might love her. I couldn't have survived the last month without her. She hasn't distracted me from hockey or becoming a father, instead she's been by my side every step of the way, always encouraging. Always knowing the right thing to say. She makes me better. On the ice and off it.

I have never felt such victory.

"I don't think I love her, Angelo." I keep quiet. I don't want Paisley to find out I love her because I'm talking to my now twelve-week-old. But he can keep a secret. "I'm pretty sure I love her. Certain of it. I want her here with me, in my home, with you. We can keep Viola, but I want it to be Paisley and me, raising you. Maybe giving you more brothers and sisters someday."

He pulls his knees to his stomach and grunts. I take that as excitement.

Either that or he has to poop.

"Excitement it is."

In the hallway, I hear the quiet sound of Paisley's phone ringing. My eyes slide to the clock above my microwave and I frown. It's just after six. So early for her to be getting a call, even for her parents who she talks to several times a week. At least her mom. They babble about nothing and love it. She has not yet told them about me though.

Which worries me.

If she's close with her mom, wouldn't she want them to

know about the guy she's dating? Unless maybe she doesn't feel the way I do? For the first time, worry filters in like a fly. Soft but annoying, I swat it away as her phone rings again.

Fortunately, Angelo is chugging the last gulp of formula and air out of the tip, so I pull it out of his mouth. He clamps his gums on it, always hesitant to lose his food source and scowls at me.

"Later, little man." I laugh at him and lift him to my shoulder. "Let's go check on Paisley. I hope nothing is wrong."

The sound of her quiet voice comes from my room and I'm outside the door when Angelo lets lose one of his infamous belches. He beat Jason in a burping contest last weekend.

"That's my little man," I tell him, patting his back. He's so loud it makes me laugh every time. I cannot help it.

Paisley's eyes are on me when we enter the room, her eyes wide but still cloudy with sleepiness. She has her hand at the top of her head, pushing back her hair.

She rolls her eyes dramatically at me and pats the bed next to her.

Angelo and I hurry there, and I settle him near the middle of king-sized bed on a blanket so he can kick and play. Then I throw a pillow on the other side of them to ensure he can't roll off.

"Mama." Paisley drawls the word.

I should have known that's who she was speaking to as soon as I heard her voice. Her southern accent always thickens when she talks to her parents. Her hand falls from her hair and onto my lap. She immediately starts drawing a circle on my thigh with her thumb.

"I know, Mama. I know. Don't be mad." She blinks at me and her green eyes clear in a second. "No. No, not today.

That's... he'll think y'all are crazy!" Her hand on my thigh digs in until I flinch.

Damn, this girl has strength behind her thin frame, and now I'm more worried. Are they talking about me?

I arch my brows in question and Paisley makes a face, crossing her eyes and sticking her tongue out of one side of her mouth. She's so ridiculous, hair messy, cross-eyed and being goofy all while I can now hear her mom's raised voice come through the phone.

"I said it's because it's new, Mama. Tell Dad to calm down." She winks at me. "And no, he doesn't need to bring his shotgun."

I fight back a laugh. She's told me her dad's protective.

With a heavy sigh, she unwraps my leg and brushes away the half-moon marks she's made, cringing. "Sorry," she mouths to me.

"I like them," I whisper back. "Give me more."

Her cheeks flush hot pink and she sighs again. "Mama, let me talk to him, okay? I'll call you back. But I'm warning you now that the answer is no. You can't come today." She scowls at the phone and yawns.

She laughs softly. Shakes her head, but even with her faces, there's no real annoyance or frustration, apart from possibly being woke up too early.

"Love you too. Tell Dad I'll call him at nine... fine, eight. Bye, Mama."

She tosses her phone to the nightstand, shoves both hands through her hair and thumps her head against the headboard. "Apparently, my father was channel surfing last night trying to find information about a NASCAR driver who was injured in a race and saw a picture of us with Angelo leaving the game."

"Oh." We walked out from the arena together and there

are always cameras. "Is that... bad?" My worry from earlier sparks.

"Well, no, not for me, I guess..." She meets my gaze and nibbles on her lip. Ah, she is worried too. "For you, maybe? It's my parents. And she called because now she says they want to meet you. Or rather, are insisting. Angelo, too. We don't have to."

"You haven't told them about me."

She makes a face that doesn't please me. "It's not that I didn't want to. At first, before you gave the interview about Angelo, I didn't know what to say and I wasn't sure what we were, so..." She shrugs.

I've made a mistake. I haven't told her how much I care about her.

"Do you want me to meet them?" It's possible I've gotten carried away with myself and my feelings for her thinking this is more than it is.

She grabs my hand in the air and kisses my knuckles. "I want. Trust me. I *want*. I want more of what we did last night, well, early this morning, and I do want them to meet you. They'll love you and Angelo."

"After your father shoots me."

"He'll only scare you." She leans forward and kisses me, laughing as my mouth drops open.

She scoots down on the bed, and I fall on top of her, her thighs widening to make room for me. We kiss until Angelo interrupts, babbling and grunting.

I push off Paisley, kissing her nose. "I want everything, Paisley. Anything and everything you want to give me."

Her look softens, more than just from the kiss.

"Call your parents back. I'll grab my schedule. Figure out a time when we both have a day off and I'm happy to have them come here and meet us." I slide off the bed. I keep the schedule printed and on my refrigerator for both Viola and Paisley even though they've both downloaded it onto their phones. "And I don't want you worrying about us. I'm all in. I care very much about you."

I'm rewarded with a dazzling smile that almost blinds me as I leave the room. That and the fact she's snuggling Angelo with as much love as a mother should.

And it hits me. If this lasts between us, she *will* be the only mother Angelo ever knows. I don't think I could have chosen better.

CHAPTER TWENTY-EIGHT

Mikah

I SCRUB MY HAIR. Water from the shower slides down my back as I dry off. Practice was killer, but the ice is where I belong. For the first time, I had a hard time getting focused. I've spent little time not memorizing every inch of Paisley's tanned skin late into the night lately. I know exactly where her bikini tan line hits at her hip even when it's covered by clothing now. She has a freckle there, on her left hip, that I've spent much time kissing.

Too much Paisley first thing in the morning made me sluggish until I found my feet. Then I worked double, skated faster, slapped the puck harder, all to prove my father wrong.

I can have more in life than hockey and still be the best.

It sometimes still surprises me how much my father's expectations spur me on even when I despise him for everything he is.

My shirt clings to my still damp skin as I tug it down and Sawyer comes up to me. "How's it going?"

"Can't complain. How's Tessa?" Every time I think of her ex-fiancé, I imagine punching him in the face.

"Struggling." Sawyer is Jason's age, and at five years younger, Tessa is still older than me by years. I can't imagine what it feels like to be screwed over by someone you hope to spend the rest of your life with. "Listen, Debbie and I are taking her out tonight. She hasn't been out much. Want to show her the city. Make her maybe think of getting a fresh start. You in? Bring Paisley. She could use some decent friends in her life right now."

"I'll need to talk to her." I'm thinking of Paisley and her freckle and what else we can be doing on a Friday night. Fortunately for me, Paisley and I have already planned a date. "I'll call and let you know."

"Sounds good. Thanks. And I swear, when we find that dick..."

"I know." Sawyer figured out weeks ago the ex-fiancé is in Nova Scotia, but since then, nothing. When we finally do find him, the team will line up behind Sawyer to get their shots in. We're family. Which means Tessa is family. Which means Will's a dead man.

Now my only worry is Sawyer going to jail for murder as soon as he's found.

We need him on defense. The regular season starts Monday.

I grab my bag and throw it over my shoulder. Gripping his shoulder, I give him a few quick shoves. "Be there for Tessa. She needs you. We'll talk later."

"Right." His jaw is tight and I'm surprised nails don't spit from his eyes with how pissed he looks.

I head out of the training facility and I'm almost to my

SUV, phone in hand to call Paisley and keys in another when a woman steps around from the back bumper.

"Hey, Mikah."

Her voice freezes every cell in my body.

Angela.

I can't believe she's here. I can't believe I ever thought this woman with jet black hair, cut sharply at her shoulders, eyebrows in high arched points above her dark brown eyes and heavily done make-up is ever a woman I thought was beautiful.

She's too perfect. Too done up. And clearly she enjoyed her Caribbean jaunt because her skin is deeply tanned.

I pull to a stop. Gaze whipping around our parking lot. So help me if there's someone out there, watching this... or my teammates who are still more pissed at her than I am.

I, after all, have a son from her extreme selfishness.

"What are you doing here?"

"I heard from Luke."

He said he finally was able to get a hold of her to leave her a message to call him and also informed me she hasn't done so yet.

"So what are you doing here?"

My body that froze at the sight of her is now on fire. If she was a man, I'd have my arm shoved to her throat and pressed against my vehicle until her face turns purple. Shame for me that I would never hurt a woman like that. The only time I lose my temper is on the ice and only when an opponent deserves it or starts something.

"I'd like to talk to you."

I step toward her. She might see the way I want to rip her from limb to limb. For the lies. For the way she's handling this because she moves quickly back on obscenely high heels to get out of my way.

"Anything you have to say to me can be said to Luke." I throw open my back door and toss my bag in. It bounces off the car seat and for some reason, seeing that seat—Angelo's seat—rattles me more than her presence.

This is his mom. Someday he might ask questions about her.

I do not want to be the guy who treats her like shit and have to deal with the fallout of that.

Plus, as I've often reminded myself, I haven't exactly done things with Angelo in the most legal manner. Which means if she wants, Angela has ammunition to take him from me.

Like hell it will happen. I'll fight to the death for him.

I close the door, quieter and more calmly than I feel and turn, facing Angela. Arms crossed over my chest, I grip my keys in my hand so tightly I feel the sting of the jagged edges cut into my palm.

"What do you want?" I might not be a dick to her, but I will not be nice, either.

"Well, how is he?" Her hands are at her hips. Then her sides. She clasps them together in front of her and then she twists them repeatedly.

She is young, only a year or so older than me. Her breasts are large, too big for her frame, and I know from experience not real. She's wearing pointed black heels and a black skirt that clings to her skin like it's painted on. And short. Purple rims the bottom of her eyes and it's the only thing out of place on her, and yet still... I can't figure out how I spent a weekend with her.

I see nothing attractive about her as I take her in and try to figure out what Angelo has from her. Perhaps her chin that is rounder than mine.

"You care how he is?"

Her round chin trembles and she presses her lips together. "This wasn't easy for me. It really wasn't. I've meant to call. I should have, but well, I can't stop thinking about him."

"You're not getting him back." I spit it out so angrily she flinches.

"I'm his mom."

"You *left* him. Did you give any thought to what would happen if I was not home? If I did not want him? Did you think of anyone but yourself?"

"I was tired. I don't have family. Or help. And he sleeps so little and cries so much and I had no help. I thought... I thought when I found out that I was pregnant that maybe, just maybe I'd finally have someone in my life who loves me. And then, it was so hard, and I kept thinking why anyone can't love me."

For a brief second, my heart hurts for her. I get her. I get where she's coming from. But she's made becoming a mom about *her*. I've been a parent for less time than her, much less considering her pregnancy she had to get used to it, but I know that when it comes to babies, it's never about you. *Everything* revolves around them.

"That is the most selfish thing I have ever heard."

If she thinks I'm going to have compassion for her, she's dead wrong. She could have made a hundred different decisions if that's what she wants from me.

"Please," she says and takes a step toward me, reaching. I toss my hands up, pulling away from her to avoid her touch. "How is he?"

"Healthy and happy. And that's all you're getting. You want more, talk to my lawyer."

"I want to see him."

"Never."

She grins then, and I hate everything about the way it twists her face. "I still have my rights, Mikah. I want to see him."

My hand curls into a fist and my blood races. I have never felt so much rage. She must be kidding.

"Call Luke then."

She taps her chin with one blood-red painted fingernail. "Or maybe I'll call your new girlfriend. Or wait... maybe you're banging the nanny?"

Ew. I at first imagine Viola but then I realize she probably has them confused. Or hasn't seen Viola. It doesn't matter. Angela will stay away from both.

I pull in a breath and step toward her. I will defend what's mine. She's a fool to think otherwise.

"Leave my girlfriend out of this."

"Or what?" She laughs and rakes over my skin like a chill. How could none of us on the team have noticed how evil she is? "What will you do to me?"

It's like she wants to be the first woman I ever hit. "What do you want?"

"Maybe I want us to be a family. I *am* his mother."

She's not. Paisley is. She can't actually be serious, except her expression says otherwise. Holy crap. Has she always been crazy and hidden it well? And what in the hell do I do?

If I say anything else, it might come back to haunt me. But oh, there is much to say to this woman.

I'm fuming, shaking so hard I can't remember the last time I've been this pissed off.

And scared.

She's his *mom*. I know how American courts are. They *prefer* kids to be with their moms over their dads and it doesn't even matter if the mom in question is selfish and only thinking of herself in all of it.

"I'll wait for your call, Mikah. Enjoy your evening."

I climb into my Land Rover, even still fighting against cringing when I see tears in her eyes. I knew Angela before we spent the weekend together. She was always fun. Up for a party. Never once did I see this side of her.

I don't like it as much as she deserves to feel this way.

My heart is still racing as I pull onto the streets and has not slowed when I enter my building. I have one thing and one thing only on my mind:

Protect Angelo and figure out a way he can be saved from that woman.

I have Luke on my phone before I enter the elevator, tapping my foot impatiently, waiting for him to answer.

"Luke Morgenson," he says.

I skip the pleasantries. "It's Mikah. I need to meet with you. Tonight. Can you come to my place?"

"Mikah. What's this about? I called Angela this morning as you know..."

"She showed up at my practice. Asking about him. She wants to see him. I told her to call you, but I need to talk to you. Come up with a plan."

"I can schedule a meeting tomorrow morning, but..."

"No. Tonight. It has to be."

My head is spinning. She could do anything. She could show up at my building. Demand to see him. She could call the cops and say I've taken him.

I have no legal claim to him and I'm not yet on his birth certificate. As far as I know, it's still processing. And it's possible by not entertaining listening to Angela for too long tonight, I've royally pissed her off.

"Please, Luke. I'm worried." And terrified out of my mind. "Please tonight."

He sighs, and I imagine the man I've met with several times running a hand through his thick, black hair, bumping his glasses as he does it. "Give me an hour. But you're paying for this."

"Anything."

CHAPTER TWENTY-NINE

Paisley

IT'S LATE. I know Mikah's schedule now like the back of my hand.

It's unlike him not to call to let me know he's on his way home. It's more unlike me I don't hear his door open and close when he does get home.

And never, in the last week especially, has he not returned one of my texts within a decent amount of time. Now, it's an hour after he said he was going to be home and I've already stopped by his place twice only to not hear anything on the other side of his door.

Which concerns me more. I've met Viola, the new nanny. She's as old as my own mom, divorced, yet never had kids and so when she left her husband and his cheating, pathetic ass — her words — she started to nanny so she could spend her time with kids.

Personally, I like the fact she doesn't look at Mikah with *fuck me* stamped on her forehead.

Still, it's strange even she isn't answering the door. She's only been there a few days, but I've seen her plenty and we've talked quite a bit. I like her.

All of this is weird. Is Angelo sick? Did something happen to Mikah at practice? I imagine having a puck flying through the air and skating on ice isn't always the safest sport in the world.

I'll give it one more try and if Mikah's not home, I'll call him again. Then Viola. I have her number since Mikah named her Angelo's emergency contact.

My phone rings in my hand, scaring me so badly I toss it in there. It flips through my hands, into the air, and again before I finally manage to catch it before it hits the floor.

I don't look at the screen, just press my thumb to the slider. "Hello? Mikah?"

"No, you hooker! It's Pippa. Your friend, remember?" I cringe. She's laughing and the background wherever she is filled with loud noises. Of course, because it's Friday. Her laugh tells me she's not upset, but I still feel that twinge of neglect inside of me. I haven't seen her in a month and I don't think we've ever gone that long without hanging out.

Between school and Mikah and Angelo, my hours as packed. But I don't want to be the girl who forgets her friends because some great new guy swoops in.

"Yes, I'm sorry. So sorry. What's up?"

"Get your sweet cheeks down to Roxbury! Maggie and I are headed there after we leave Duckworth's Grill and we want to see you."

My eyes go to my door and I frown. The week has flown by despite being more tired than I've been in a long time. Late nights and early mornings with Mikah have me dragging by late afternoon and yet invigorated by evening. I've been so lost in wanting to spend as much time with him as possible, I've been more focused on my research too which is a bonus.

Even Ms. Felarky was impressed earlier today with Maggie's and my progress.

"I... I don't think I can. Mikah and I, we were going to go out."

Our first official adult, alone, date. Last night we grabbed gyros from a street truck and pushed Angelo in the stroller. The night before we grilled out on the rooftop deck. It was a gorgeous evening, cloudless sky and we stayed there past the sunset, just talking and laughing, and playing with Angelo. It was absolutely beautiful. And easy. And fun.

"Fine. Ignore us for the hottie, but we miss you," she says, drawing out the second half and laughing at the same time.

She's beautiful and overdramatic. Gives men boners as she walks by and then drives them insane with her over-the-top personality.

"Maybe tomorrow?"

"Fine, hooker. Tomorrow." I take no offense to the hooker comment. She says it to everyone she loves.

"Bye, loser."

I hang up and glance again at my door. I need to figure out what's going on before I lose my mind.

Grabbing my keys, I lock my door and take the few steps over to Mikah's. It opens before I even lift my hand to knock so I'm smiling, assuming Mikah saw me coming. Then he becomes a cement brick in front of me. It takes a second to register what I'm seeing as he stands in from me. Unmoving. Eyes glazed. Hair messed. His shirt is wrinkled, and I'm not sure he notices he has spit-up on his shoulder.

I'd tease him for wearing Angelo's puke if he didn't look at me like I was a stranger.

"Mikah? Everything okay?"

"No."

Instead of opening his door for me to enter, he glances back into his apartment and shuts it behind him as he steps toward me into the hall.

"What's wrong? Is it Angelo?"

I peer at his door over my shoulder. He's never shut me out. I feel it now, in the closed-off expression on his face and the door he shut behind him. He's shutting me out of more than his home.

Dread fills my stomach.

"Angelo. Angelo is fine." He presses his hands to his hips and squeezes his eyes closed. When he opens them again, he looks tortured. "I cannot see you now."

I stumble back. His words come like a whip, stinging my cheeks. Perhaps that's the tears already falling. "What? But we had plans."

In a move I've never seen him make before, he pinches the bridge of his nose, dropping his head. I stepped toward him but stop when he lifts his head.

He might as well be on a different floor of the building for as much distance his look puts between us.

"I cannot see you now. Or anymore."

"Why?" It rips from my throat before I can stop myself. This makes no sense and the floor wobbles at my feet. Just this morning we made love before I left for class. He reminded me Viola is staying *late*. Which means after we go out, we can spend time at my place before heading to his. We've had it all planned for days.

"I can say no more but that it is over. It is for the best. Thank you for your help with Angelo."

Tears swell and he blurs in front of me. My jaw unhinges and I'm too slow to move because he really does become a blur of movement when he turns quickly, and disappears behind his door, slamming it shut.

I follow him, pound on his door. This is crazy. Unfortunately, I pound a few more times and get no response and I give up.

The noise could be scaring Angelo.

My fist is sore as I slump back to my own place. My heart is hurting worse. Something has happened. Something horribly wrong.

Mikah would never treat me like this. And I will figure out exactly what's going—

After I get really, really drunk to forget this sensation of feeling like he's just shredded my heart into unrecognizable pieces.

THE ROXBURY IS NOT where I want to be but it's the perfect place to forget the shitstorm I left behind an hour ago. I've been morose through dinner and thank goodness for Pippa and Maggie who have done their best to keep my mind off the story I told them. None of it makes sense and I keep replaying it in my mind, flashes of him and his expression flicker through as brightly as the strobe lights on the ceiling above.

I usually love the Roxbury, the 80s and 90s club where the music is loud and the drinks are cheap and tonight since it's still relatively early, even cheaper. Maggie found a coupon on Facebook, so we not only get free cover and get to skip the line, we're given one free drink when we get inside.

Pippa has her arm looped through mine and pulls me through the quickly crowding dance floor to the back. The second floor is filled with tables as well as a VIP seating area. Even been there before for birthdays in college. It's where we celebrated Maggie's because she's a fiend for 80s music. Odd considering none of us were born before 1997, but whatever. Tonight, she's left Asher at home and she's trying to do her best to pull me out of my funk. Which I've now explained in full, along with how I originally met Mikah.

It feels like a relief to finally be able to tell my friends everything, and yet at the same time, it's a dull stab to my chest at having to relive it with how the night has gone.

But I'm determined to push past this. I don't know what's gotten into Mikah, but I know how he feels about me, and I know I love him.

Whatever is going on with him, I'll give him space and then try to talk to him.

We'll work it out, we have to.

"Drinks!" I shout and throw my hand in the air. First, I need to forget it ever happened. Drink my way into oblivion. Tomorrow, I'll deal with everything that happened.

"That's my girl!" Pippa yells and we meet Maggie at the bar who already has three shot glasses lined up.

I roll my eyes at the thick foam on top of the small glasses and arch a brow at her. "Really?"

"You know nothing gets the night started right like a really good blowjob."

"Hell yeah!" three guys to the left of us cry out, eyes widening but glazed showing this is definitely not their first stop of the night.

I ignore them, pick up my shot, and toss it back. I will take the shot, but not without hands like it's supposed to be done. Maggie and Pippa follow and then we order another round of drinks. Vodka club soda for Pippa, rum and Coke for Maggie. I grab another shot, tequila this time, and wash it down with a Long Island Iced Tea.

At my drink order, Maggie arches her brow at me. I take the shot without salt or lime and take a large sip of my Long Island. "I said I was getting drunk."

"Yeah, but there's drunk and then freshman-sorority-girl ugly drunk."

"I'll slow down with this. Promise." She's right. I want to get drunk and dull my pain, not end up puking in the rundown bathrooms by eleven.

"All right. Dance time?"

"You got it!"

We weave through the crowds, drinks in hand, sliding single file into the middle of the dance floor. I'm glad I called them back. I might not really want to be here, but there's no way I could have survived the night so close to Mikah, so far away, spending it by myself and being miserable.

I needed my friends. Good music where we can dance like fools.

We circle together, and shout along with lyrics, laughing at the ridiculousness of some of the people, both women and men, who come dressed for the appropriate decades. Bright colors, bangs so high they never should have existed, scrunchies galore adorn wrists and high ponytails and shirts tied at the waists making them more crop tops.

There are leather gloves on hands and red leather jackets, a la Michael Jackson, acid wash jeans. The best part is from the wedding parties that are dressed in elegant gowns to the ripped jeans and blue eyeshadow, everyone is out to have fun, so the vibe is perfect.

I'm halfway through my Long Island, sweat gathering at the back of my neck when I tell Pippa and Maggie, I need to take a quick break. My thighs might not be able to take any more if I don't rest so I scoot my way back through toward the bar where it's a bit quieter and I can wait for another drink when someone steps in front of me, hand on my shoulder.

I immediately jolt back, shaking it off, until I recognize him.

"Paisley. I thought that was you."

Jason Taylor. The sight of him alone has me panicking, and I quickly scan the area around. No way. There's no way Mikah broke it off with me and then came out with his teammates.

"Paisley?" he asks, and his head falls, tilted to one side. "You okay? Sawyer said you and Mikah were going to meet us out later, but no one's heard from him."

My chin wobbles. Oh God. What is going on?

"I wouldn't know," I say, fighting through the pain. Darn it. For one blessed hour, I was faking doing so well. But now there's a tremor threatening to erupt starting in my gut. "He ended things with me."

"What? You're shitting me."

I wrap my lips around my straw and take a huge sip. Screw it. I toss the straw to the floor and drain the rest of my drink. *Sorry environment. I'll recycle more tomorrow.* "Not shitting you and no offense, but I'm here with friends."

I go to move around him, but he steps in my path. "Are you okay?"

"No, Jason." I laugh. The Long Island has made me a lunatic. "I am not okay. And worse, Mikah isn't and totally shut me out. I thought... I thought..." Oh God. He's turning blurry. Which means I'm crying. In a freaking bar.

Sign me up for freshman-sloppy-drunk girl.

I slam my eyes closed. Maybe he'll vanish. Maybe my

alcohol brain has made him appear and when I open my eyes, he'll be gone.

Instead, a freakishly large hand wraps around my biceps and he tugs me through the throng of people to the stairs.

"Where are we going?"

"To the team. Where it's quiet."

"No." I try to shove my heels to the floor, but it's useless. Jason's way bigger than Mikah and probably stronger. Plus, the floor is slippery from spilled drinks. "I don't want to see them."

"Well they're going to want to hear this. Sawyer talked to Mikah right after practice, said he'd talk to you about meeting us and headed out."

My heart shouldn't flutter he said that. But it does.

Then I remember the slammed door in my face and the distance he put between us before that. The tortured way he looked at me.

I give up the fight. If I manage to pull free of Jason, I'll probably end up with my ass on the floor, soaked with beer and whatever else. So I stay quiet until we're up the stairs, in the VIP area where it's quieter and I let him drag me to near the back where it's even quieter and several faces I recognize all look at me with surprise.

"Paisley!" Katie cries and jumps from her seat. "You made it! We were wondering where you two have been."

If someone could rip into my chest and pull out my heart, I'm not sure it could hurt worse.

"Mikah broke up with her," Jason says, dropping the bomb. And God... it sounds so much worse hearing it than saying it. "Jude. Newman. Let's go."

"What?" I spin, wobble on my legs a bit. I blame the dancing. It's probably fifty-fifty that and the drinks.

Maybe seventy-thirty drinks to dancing. My head is swimming a bit and I barely register the other guys moving.

"What? No. No, no, no." I reach for Jason, but he's already talking to Sawyer. Next to him is Tessa, who looks as pale-faced as I feel. "You can't."

Oh my God. He'll think I called his friends. Cried my eyes out to Katie or something. How *humiliating*.

"Jude," I say, because he's closest. "Please don't. It's a breakup. I'll be fine."

Jude glances at Katie before meeting my gaze. "He cares about you. Talks about you all the time. He likes you. A lot. No way he'd do this. Not without something going wrong. We'll figure it out. You here with someone?"

"Friends." I point my thumb toward the dance floor and then... *Oh shit*. I've just ditched them. I slap my forehead and groan. "I need to get back to them."

"No need," Katie says, and she's laughing. "I think they found you." She points behind me toward the stairs that lead to the upper floor. I spin slowly so I don't get dizzy, but it still doesn't help.

I should sit. I don't drink much. Long Islands might not have been a great choice. I make a mental note to listen to Maggie in the future and then see them both, waving their hands in my direction, behind the roped-off area. A bouncer the size of New Jersey prevents them from entering.

"I'll go get them," Katie says and gives me a quick hug. "The guys will figure things out and I'll call you when I know more. Okay? Jude's right. This doesn't make sense. I've seen the way he looks at you."

"Oh *wow*. The Ice Kings." Maggie says it as she reaches me, collapsing into my shoulder. I throw my arm around her waist before we both topple over. "They're so *pretty*."

Katie laughs and I introduce my friends to them. Jude,

Jason, and Newman are gone before I realize it and Katie scoots down, making room for us all.

I finish my drink and switch to water.

This night didn't turn out the way I'd planned at all, and yet with Jason and Jude so pissed, the smallest flicker of hope grows.

They agree with me.

Something happened.

And before another song kicks in and Maggie starts shimmying in her seat next to me, one word—one person comes to mind.

Angela.

It has to be about Angela.

CHAPTER THIRTY

Mikah

MY HOUSE IS QUIET. Too quiet. It's torture. Everything from the moment I stepped outside the arena earlier to now is an ugly blur of worst-case scenarios and the fear I've had about Angela coming back. How in the hell can she leave our son with me with a note saying she promises she doesn't want him back and then show up, demanding to see him, demanding that she'll go to the police for kidnapping if I don't allow her to see him?

That was the exact threat she gave Luke when he called her. She didn't even say hello and I know because he had her on speakerphone from my living room.

Let me see him or the golden boy of hockey will be arrested.

What else was I supposed to do?

Every second I spent waiting for her to arrive, Luke and I planned. Give her what she wants. Keep her happy and calm. This will give Luke time to figure out what her real plan is so we can determine how to proceed and not only ensure she doesn't get custody if that's what she wants, but that she has absolutely nothing to do with Angelo.

It killed me. I have never felt a pain so fierce as I did the moment I told Paisley it is over. But Angela was inside my home with Luke, fawning over Angelo. She'd already mentioned Paisley once and as soon as she did, realization struck.

She'd been watching me. But for what end?

That was when I decided. Paisley would have nothing to do with this, not until Luke knows what's going on.

His theory? She wants money.

My theory? She's a vile, evil witch. I'm beginning to suspect she planned this all along. Especially when I think back and realize many of the condoms we used that weekend were hers. What if she did something to them to get pregnant on purpose? What if that's why she was always hanging around the team?

My mind is racing, and has been, for the entire evening and Angelo must sense my anxiousness because he's been grouchier than normal, taking longer to get down.

Luke left several hours ago. He's going to have his investigator widen his net to see what else we can discover about Angela. Earlier, she refused to sign away her rights. She didn't even ask for money. Acted offended when Luke offered.

"I've realized my mistake. I want him." She said it like she expected me to believe it.

I don't and we need to figure out what she wants because I'm already dying inside with what I've done to Paisley. As soon as Angela left, I ran to Paisley's. I can't bear the look of pain on her face when I think about what I said to her earlier. But she either took off or refused to answer her door. Not that I blame her. I've run different scenarios in my head, but none are good. There's a chance we can stay together, but only indoors and then that makes her feel like my dirty secret. I do not want her feeling that, either.

It's now going on eleven. I am exhausted. My brain will not slow and my heart will not stop racing.

A knock hits my door and I hurry to it.

Paisley. I will fall at her feet. Explain everything. Apologize forever for hurting her so deeply earlier it's possible it hurt me more.

I open the door without thinking and immediately a hand hits my chest and I'm shoved backward.

Jason.

"What are you doing here?"

"I think the better question is what the hell is wrong with you?"

"What?" Behind him are Jude and Newman. This has the makings of a beat down even if they won't raise fists and I'm confused, because the expressions on their faces are all the same. Furious. I focus on Jude. "What have you heard? Did she call Katie?"

"No. Saw her getting trashed at Roxbury with her friends where you were supposed to bring her."

"Trashed? Is she okay?"

"I think we're all more concerned with what happened to you tonight."

They step in and fan out. Newman is smart enough to not let the door slam, though. He catches it at the last second and asks, "Angelo?"

"Sleeping. But I just got him down so don't yell at me too loud."

"What happened?" Jude asks. "And don't say you fucked up. All men do that."

"I fucked up."

"I just said—"

"I know. But Angela is back. She wants Angelo. Or she wants *us*, I think. Her motives aren't clear yet."

"And you'll give her that?" Jude's teeth grind together. "After she abandoned him?"

"I will let her think whatever she needs so she doesn't steal my son back from me. Yes."

"Have you called Luke?" Jason asks.

"I did." I explain everything from the moment Angela surprised me outside the rink. The men curse. Repeatedly. More questions with *What the fucks?* And *That bitch* than I ever heard us say. "I can't... the night he came, we should have called the cops, but I didn't want a public record. Luke said we'd handle it privately and it all seemed so easy. She said she promised she didn't want him, so..." I screwed up. I've been doing it since the beginning.

We should have suspected she had something in the works when she was so elusive after stating she was easy to find.

"Let me figure out what I can." All of us turn to Jason.

"How?"

"Angela. She has friends. She's not the only puck bunny around and she used to come to the clubs with a few I spent time with." By spend time with, he means screwed. Probably more than once.

"And they'll tell you something?"

"Please," he scoffs. "A promise of a night with me and they'll be singing like canaries."

"Until then?" Jude asks. "You really going to stay away from Paisley? I thought you loved her."

"Perhaps because I love her is why I should stay away." We haven't even been together long. Is it possible we have moved too fast anyway? What twenty-two-year-old graduate student wants to be raising another man's baby?

She has never said these things.

It's Angela's voice in my head, casting doubts from earlier.

It still worked, even if I'm eighty-five percent sure she can speak nothing but lies.

"You're an idiot," Jude says, and he points at my door. "Even I know that, and I'm not the sharpest tool in the shed. But that girl loves you. She'd do anything for you. All you have to do is tell her."

"I will. When I can." When I have my head on straight and know what I am doing with Angela. "Paisley. Is she okay?"

"She cried in my arms if that tells you anything," Jason says, still frowning at me like I am an idiot. I might be. "But Katie's there and she's with friends. She'll be fine. I'm sure someone will take care of her."

I don't like the implication that it's not me, but I caused this. If he expects me to shove past them to go get her, I will not. I don't want to use her and pull her back and forth, and I definitely do not want her to have to deal with Angela.

Jason shakes his head like he can't believe me.

Newman rolls his eyes.

I look back at Jude. "You all three came all the way here to yell at me?"

Jude shrugs. "We're brothers. It's what we do."

DAYS HAVE FELT LIKE WEEKS. For a month I looked forward to the first home game of the regular season, looking into the stands and finding Paisley. Right where she was supposed to be. Instead, her seats stayed empty. Jude had skates filled with nerves and it took him until the third period to shake them off. Who can blame him considering we were playing the team who busted his knee last season. Selkin, the guy who took him out, took to the ice like he was out for blood all over again.

Me? I had a head filled with a beautiful blonde who should have been the woman sitting in the seats in front of Katie, holding my son. Instead it was Viola. And even though I really like her, like she treats Angelo like her own son or grandson and yet does not mother me, she is not the woman I wanted cheering for me.

I wanted my family. The one I threw away. Every day we wait for news on Angela, for Jason to find out what he can from his former lovers and for Luke's private investigator to get back to us.

It's been seven days. One week. Seven weeks.

It does not matter. Every day I spend without Paisley, playing along with Angela's games so I don't end up arrested is killing me.

All I want is Paisley. And now, I am packing to leave for California for three days and two games. One in Los Angeles and then San Diego. It's not the first time I've had to leave Angelo. It's the first time I haven't known Paisley will be watching and cheering for me even if she doesn't understand the simplest rules like the difference between icing or off-sides.

I grin, shake my head, and go back to packing. I'm already in my suit I wear on the airplane. The coat is off to the side of my bag. I only need a few casual clothes, toiletries, so it's not difficult and I've traveled enough it usually take me minutes.

I'm stalling.

I don't want to be an entire country away from my son, and I want Paisley to give me a goodbye kiss.

I want all the things I cannot have with her and it's eating away at me, ruining my focus on the ice.

Perhaps my father was right after all. All hockey. Nothing else. It's the only way to stay on top.

My phone rings with the tone for the concierge desk downstairs. Viola has permission and her own key to come up and she should be arriving any minute. But it could be Luke.

Maybe.

Hoping I'm right, I answer the phone. "Pierre?"

"Mr. Lutzgo, yes, this is Monsieur Pierre. I have someone for you, someone demanding to be sent up—"

"Lutzgo. Jaxon Hayes. Tell him to send me up."

I'm thrown by the voice and the abrupt change. "Who?"

He sighs, as if annoyed. "Jaxon Hayes. Security Specialist. I got news for you, and Luke is in Georgia. You'll want this. Send me up."

"The investigator?" My heart races.

I receive another sigh as a reply. "I'll wait for you to call Luke if you want. Or call Beaux Hale. Hell, call Gage Bryant, he's married to my sister. I'm legit. I'm also in a hurry 'cuz I just drove my ass down here from Raleigh and I'm tellin' you, you want to hear this. And not down here."

Beaux Hale. Quarterback for the Raleigh Rough Riders.

And Luke is in Georgia. He let me know this week he had to leave town for a few days for his niece's wedding. Plus, he also told me Jaxon's office in Raleigh came recommended from the team.

"No need. Tell Pierre to send you up. And thank you."

I get no response except the click of the phone hanging up on me, but I pick up Angelo from where he's in a bouncy chair by my bed, kiss the top of his head and hurry to my door.

I've become obsessive about checking the peephole. Once, I almost left when Paisley was in the hallway and I barely stopped myself from throwing myself to my knees and begging for her mercy.

The elevator door slides open and I throw open my door, meeting Jaxon in the hallway. As he reaches me, my hellish nightmare continues because so does Paisley's door.

She spies me and freezes, eyes sliding from me to Angelo and the Jaxon. They widen when they meet him, but who wouldn't. The man is built like an ox, dressed in military fatigue-style pants like he's set to be deployed immediately and he has sunglasses over his eyes.

"Paisley," I call her, and her hair whips in the air as she turns to me. Her skin pales and she licks her lips.

I want to kiss her and apologize and make everything better.

She blinks. "Mikah." Then she turns, scoots by Jaxon who hasn't changed his expression as she comes closer, and then she's gone, slipping into the elevator as the door closes.

"Damn." That couldn't have gone worse. Or maybe it could, if she would have slapped me.

"That was about as icy as the Arctic," Jaxon says and holds out his hand. "Jaxon Hayes."

"Thanks. And yeah, that was... well, that was..."

"Paisley Hughes. Yeah, I know."

I should be surprised, but I'm not. There's a reason Luke hired him. I told him to find the best.

"Come on in."

I turn back and enter first as he says, "If it's any consolation what I'm about to tell you will probably help smooth things over with the neighbor."

"Yeah?" I bounce Angelo in my arms. He fusses a bit and I check my watch. Viola should already be here. It's not like her to run late. "What is it?"

He reaches behind him and without saying a word, hands me a folded piece of paper.

"What is this?" I'm already reaching for it, but with Angelo fussing it's not easy to open.

"Termination of Parental Rights Request."

I almost drop Angelo and I'm shaking so I lay him on his playmat on the floor before I do. "I'm sorry. What?" I tear open the paper and see for myself.

"You'll need to go to a judge. But I've filed the work already. Got that done as soon as she signed. And with the information I found the judge will give it."

"What... what information, and how..."

"One, it's my job and you sure you want to know? Because not everyone does. And the good news is she's out of your life. Guaranteed. Slippery, but I got it, and witnesses to her deceit."

"Deceit." I whip toward Angelo.

"Don't worry. He's yours."

"Tell me."

"She didn't know whose he was. Process of elimination. Two other guys she went to, them for money, they refused, but they weren't as rich as you. A dentist and some guy who owns a contracting firm. He's also married, so, well, he wanted her gone, but also wanted the kid."

"Are you... she slept with..."

He finally changes his expression from stone to something like a sneer. Slowly, he slides his glasses off and tucks them into the front of his black shirt. "Got knocked up. Didn't know whose it was. I figure, by the time she got to you, she was tired of actually fucking guys with a moral conscience and the smarts to determine they're actually the father before handing over stacks of cash. Your girl isn't too smart. Probably started with less rich guys first in case he *was* theirs. Didn't want to risk losing your money pot."

"She's not my girl," I snap. This woman. This damn, evil.... My living room spins, I'm in such shock. I might need to sit.

I really need Viola to get here. If I go down, no one can help with Angelo because Paisley is gone... from the building and my life. *For helved. Pis.* Shit. I have screwed everything up.

Jason was right.

I am an idiot.

"So me... why did she leave him?"

"She wanted the vacation. Got back, has no money, watched you for a few weeks. Was going to come back but then waited until you went public, figuring you'd have to eventually and she'd get more money than from you."

"All of this, screwing with my life... with Angelo's for money?"

"Three million."

Stupid. She should have just said it last week. "Had she asked I would have given it to her to get her to go away."

"That's what I told her. Needless to say, she's not thrilled with me or my tactics to get her to sign, but it's done and filed. Nothing she can do about it now."

"He's mine." I scan the paper again. It's a copy, like he said, but it's still stamped. Upper right corner with the day's date. "I'll email another copy to Luke but like I said, knew you'd want this, so I figured I'd hand deliver it. No tellin' with his family thing when he'd see it. Thought you'd want to know."

"I did." I correct myself. "I do. Thank you. Whatever I owe you, I will double."

Jaxon grins. It looks like it doesn't belong on him. Like he rarely does it. I can relate. I cannot remember the last time I've smiled. "No offense, but you've already paid me enough. I'm sorry we couldn't figure it out sooner while she was out of the country. Would have loved to have messed with her there, make her think she couldn't return."

I smile. Anything to make her pay for this makes me happy, even if it's only a thought.

"Thank you. Again." A huge breath falls from me and my body temperature drops ten degrees. Finally. It's done.

"I'll let myself out. Know you got a plane to catch."

As he heads that way, the door opens, and Viola enters. "Oh." Her eyes widen when she sees me and then she notices Jaxon. "Oooh. Well, aren't you a big boy."

"Never skip a bowl of Wheaties," Jaxon says, and Viola's eyes pop wide. He tips his head toward her, gives me a low wave and heads out the door Viola has just entered.

"Who was that?" she asks. "And I apologize for being late. I wasn't feeling well last night, so I took cold medicine. Slept in."

"Are you sick?"

"Oh. No. Nothing. Just a cold. Or allergies. I'll be fine though." She coughs into her hand and I frown.

"Are you okay being sick around Angelo? I can find someone else for this trip?"

"No no, Mikah." She coughs again and gives me a weak smile. "I will be fine, I'm certain of it. Besides, if it is a cold, Angelo has already been exposed to my germs, and he's healthy so he should be fine."

"Are you sure?" There's no way I can't get on this plane, and I need to get going. I spent too long waiting for Viola before I started packing. And then Jaxon. Which reminds me. I shake the paper at Viola. If she says she can watch Angelo, I trust her. "Look at this."

"What is it—*oooh*—" She grins up at me. "She signed it?"

"Yes. Finally."

Her face lights up like a Christmas tree. "Well, that's wonderful. You can call Paisley again."

"Maybe. When I get back. I must go."

"Oh. Right. Of course. Okay." She folds the paper and hands it back to me, her bright happiness diminishing. "Well then, play hard, skate fast, you know... all of those things. Angelo and I will be just fine. I promise. And call when you must."

"I will." Viola laughs at me because I call all the time. When I wake up. Before a game. After the game. Before I go to bed. Nothing changes except that Angelo has pooped again or eaten, but I like knowing his day when I'm not here.

I throw the rest of the things in my bag, slide into my suit coat and spend more time than I have, holding and kissing Angelo and telling him how much I love him, before handing him to Viola.

My gaze holds on Paisley's door as I pass it. If only I had the time to go to her, I would.

But I will make things better and somehow, I will get her back.

As soon as I return.

CHAPTER THIRTY-ONE

Paisley

IF MY OBSESSION was borderline stalkerish before Mikah and I met, I've now passed unsurmountable levels of psycho. I check my door before I leave. Peer through my peephole when I hear a noise. I'm aware of how well he played on his first home game because yes, while I didn't go, I watched from home even though I don't understand anything, and he moves so fast on the ice I can barely keep track of him.

And I shouldn't have gone out earlier. I should have stayed inside until the voices in the hallway vanished. Curiosity killed the cat and all that.

Except this time, curiosity stomped all over my still shredded heart.

One glimpse of Mikah holding Angelo and the pain of him shutting me out and then not answering the door the day after when I tried to talk to him revved into overdrive.

Which pathetically explains why I'm shoving my face

into a carton of cookie dough ice cream, research for my paper and another class spread in front of me. I'm pretty sure they're stuck together with melted ice cream.

I've become the girl who falls apart when a boy breaks her heart, and there's still a stupid tiny part of me who knows there's something else going on. Adding insult to injury, I feel like I've lost a whole new set of friends I was really beginning to care about. It's not like I can call Katie up and bitch about him when she's engaged to his team-mate. I can't whine to Tessa, who is somehow now *living* with Jason instead of going home to Toronto, or Hannah.

"Screw it," I mutter around a spoonful of ice cream. People lose friends during break-ups all the time. Sure, they don't always have the *awesome* luxury of living next door, or across the hall, from said break-up, but I'm being way too overdramatic here.

A couple months we dated, not even.

So I had a crush on the guy for months beforehand.

So I envisioned us raising Angelo together. Things don't work out for whatever reason and even if I ever get an answer to *why* he did this... does it matter?

In the end, Mikah didn't trust me enough to handle it with him. Us together. Pippa said it best the other day when she called to check on me. *A man who doesn't trust you enough to go through hard times isn't worth hanging on to for the easy ones, girl. You're stronger than this. And if he's not it, no matter how great he is, there's better for you.*

"She's right." Girl power. All that jazz. I've got this. Stabbing my spoon into the carton, I take it all to the kitchen where I clean up and wash the melted ice cream off my face and good grief, there's some dried to my chin and drying on my shirt.

I will not become a wreck over a guy. Other fish in the

sea. I channel Pippa's ooh-rah fierce-woman power speech and blow out a breath.

After a quick change of clothes into a lightweight sweatshirt where one shoulder dips to my biceps and my coziest pair of wide-legged yoga pants, I sit down on my couch, turn off the stupid romance movie I was watching and clean up my research notes.

I was right. There is ice cream sticking to them, so I put those to the side. I'll have to redo them for my Advanced Techniques class but so what. Not like I have more important pressing matters on my to-do list. I'm in the midst of separating my disastrous mess when my phone rings next to me.

Viola.

Her name shines on the screen and I hesitate. She's called me twice. Both times I answered, only for her to offer to bring Angelo over for a bit. I declined. It'd hurt too much to see him. I don't want to tell her to no again.

You are a strong, independent woman who can move mountains and screw men who don't treat you like you deserve.

Right. I almost forgot.

"Hello?"

A cough, a wretched sounding cough comes through the phone. "Paisley?"

"Viola? Are you okay?" Without thought, I'm scrambling off the couch.

"Yes. Well no. I'm sick. Really sick." Another cough. "I told Mikah it was just a cold, but I think I was wrong and now I have a fever and well... I'm so sorry. I know things aren't well for you two but can you... can you come help? I don't know if I can take care of Angelo."

"Viola." I cringe as she hacks so loud I swear I can hear

her through the thick walls. "I don't know if Mikah would want that."

"I know. I know you think that, and I know why, but Paisley—" she coughs again, and I yank the phone from my ear, cringing— "I'll just, call the service then."

Visions of Leah flash in my brain and I cringe worse than hearing Viola hack up a lung. Last I checked, we still needed two of them.

"Okay. Okay. I'm coming over, but give me a few minutes to grab some things, okay? I'll be there in ten."

"Thank you. Thank you, Paisley. I'll let Mikah know and clear it with him. Okay?"

"If he hesitates at all..."

"He won't. He was worried when he left."

"Okay. Be there in ten."

She hangs up and I frown at my phone. She sounded okay, but that cough... I shrug off the weirdness and pack a bag. Tomorrow is Saturday so I can spend the night and get caught up with schoolwork this weekend while I stay over there but it's not like I can't run back here if I forget some-thing. For now, I grab my pajamas and book bag and phone charger.

I've spent so much time at Mikah's anyway, I have most of my necessities.

I shake off that thought.

This is for Angelo and Viola. Partly for Mikah. But that's it. I'm now his neighbor, and I'll have to go back to remembering that.

Which I should have done from the very beginning.

<hr>

IT'S Saturday afternoon and Angelo and I have just

gotten back to Mikah's after a walk around Uptown. I took him out early this morning and swung through the farmer's market, something I've never done but will definitely be doing again. It wasn't even the fresh fruits and vegetables from local farmers that I loved so much, but the energy in the streets. Bright flowers seemed to be on every third stand. There was live music. People, happy to be out and about sipping their coffee drinks from local coffeehouses, getting early morning exercise. Kids of all ages ran around and I stopped and petted so many puppies I'm now itching to get to a rescue event and get myself one.

Ha. Uncle Trent would kill me. But what he doesn't know....

Regardless, it was a great morning. I spent the rest of it working while Angelo napped and after lunch, I took him to the rooftop where we walked around some more. I pushed him in the lone infant swing. We saw more puppies in their dog parks and then watched a foursome play some incredible competitive tennis. By my count? The losing team is now down several hundred dollars.

I'm feeling refreshed and tired, the perfect early fall combination when we return to Mikah's. I've fed Angelo again and he's happily sitting in his swing while I clean up the living area. The last thing I want is for Mikah to return Monday and have his home be a mess. Mid-folding a blanket from Angelo's laundry I started this morning, my phone rings with the FaceTime sound and it takes me several seconds to realize I'm staring at Mikah's face. And why I'm staring at his face.

Of course. He probably wants to check on Angelo.

With trembling hands and a buzzing sensation of nerves sliding up my arms, I grab my phone and swipe right. It takes a minute for Mikah's face to appear, and when he does, he looks wrecked.

His hair that's usually styled nicely is a disaster. His scruff is longer, making him look like hasn't shaved in days.

"Paisley." He says my name on a gasp and then his eyes narrow. "Why are you in my home? And where is Viola? Is everything okay? I have been trying to reach her and she's not answering and Angelo... oh God. Angelo... is he okay?"

"Woah—" I hold up a hand to stop him before realizing he can't see it. "Viola's sick, Mikah. Didn't she call you?"

"Sick. She had a cough. Said it was a cold."

Oh. This is bad. This is *bad, bad, bad.*

"Mikah." I try to soften my voice. "She called me last night and her cough was bad. She said she had a fever and asked if I could take over. I'm sorry. So, so sorry. She said she'd clear it with you."

"She did not call. She is okay?"

"She didn't look that bad." But that cough. I shiver at that wretched sound. "I haven't talked to her but I can call her."

"No. I will." His stressed features seem to ease, and he pulls in a large breath. "Angelo. He is okay?"

I turn so Angelo is behind me, over my shoulder. He has one thumb in his mouth and his other hand is reaching for a duck that spins around over his head.

"He's good. He slept well. I've taken care of him. We went to the farmer's market this morning and then to the rooftop this afternoon. I'm taking good care of him, Mikah." I'm not sure why I feel the need to reassure him. He's seen me with him.

There is a pause, a long one, too long, where he stares at Angelo on the small screen before he closes his eyes.

Oh no. He's not going to tell me to leave, is he? He can. He can call the nanny service and get a replacement.

"I like you in my home. With him."

"Don't." My word comes out harsh and my cheeks start to burn. "Don't say that to me."

His blue eyes, so dark and vivid even through the small screen in my hand burn straight to chest. "I am sorry, Paisley. So sorry. I did... what I did... that was wrong."

I shake my head. I can't listen to this. Not now.

"Mikah—"

"I will explain when I get home. But I like you there. With him. It is as it should be. As I wanted...as I want." His brows furrow as he corrects himself. I can tell he's now leaning forward, almost like he's trying to plead with me through the phone to believe him.

"Stop."

"It was Angela. She came back. And there were threats, and I did not want you involved."

I knew it! I'm not surprised by this, but not ready to hear it. And he has me trapped.

"I can't do this, Mikah. I'll watch Angelo, I'm happy to this weekend, but what you did... how you hurt me..." But oh, how I want to hear it all. It doesn't make me happy to know I'm right. Not while I'm staring at Mikah's face, so sad, so serious. "You shut me out."

"And it will never happen again. Take the time you need but I swear, and I mean it more than I have ever meant anything. Give me a chance to explain and make it right and it will be the best risk you have taken ever."

"Mikah—"

"Think on it. I will give you time."

Oh God. My heart. For him. Angelo. I want to hear him

out. I should. I *deserve* the reason for his sudden change in demeanor.

"We'll talk," I say, and it's barely a whisper because I'm quickly losing it.

"Thank you. Angelo is okay? I need to get going but I had to see him and Viola not answering had me worried, so I called you..."

"He's fine, Mikah. See?" I hit the double arrow button on my phone to spin the screen around and move close to Angelo. Then I laugh to myself as Mikah talks to his son, his face probably overtaking the screen I have it held so close. Angelo smiles. His whole face lights up as Mikah says he loves him, and he'll see him soon and to keep being a good boy. To sleep lots for me. *Yes. Please, Angelo. Sleep a lot.* Then I hear, "I am done being a fool on the phone for him. Can I see you again?"

I flip the phone back to my face and Mikah is smiling. "Beautiful. Always so beautiful. We will talk soon."

The screen freezes, his face on a grainy smile as he disconnects. It disappears and I realize I'm smiling.

Always smiling for him.

The question is does it make me being the one who's acting like a fool?

CHAPTER THIRTY-TWO

Mikah

I skate better against San Diego than I have ever skated in my life, ending the game with a hat trick, something I only accomplished a few times last season. My grip is tight, my feet are quick, and I imagine at any moment I will receive a call from my father telling me everything I've done wrong despite my success and my teams.

We are off to a great start for the season.

I don't care about any of it. My foot taps on the long plane ride home on Monday. Thankfully, we leave early, but I still won't get there until half the day has passed. I want to get my hands on Angelo and see him. I want to smell his clean baby smell and hear his giggle.

I want to get my mouth on Paisley and hear her tell me she forgives me for being a massive idiot. For not trusting her. I want to show and tell her everything and then I want her to come into my arms so I can take her to my bed.

I have never realized how impatient I am until I have people waiting for me at home. The elevator comes to a stop and I'm moving before the doors open, almost running straight into them. I've called Paisley this morning to tell her I was at the airport and she said that Viola showed up to take care of Angelo so she could go to school.

Must have been a twenty-four-hour thing, because she looks great, she said to me on the phone.

So I am expecting to open the door to my home and see Viola, but she surprises me at the door.

"I think you want to go that way first," she says.

I will get there, but first, I am worried about her. About Angelo. She looks healthy. Her blonde hair with grays at the temples is pulled back into a ponytail and she is wearing the typical clothes she does at my house. Yoga capris and a short-sleeve shirt. She dresses simple, but it's easy to see she was once beautiful. I would admit she still is if I was twenty years older.

"How are you feeling?"

She flips her hand in the air, smiling like she hasn't been sick at all. Perhaps Paisley was right. I'm beginning to learn she usually is. About everything. "Oh, I'm great. Healthy and hale and Angelo is napping so if you want to go back and get your girl..."

"I want."

This woman. I wish my mom could have been like her. Or maybe I wish for a cool aunt like Viola. I'm at Paisley's door, lifting my hand to knock when Viola calls my name again.

"Yes?"

She coughs into her hand and winks, smiling behind her fist. "Have fun."

She disappears behind the door to my condo and it takes a second for what she's done to register.

That woman.

She played us.

I shake my head, laughing and knock on Paisley's door. Nervous as the day I was when I signed my first contract with the Ice Kings, I swipe my sweaty palms down the front of my athletic pants.

The door unlocks and slowly opens.

"Paisley?"

She only opens the door a few inches, enough for me to see her face, but I want to see more. I can't read anything from her expression.

Her cheeks are flushed, hair down, but it's her green eyes that pull me in and make my nerves scatter wildly.

"Mikah." Her gaze slides to the left, toward the door of my home and back to me, and the top curves of her cheeks darken. "Hey."

She steps back, bringing the door with her and then I see why she only opened it a small amount.

She's dressed in a towel. And from what it appears, only a towel.

I grab the doorknob, forcing her farther back, the door opens wider so I can finally enter and then close it behind me.

"Do you need more time?"

"No." Her hand goes to the top of the towel where one end is tucked in, holding it up. I stop her before she can undo it.

Her hands are trembling. She's nervous, possibly scared. She has no reason to be either.

"We will talk after. I will tell you everything."

"You will. And I'll still end up forgiving you for acting like an idiot."

"You're so sure of that?"

She shrugs and her tongue brushes over her lip. "Yeah. I mean, I love you. So that's what you do for people you love."

"You love me." It hits me like a puck to the chest, slamming into me and stealing my breath.

"Possibly from the first moment I saw you." Her lips quirk and her hand swipes down the length of her body. "Dressed in something like this, if I remember correctly."

"You love me."

"I do."

I drop her hand I'd taken earlier and pluck the edge of the towel. It falls to the floor, but I don't remove my gaze from her eyes. "I love you, too."

She flies at me and I catch her, falling back a step before I steady her. My hands settle on her ass and her breasts are pressed to my chest. I revel in the feel of her body in my hands once again for only a moment.

And then I press my lips to hers. "I love you," I say again before chasing my words with a kiss. "I mean it and I'm sorry for hurting you, *skat*. So very sorry."

"Sket?"

I didn't realize I'd slipped in language and I smile at her. "Close enough. *Skat*. It means, sweetie, or treasure."

"Oh." She presses her lips to mine. They're turned up in a smile. I didn't think I would see that from her today. At least not yet. "I like that."

I've made it to her room, and I drop one hand from her ass to place it on her bed. She clings to me as I place one knee then the other on her mattress and move up until I can lay her down in the center.

"I will show you other things you like more," I tease,

humming against her throat. My dick is already hard. Her nipples are too, light brown hardened points that raise and fall with every breath she takes.

I want to make this good for her. Slow. I want to spend the evening and night showering her with my love through my body to begin proving how much I love this woman.

She swept into my life when least expected and most needed.

She's been nothing but gracious and kind and loyal, and when I needed help the most, I turned her away instead of drawing her closer.

It was a mistake I will never make again.

I bring her to her first climax slowly with my fingers and mouth, and then I slide deep inside of her, fully seating myself in her before I realize what's different.

"Paisley." Her name tears from me on a tortured groan. She's tighter and warmer and wetter than normal. "Condom."

"Birth control," she whispers. Her fingers are on my ass, holding me against her as she grinds her clit to my pubic bone. "You know I'm on it."

"Are you sure?"

She wraps her legs around my hips and hooks her ankles together. Grinning up at me, she gives me a jaunty wink. "Show me what you've got, hockey star."

EPILOGUE

Paisley

"MOM. HE WANTS TO MOVE."

"Oh that's silly. He loves being with his grandma."

In my mom's arms, Angelo kicks and squirms. His face is squished with frustration as he flails his arms. My mom is now a certified lunatic. At least I know where I get it from. From the moment she first met Angelo way back in October, a couple of weeks after Mikah and I got back together, I've seen her more than I have since high school. She *loves* having a baby to play with so much I'm not sure Viola is necessary.

But I can tell Angelo wants to get down. He rolls all over the place nowadays and can sit on his own too. My mom refuses to allow him out of his arms which means he's constantly wiggling in her arms.

Even more strange is that when Mikah first met my parents, he introduced Angelo to them as their grandson. Their eyes widened briefly before grins broke out. I'm not sure there was a better way he could have let my parents know how serious we are outside of gifting them with that title from the get-go.

But really, it makes sense... what else is he supposed to call them? Mikah's already started calling me Angelo's mom, which was *weird* the first few times until I talked to him about it.

"You and I will be together forever. That is a matter of time. What else is he supposed to call you? Then we change it? Does that make sense?"

Logically, I got it. But... "Mom?" I'd asked.

Mikah cupped my cheeks with his palms and kissed me. "Someday, you will be. Yes?"

Oh, I'd be that in a heartbeat. All Mikah has to do is ask. Still, it is soon... "Mikah..." Apparently, I can only say his name when I'm flustered. He doesn't seem to mind.

"Someday." He seals his promise with a kiss and silences my fears and nerves by carrying me to bed. Hours later, I don't remember what we were talking about.

Now, it's Thanksgiving. My parents are here and my mom, outside of stealing Angelo from the moment she walked in has also taken over cooking a massive meal in Trent's apartment... which is now vacant except for when they visit.

I haven't officially moved in with Mikah, but all my things are at his house. It started slowly, then he cleared a drawer and space in his closets. The only time we go to Trent's is when I need something or when we need a few more moments—hours—of privacy on date nights.

It's essentially our sex pad. We make sure the sheets are cleaned before my parents come into town.

"No!"

"I do not get the fascination."

This comes from my dad and Mikah who are camped in front of the television. It's Thanksgiving after all. It's the American way to watch the Detroit Lions game before a meal apparently. I think it's the only time my dad pays attention to the sport but you don't mess with the religion of a Turkey Day football game. Mikah is the one who now is confused. He wants to watch hockey, but that's not until later.

Tomorrow, he takes off to Minnesota for a quick overnight game before being back in town for five days.

His schedule is insanely grueling and the more I get used to it, the more I respect everything he and his team does for a living.

We only see each other a few nights a week and most of those nights are spent with Angelo. I've practically become a mom years before I was prepared and somehow, Mikah and I have done it all together, figuring it out with us being a team from the moment I saw Angelo on his doorstep.

Except for that week we were separated, we've done it all together. And the day Mikah came back, and he told me everything, I only had the lingering anger to release before I fully forgave him. He still should have been honest with me. I would have stepped back until he figured things out. But I love him too much to hold it against him so it didn't take long for me to forgive him.

Angelo makes a fussy noise and I can no longer see him look so frustrated.

"Mom. Hand me the boy." I walk to her slowly as if she has a bomb strapped to her chest. Sometimes if you move fast, she whisks him away to spend hours reading to him. I mean, I knew my mom was crazy, but she's taking being a grandma to a whole new level.

"He's fine."

In response, Angelo slaps her cheek and yells.

"Oh, see, that's just your way of saying how much you love your grandma, huh, isn't it you perfect little angel."

She blows a raspberry on his covered tummy and squeezes him.

"Mom." She's nuts. Absolutely nuts. I turn to Mikah for help, but he and my dad are having a beer, watching the game. I'm forgotten and on my own.

"I think the turkey's burning," I say and it's the only thing to get my mom's attention. She swoops toward the stove and in her haste, I grab Angelo from her. She's so worried about the meal being perfect she doesn't remember she only put the turkey in the oven an hour ago.

Still, with Angelo safe in my arms, I take him to the family room where I spread out the blanket and lay him down. He stretches with relief and promptly rolls to his stomach, starts doing an army crawl maneuver straight for my dad.

I fill a glass with wine and head back to the living room. I don't bother offering to help my mom cook. I already did and she let me know she doesn't feel like calling the fire department today so I slide easily next to Mikah on the couch, curling my knees over his lap while he drapes an arm over my shoulder.

"You rescued our boy." He kisses the top of my head.

I get a shiver of happiness every time he calls Angelo *ours* and not *his*. As the paperwork showed, Angela relinquished her parental rights. A couple months after that day, apparently Jaxon Hayes did a check up on her and let Mikah know she had moved to Michigan where she was originally from. Good riddance. Since then, it was easy for Mikah to have his parental rights declared.

He's officially been Angelo's father for a full month, so I'm thinking we have lots to be thankful for this year.

I hum with happiness at the thought.

"What's that for?" Mikah asks.

I grin up at him. "Just thinking...we have a lot to be thankful for this year. Angelo. Us. The season you're having so far."

"All good things." He kisses my cheek and then my legs are being moved so he can slide out from beneath me.

"What are you doing?"

"Grabbing Angelo."

I glance to see he's on his belly. His little fingers are fiddling with the laces on my father's shoes. My dad keeps moving his feet away, making Angelo giggle and grunt and reach for them.

Since Mikah is on the floor with Angelo, dragging him back to the blanket, it takes me a second to realize once he's in front of me, he doesn't get back to the couch.

"Mikah?"

He's on a knee. Angelo is bouncing on the other knee, facing me, arms flailing and clasping together. And then...

"Shut up," I say.

He's holding a box.

Mikah laughs. "I have not said anything yet."

"But..."

Oh my God. Next to me, my dad has gotten off the couch. He's now standing off to the side. My mom is next to him. Crying.

"You're... what is going on?"

An idiot would understand faster than I am.

Mikah reaches out and squeezes my thigh. I cling to his hand. I'm shaking. Hot. My heart might explode. Oh dear. It's been a while since I've had these symptoms.

"You are right," he says, and his laughter has died and his face has gone somber. So serious. Such a deep, rough voice. "We have much to be thankful for this year. My team. A good family," his eyes flip to my parents and Angelo and then back to me, "and Angelo. Becoming a dad. But you... you are what I'm most thankful for."

"Mikah—" His name lodges in my throat. I can't believe he's doing this.

He raises up Angelo's pudgy arms still holding a small box. "There is only one thing that could make me more thankful, and that is marrying you. Will you be my wife? Become Angelo's mom legally?"

"Oh my God. Today?" I cry.

Mikah laughs and takes the box from Angelo's hand. It's now wet from his drool. Apparently, he thinks it looks delicious. "I think we cannot do it today, but as soon as you want. As soon as you're ready. I love you and as far as I'm concerned, our forever began the day you brought this boy into my life." He pops open the box and I think my heart stalls.

Oh dear. I really, really should have gone to the doctor to get help for this heart condition I have.

"I love you, Paisley. And I want all of us to be a family. Forever. Marry me?"

"Yes!" I cry, slide off the couch and tackle both Mikah and Angelo. My parents laugh. I've forgotten they're here and I must look a fright, straddling and kissing Mikah and Angelo while wearing a dress.

Fortunately, we're all a little bit crazy. My mom cries. My dad whoops. And I keep kissing Mikah and Angelo, tears streaming down my cheeks until Mikah sits up and finally, *finally* slides a gleaming diamond onto my finger and kisses my hand.

"I never knew I could have more in my life than hockey, but winning you feels better than any goal I have scored. Thank you for loving me every day. Every minute. I will always do the same for you."

Silly man. He's done that since the day we first met. But I can't wait to show him how good I'll be at it for the rest of our lives.

THANK you for reading Scoring Off The Ice! Hooked On Her, Jason Taylor's story, will release later this summer. Want to be notified as soon as it releases? Subscribe to my newsletter by visiting my website: www.staceylynnbooks.com

ACKNOWLEDGMENTS

HUGE thank you to Hilary and all of Social Butterfly PR for throwing your full enthusiasm and support behind each and every book I write. I have loved working with all of you and can't wait to see what's ahead! Hilary, I miss you most of all. ;-)

Ellie and Virginia, as always, thanks for putting up with my mess and spit-shining each manuscript until it sparkles.

Shannon, you're the best. Always. Forever. Your talent is astounding and I'm thankful I can call you a friend.

Special, enormous thank you to my family who is always here, cheering me on and being so patient when I'm in my office. Your support is everything to me and I love you all with all of my heart.

To my Sweeties! I love you ladies and your excitement for my books! Special thanks to you this time for coming up with Brenna's name for me. It fits her perfectly.

To Lauren and Tamara – I'm so thankful our moves brought us into each other's lives!

To all the bloggers who devote their time and passion into reading books, book tours, release events, leaving reviews, promoting and pimping – you are all rockstars! Thank you for all the love over the years.

My family— I love you all to the moon and back. I don't know what I would do without you in my corner, cheering me on every step of the way.

And last but definitely not least – to you the reader. I'm blown away with every release how much you adore my books. You have made my dream a reality and I hope I can cheer you on with yours.

OTHER BOOKS BY STACEY LYNN

Ice Kings Series

Playing To Win

Scoring Off The Ice

Hooked On Her – summer 2020

Hard Checked – fall 2020

The Luminous Series

Dominate Me

Crave Me

Long For Me

The Rough Riders Series

Dirty Player

Filthy Player

Wicked Player

Cocky Player

Love In The Heartland

Captivated By You

This Time Around

Long Road Home

Before We Fell

Crazy Love Series

Fake Wife

Knocked Up

28 Dates

Weekend Fling

The Fireside Series

His to Love

His to Protect

His to Cherish

His to Seduce

Tangled Love Series

Entice

Embrace

Enflame

Just One Series

Just One Song

Just One Week

Just One Regret

Just One Moment

The Nordic Lords Series

Point of Return

Point of Redemption

Point of Freedom

Point of Surrender

<u>**Standalones**</u>

Remembering Us

Don't Lie To Me

Try Me – A Don't Lie To Me Novella